"Who is there?" Margaret called out.

She thought she detected a faint intake of breath, a tiny shuffle.

"I am armed," she said boldly. The cutlass was rather heavy, not to say unwieldy for one unaccustomed to its use.

There was no response.

"Ah!" She spoke involuntarily. She could now see the shape of a person crouching near the chair where she'd found the chicken head.

Neither of them moved, but Margaret's heart was still beating rapidly.

Suddenly, the person sprang at Margaret, and she saw only dark clothes, a dark face, a dark head. The person grabbed the wrist of her hand holding the cutlass. She released the big knife, and the blade clattered loudly as it hit the floor.

Also by Joyce Christmas
Published by Fawcett Books:

Lady Margaret Priam mysteries:
A FÊTE WORSE THAN DEATH
SUDDENLY IN HER SORBET
SIMPLY TO DIE FOR
A STUNNING WAY TO DIE
FRIEND OR FAUX
IT'S HER FUNERAL

Betty Trenka mysteries:
THIS BUSINESS IS MURDER

A PERFECT DAY FOR DYING

Joyce Christmas

FAWCETT GOLD MEDAL • NEW YORK

For Larry,
my constant reader

A Fawcett Gold Medal Book
Published by Ballantine Books
Copyright © 1994 by Joyce Christmas

All rights reserved under International and Pan-American Copyright Conventions. Published in the United States of America by Ballantine Books, a division of Random House, Inc., New York, and simultaneously in Canada by Random House of Canada Limited, Toronto.

Library of Congress Catalog Card Number: 93-90717

ISBN 0-449-14703-7

Manufactured in the United States of America

First Edition: February 1994

Prologue: Dayclean

*T*ap, *tap*. Tap.

Dayclean. Dawn came quietly and gently to Boucan, touching first the tops of the coconut palms along the road to the harbor on the Atlantic side of the island, then gilding the tall windows of the big house called Indigo Hill, and finally brightening the foam of the waves that rolled in on the Caribbean side and broke on the golden sands of Arawak Bay.

Tap, tap. Tap.

The only sound was the old pipe striking a nail head somewhere deep in the overgrown gully.

It was almost a carnival rhythm; a calypso beat, a soca beat. Ska. Reggae . . .

Tap, tap. Tap.

The unexpected sound puzzled the small boy who stood in the cover of the great crimson bougainvillea that Mamee Joe had planted a hundred years ago (she said) to mark the edge of her property. From there a rough road wound upward to a cluster of wood and cement-block houses that looked down on Chatham town and Boucan harbor, and off to the steep hills in the middle of the island.

The boy waited, shifting from one foot to the other in his too-big sneakers inherited from his Uncle Derrick.

The sound had come from the bottom of the gully where a big, big old mango tree stood, raising its heavy branches above the tangle of breadfruit trees and broad-leafed banana plants.

Who would be down there? Nobody liked to go to the gully, even in full day—and then only bravely, quickly with others, to collect mangos. Bats flew about in the darkness and people threw the bodies of dead animals into its depths, where scavenging land crabs and other wildlife stripped the bones clean. The older boys whispered that a man had been killed there long ago.

Mamee Joe said it was just big talk. "Some girl kill a no-good boy's romantic ideas, is all," she would say. "Foolishness."

Silence. Not even the sound of someone moving away through the bush. The boy shivered, caught between the thought of investigating and the wild stories the boys told.

Coo-Coo St. Joseph scratched his head. If he braved the bush and the steep hill to discover the source of the puzzling noise, he could meet some unknown danger. A jumby could steal him away. The ghost of the dead man could rise. He shivered again.

Then he took a deep breath and considered more reasonable possibilities: he could meet some ordinary grown-up who would want to know why he wasn't ready for school. School was not on his agenda today. No starched shirt, no boring schoolbooks, no long day in the cramped schoolroom. Christmas holidays were coming just now, and Coo-Coo was planning on walking up by Indigo Hill to see when m'lord was arriving on Boucan from England. And better yet, m'lord's green-eyed laughing daughter, Miss Georgina. Even at eight years, Coo-Coo already had an eye for a pretty woman, and never mind she was a big grown woman, twenty-five years at least. Then he was going over to Arawak Bay to help the fishermen pull seine.

Still, he hesitated. Who could have made that ringing sound from the gully so early? The sky was faintly blue, and the bellies of puffy, drifting clouds were touched with streaks of pink. Up on the hill the coconut palms were black silhouettes against the pale sky. It was not even six yet.

But the island's day was beginning now. Suddenly there were other sounds: A rooster uttered his morning announcement of feathered male dominance, and across the hills, another answered, and then another. Hero barked once, twice up at Coo-Coo's house on the hill. The faint sound of a Trinidad calypso from a radio hovered on the edge of hearing. Coo-Coo heard a lorry speeding along the main road. His dark fears faded, and his curiosity won.

Coo-Coo made his way carefully down the slope through the tangle of brush and vines. He stepped gingerly over a whitened skull of some small animal, a dog or an agouti. The place smelled of damp earth and rotting wood. Only a few pale rays of light reached the ground through the thick overhead growth. At the bottom, he peered into the clearing near the mango tree. The weeds around the foot of the tree had been trampled a bit, but he saw no one.

But there was something to be seen. He looked up at the thick trunk of the mango. A rectangle of paper had been nailed to it. He squinted. A picture, a colored snapshot of a woman with her face disfigured by nails that had been pounded into the paper.

It looked like a white woman, but was unidentifiable, even as one of the few white women Coo-Coo knew.

Coo-Coo caught his breath as a shiver of fear raced

through him. A trickle of blood came from the photo, as though the life of the lady in the picture was oozing away. Then he saw it was only a thin strip of red cloth that had been nailed to the woman's forehead.

This was bad. Some kind of obeah, for sure. A spell cast to harm the woman.

Coo-Coo backed away. His mother said that spells and magic were stupidness, and the Lord on high forbid it, but still . . . this business was nothing he wanted to know about. He wanted to see the nets full of silver bonito and flying fish spilled out on the damp sand. He wanted to sit in the shade of the seagrapes with the old fishermen and listen to them talk of the storms they'd conquered and, indeed, the big fish that had got away. He wanted to watch them grill fat filets on sticks on an open driftwood fire right on the beach.

He started to run. One of his shoelaces caught on a twisted root that had thrust itself up from the earth. He staggered and fell to his knees. As he tried to untangle the lace, he saw another piece of the red cloth, half-buried in the muddy ground. He pulled at it, and uncovered a bundle that contained something hard. He started to breathe heavily as he got to his feet. More obeah? He looked around, fearful that someone was watching him from deep in the gloomy bush.

"Ellis! Where you at?" His mother's voice reached him from way up the hill. "Schooltime. You come now, you hear me?"

Coo-Coo heard her. When she called him by his given name, she was mad. He thrust the red cloth bundle into the pocket of his shorts, and looked back one more time at the terrible photo nailed to the tree with nine long nails. Then he was scrambling up the other side of the gully toward the abandoned sugar mill, its gray stone blocks overgrown with vines. It was a remnant of the big sugar plantation of the last century where Coo-Coo's ancestors had cut the cane.

He stepped in through the open round doorway and startled the green lizards that climbed the walls. The stone walls were comforting: old and solid. The place was empty except for ends of cigarettes from courting couples, and old fertilizer and seed sacks left by the local farmers who sometimes stored things there, some broken boxes, a pile of dried coconut fronds.

Coo-Coo peered back out the door. The mango rose majestically above the other trees growing in the dim gully. A king of the woods flew from one branch to another and cocked his bright green head warily at the sight of Coo-Coo. Everything seemed perfectly normal. He knelt on the floor and fumbled with the knot of the white cord used to tie up the bundle. Suddenly it loosened, and the cloth fell open. He saw the glint of gold and the sparkle of gems, and to his horror, what appeared to be a lock of dark hair. Another magic sign for sure.

He frantically retied the bundle and looked around. He saw a chink in the stones of the far wall, big enough to thrust his hand in. He quickly stuffed the red cloth bundle as far back as he could until it disappeared from sight. His heart was still beating fast, but he sighed with relief.

"Fllis!" Coo Coo headed away from his mother's voice. "You come here now!"

He took the path through the coconut plantation that had replaced the fields of sugar cane and was now part of the Indigo Hill estate. He crossed a field where a farmer was already at work pulling up tall slender cassava plants and piling the tubers in a basket for the market. In the next field, another farmer was cultivating rows of aubergine. Coo-Coo avoided them both.

It took him barely fifteen minutes to reach the foot of the steep path up to the big house.

Indigo Hill, at the end of a long climb, was another kind of world from the ramshackle cluster of houses where Coo-Coo lived with his mother and sisters and aunts and cousins, Uncle Derrick, and the matriarch, old Mamee Joe. Indigo Hill was always orderly. The big house was always freshly painted white with lacy blue fretwork and louvered shutters. A row of guest bungalows was hidden behind ixora bushes heavy with red blossoms and lantana shrubs covered with pinkish flowers. The grass on the lawns and along the drive was trimmed, and the hibiscus bushes were always cut back just so. Someone raked the gravel drive every day, and cleaned the pool down the hill above the sea, whether or not Lord Farfaine or others were in residence.

Tante Marva, the English lord's island housekeeper, was wielding a dry coconut broom to sweep the pounded earth around the cookhouse and the household storage sheds half-hidden behind a wall of flame red poinsettias. She shook her head at the sight of him.

"Boy, you missing school again today? How you going to be a big man on the island you can't read your lessons?" But Marva laughed. She was a cousin of the father Coo-Coo hadn't seen since he went off to work in Canada three years before, and an easygoing woman except when she was managing matters pertaining to m'lord's household.

"Going to pull seine," Coo-Coo said. He hesitated, then said, "Tante, I saw . . ." He stopped. Suddenly he didn't feel well, as though the terrors of the gully had sent a fever through him that stopped his voice.

"Something painin' you?" Marva asked. She bent down and scrutinized his face.

"No big t'ing," he said, and looked away. The feverish feeling passed. "Got to get to the bay." He knew Tante Marva would understand about the obeah, but now he couldn't bring himself to tell about the picture and the nails and the red cloth bundle he'd hidden at the old sugar mill. Gold was valuable, you could buy all kinds of things with gold, even boats like the ones the men at Arawak Bay had. But if the gold was protected by a spell . . .

Marva gently felt his head for fever. Coo-Coo liked the way she always wore a gray dress and white apron, like a uniform to show her status at the house. Her silver and gold bangle bracelets, beloved by local women, clanked musically as she stood up. "You get yourself fit, you hear? M'lord coming soon, after the new year, himself and those fancy friends from London and New York. Plenty of surprises comin' this year, boy," she said and laughed. She could have been young or old. He knew she was older than Derrick. She'd been at Indigo Hill since she was a girl. Her face showed no wrinkles, but she had wise, dark eyes. "I'm going to ask m'lord to take you on to keep the pool clear of leaves to earn a few coppers. The man always glad to do these little favors for me. You like that?"

"I guess," Coo-Coo said. Derrick worked all the time for Lord Farfaine, minding the estate, and he earned plenty of money, which he put into the guest house he owned near town.

The guest house. A woman had come to stay there a few days ago, a white woman like the one in the picture. Derrick said she was writing a book or some such thing. Coo-Coo had seen her once at the market. Coo-Coo froze. Never mind the woman at the guest house. Miss Georgie was coming from England, maybe stepping right into the middle of a terrible danger.

"Ellis St. Joseph," Marva said, "there is somethin' bad troubling you."

"Is nothing. Nothing." He started to shuffle backwards, to get away from Tante Marva's sharp eyes. Then he blurted out, "Is true you can kill somebody with a spell, Tante? The boys say . . ."

Marva laughed. "Is that what's bothering you? What have those fellows been saying now? Boy, you kill somebody with a gun or a cutlass, you don't go worrying about obeah. Put it out of your head. People try all kind of nonsense. It is nothing." Coo-Coo relaxed. "That's better," Marva said. "And if you bring me a nice fat bonito from the beach, I won't tell your momma you missing school again."

"She knows," Coo-Coo said ruefully. "I gone." Then he was skittering away, feeling immeasurably better, and safe for a day from the confining walls of the schoolroom.

Marva watched thoughtfully as he raced past the chaconia trees heavy with bright red blossoms and the pink oleander hedges, past the big white house and the bungalows. He was soon out of sight, scrambling down the steep path toward the beach, where a line of seine pullers was starting to haul in the huge curved net, step by step, pull by pull. He left his sneakers high on the beach, and took his place at the end of the line.

The waves swirled around his skinny dark legs as he pulled and pulled, and soon he was standing ankle-deep in the mass of fish the net had brought ashore: flying fish, bonito, some jacks, a baby barracuda that had strayed away from its coral reef.

"Is a good catch, man." The fisherman in charge squatted beside the mound of fish and quickly gutted a bonito. He threw the entrails into the sea, and tossed the fish into a basket.

The memory of the mutilated picture nailed to the tree flitted through Coo-Coo's mind.

Maybe he had stopped some bad magic by taking the

red bundle from the gully. He wished he had it now so he could toss it into the sea like the fish guts and it would be gone and forgotten forever.

"But what t'ing is this?" The fisherman paused in his work and stood up. A man some distance down the beach was shouting and waving his arms frantically to get their attention. The village women who had come to buy fish fresh from the sea stopped their gossiping and looked.

"Coo-Coo, see what the man want," the fisherman said. "Run."

Coo-Coo kept to the damp sand at the water's edge so he could run faster. He passed a line of brightly painted fishing pirogues that had been drawn up on the beach, waiting for their bottoms to be scraped. He was nearly out of breath when he reached the man who had signaled, an old man from the tiny village at the end of the beach.

"What . . ." Coo-Coo stopped short at the look on the man's face.

Then he saw a person lying on the ground under the seagrape bushes, half-hidden by the drooping branches. He took a step closer. It was a woman, light-skinned but not white, an island woman he didn't recognize. He could see the blood on her face and throat.

"Go back, boy. Bring the men. She dead. Someone cut she with a cutlass."

"Who . . . ?"

"I never saw she before. She not from here, boy. *Go*, I'm telling you. Fast, fast. Have them run up to the big house, call the constable."

Coo-Coo ran. His heart was pounding and he felt weak with the fever and the memory of the dark gully.

The Caribbean was blue, blue. Green-blue, pale blue, and aquamarine. The trade winds blew gently from the east across Boucan, and today there were no rain clouds in the clear sky.

Chapter 1

A cluster of silver bells jingled softly as Lady Margaret Priam considered where to place the last blue ball on her small but incredibly expensive Christmas tree.

Back home in England at Priam's Priory, old Potts would have gone off and chopped down a decent tree somewhere on the estate, and it wouldn't have cost a penny. New York was different in that respect, especially in her high-priced Upper East Side neighborhood, where today it was grim and gray with the promise of snow.

"Of course I know Lord Farfaine," she said. Her back was to Prince Paul Castrocani as she answered his question. "Everyone does. Everyone in England, that is to say, and quite a few here."

Paul was sprawled in one of the overstuffed, chintz-covered chairs of the living room in Margaret's apartment. He was listening intently to what she had to say. ("The darkly handsome young prince," according to the New York social columns. "Totally awesome," according to young women who passed him on the street or came face-to-face with him from behind a shop counter.)

"Jimmie's completely dotty," Margaret added. "I haven't heard much about him for a while. That's what happens when you take the expatriate route as I did and get lost in New York. He was an acquaintance of my father's. The family name is Hose-Griffith, the title is scarcely ancient." The Priams and their titles went back to the days of the Tudors. The Hose-Griffiths' did not. "Daddy actually couldn't bear him, but they'd been to the same public school, different decades. You know the old-school thing."

Paul didn't. His schooling had been erratic, starting in Italy, moving on to Switzerland, and ending with two terms at a Texas university. He certainly hadn't been admitted there on the basis of a remarkable academic record, but his mother Carolyn Sue, now Mrs. Benton Hoopes of Dallas and once married to Paul's penniless, charming father Prince Aldo Castrocani, was very, very rich. Paul suspected that she must have paid for a building.

"Why the interest in Jimmie Hose-Griffith? He doesn't strike me as your sort. I say, could you use more eggnog?" Margaret waved toward the kitchen. "I have it here around the holidays. . . ."

"It's the rum they like," Paul said. "If I take this job Lord Farfaine is talking about, I shall be awash in rum. It would be the local drink, I assume."

"A job with Jimmie? On that Caribbean island of his? Is that wise?" Margaret opened her blue eyes wide and ran her hand through her short blond hair. In her mid-thirties now, she was a good ten years older than Paul, and had always thought of herself as considerably wiser. This seemed a moment to remind him of that. "Life in Lord Farfaine's orbit," she said seriously, "would not be smooth sailing. The whole Hose-Griffith family has always had a rackety reputation."

"I thought you would say something like that," Paul

said. "But I have a great fondness for the tropics, and I do need a job, since my mother has chosen to limit my allowance. It is not 'his' island. He merely owns a house and some land."

"What's the island? Boucan? Off the beaten track rather, but I hear that amusing people drop by to see him."

Margaret stood back to admire her tree. Her significant other, Sam De Vere of the New York City police, would surely find it too, too aesthetically precious, but Margaret liked the silver-and-blue motif, with a few crystal ornaments among the tiny white lights.

"I hope," Margaret said finally, "that you are not asking *me* for permission to accept."

Paul shrugged, an eloquent Italian shrug, learned at his father's Italian knee.

"Go ahead then, but keep a return air ticket with you. Have a lovely time. I myself wouldn't turn down a chance at the Caribbean in winter. I understand that Jimmie's place is divine."

"Indigo Hill," Paul murmured.

"The tiniest delicious hints of decadent goings-on have reached my ears. He's famous for his parties. . . ."

"I need only keep social arrangements in order for two months," Paul said. "It does not sound decadent to me. It sounds like a place where nothing worse than a bad sunburn happens. It is said to be quite a beauty spot."

What Lord Farfaine had said to Paul was, "Absolutely idyllic. Love it. Always have. Family goes back years in that part of the world. Sugar. Copra. Indigo. Spend at least two months there every year. Princess Margaret drops by from Mustique, time to time. Rent it out otherwise. Make a fortune. Big party planned. Need a fella like you for the festivities, what? Good looking, got a title, all that. Pay you well."

How could Paul resist?

"There is to be some grand celebration," Paul said. "An anniversary of Lord Farfaine's current marriage." Paul was not certain if it was the second, third, or fourth year of the union, but Lord Farfaine didn't appear to be certain either. At the age of sixty-five, perhaps it didn't matter, although it surely did to his bride, who was said to be some forty years younger.

"That would be the third wife," Margaret said absently. Her tree looked a bit lopsided, and she wondered how she could straighten it without disturbing the decorations.

"Jane," Paul said eagerly. "She's American, not English. I have not met her."

Margaret said, "Sophie was his first. Mummy knew her well. Jimmie was so impossible that she bolted twenty years or so ago. Now she's an Austrian countess or something. I know the son, Anthony. He was a bore even as a callow youth. The Honorable Georgina has the usual genteelly lurid rumors trailing after her. Nobody really knew the second wife. Odd, arty, definitely not cut out for English country life. She lasted only a short time, with silly rumors galore about why Jimmie got rid of her—a lover, selling off family heirlooms, mistreating a horse. They said that she tried to kill Jimmie, or perhaps it was the other way 'round." Margaret shrugged. "I know nothing of the present wife, although Poppy would have all the sordid details."

Poppy Dill wrote the printable gossip in her "Social Scene" newspaper column, and kept the unprintable stuff in her head. Indeed, "darkly handsome" was Poppy's contribution to Prince Paul's social persona.

"Lord Farfaine appears to be very rich," Paul said cautiously. "I hope this would mean that the daughter would be . . ."

"Aha! Potentially rich as well. Georgina would be about your age." Margaret grinned at her friend, whose Italian-Texan good looks and social graces most young women found highly attractive. "I wonder if she would consent to consort with the hired man."

"I am a prince," Paul said with some dignity. "I was for a short time an international banker, before United National chose to dispense with my services because of that recession business."

"And you are also the son of a prince and of a woman whose personal wealth and social reputation are legendary." Margaret was fond of Carolyn Sue, who managed to keep her Maud Frizon-shod feet firmly on the ground and remain unblinded by the dazzle of the diamonds she was so easily able to afford. "Perhaps the Farfaine lassie would find your credentials as appealing as your Roman nose and those dark Mediterranean eyes. Does that help you decide on whether to take the job?"

"Georgina is said to be a beauty. I have already accepted the position," Paul said sheepishly.

Margaret paused. "Have you indeed?" She frowned. "I hope it is a limited contract. If matters turn messy, you wouldn't want to have to extricate yourself from long-term servitude. Jimmie is not known for being entirely beyond reproach in his business dealings, although bless him, he does seem to have a lot of money to support his life-style. Daddy always referred to him as an old pirate." She rearranged an ornament. "Keep me informed. Postal cards with scenic views on the one side and the goings-on on the other. You can ring me if you're at a loss on some point of upper-class etiquette. I suppose they do have the telephone in that part of the world. And if you're here in the city next week, come meet De Vere and me for Christmas Eve."

"For Christmas I go to Dallas to my mother. And

Ben, of course." Paul did not hold his stepfather in especially high regard, since he had been instrumental in cutting short Paul's carefree years of junior jetsetting. "Then I shall be occupied with my wardrobe for the tropics. I leave immediately after the first of the year. I hope to persuade my mother to give me access to her Neiman-Marcus account. I should look my best."

"The old problem of *bella figura*," Margaret said. "Fine plumage to attract a mate."

"I must attend to my future," Paul said stiffly. "I have always said that finding a wealthy wife would be carrying on the Castrocani family tradition." He looked up at Margaret from his comfortable chair. "Will you and De Vere ever marry?"

Margaret smiled sweetly. "Do you ever ask him?"

Paul and Sam De Vere had for a couple of years shared a rather fine duplex apartment in the Chelsea neighborhood of New York, in a building fortuitously owned by Paul's mother. The rent was therefore reasonable. It was a satisfactory arrangement, since Paul and De Vere maintained vastly different life-styles and hours of waking and sleeping.

"I would not be so bold as to ask him," Paul said, "although my mother has. She is unable to hold her tongue when she feels she is entitled to know something."

"And what did De Vere have to tell Carolyn Sue?"

"I understand that he assured her that she would be the second to know. You, presumably, would be the first."

"Perhaps," Margaret said, "if I get through an extended period without coming upon a dead body, De Vere might consider taking on a quiet, retiring woman who has spurned bad habits like murder."

Paul shuddered, remembering past incidents involving murder, Margaret, and occasionally himself.

"Although," she added, "I might choose not to accept." She finally found the perfect place for the last ornament, and decided not to risk a catastrophe by trying to make the tree stand exactly upright. "Possibly a challenging position with Lord Farfaine will be a character-building experience for you," she said. "Ben Hoopes should be pleased that you are earning money."

Paul considered this. "I believe that my stepfather barely approves. He dislikes seeing me without a job, but I do not think this is the job he had in mind." He sighed. "It may be that the position will assist me in putting myself in touch with my inner self. Teach me who I am, test my inner resources." Paul stood up and paced about the spacious room, pausing at a window to stare out at the Manhattan high-rises against the cloudy sky.

"Several attractive young women I have met recently at parties seemed very interested in inner resources," he said. "Finding the inner child. Revealing the inner man. At the time I found myself agreeing with them. They were quite stunning." He gestured to indicate a certain voluptuousness on the part of the young women.

Margaret laughed, but without much mirth. "Darling Paul, don't be misled. The job may teach you about living for a time on a tiny island where you are white and upper class, and most of the population is black and likely living at subsistence level. Lord Farfaine's family and guests will be petulantly overprivileged, and wealthy in fact or merely in appearance. Thoughtless luxury on the one hand and resentment on the other. There's a bit of that in New York, but on Boucan it will be concentrated on a spot of land surrounded by miles of water. You will have to be the liaison between those two worlds. Can you do that?"

"*Certo*. Certainly," Paul said confidently. "You remember that I have known both wealth and poverty. I have no doubt that I can do it.''

Margaret smiled, and took his glass to refill it with her top-quality holiday eggnog. She wasn't going to be the one to destroy his confidence.

Besides, simple excess in one's style of living was nothing to worry about, and if that was the worst one could say about Lord Farfaine and his family . . . Actually, wretched excess was more accurate.

Then why am I worried? she asked herself, and answered her own question: Because my father called him worse than a pirate. The word he used was ''criminal,'' although it seemed incongruous when applied to the jovial, plump white-haired man she remembered.

She handed Paul his glass of eggnog. ''You must tell me about the plans,'' she said.

''Lord Farfaine will be faxing the details, the guest list, and so forth.''

''Plenty of expense money and all that?''

''There is an account in the bank in Boucan to draw on.'' Paul shifted uneasily in his chair. ''I expect he will explain how I am to do that.''

''I expect so,'' she said. ''He's in London now, is he?''

''Somewhere for the holidays,'' Paul said. ''He travels about quite a bit. He has many business interests. I understand his son is involved in his affairs.''

Margaret grimaced. ''Quite a pair. The eccentric shark and his tedious and conventional son.'' It was beginning to seem like a good idea to persuade Poppy Dill, who really did know everything, to share her files on the Hose-Griffiths. ''I'm sure everything will be fine, but you will ring if there's a problem.''

''Do not be such a . . . a mother hen,'' Paul said. ''This is one job that I can do.''

Chapter 2

Two weeks later, Paul sat at a desk in his mother's obscenely large house in North Dallas and muttered to himself, "I can do it."

Christmas was behind him, the new year a few days ahead. His bags were ready to be filled with a new tropical wardrobe. He had in hand a ticket to Boucan by a complicated route through the Caribbean, bringing him eventually to Boucan's bigger sister island, where he would catch a local plane to Boucan, ten minutes away by air. He would be met at the Boucan airstrip by a Mr. Jackson. ("Old Derrick's an island boy, but he's been about the world a bit. Couldn't manage without him. Grand fellow," according to Lord Farfaine.)

He again read through the mass of faxes from Lord Farfaine that had been pouring into Carolyn Sue's house through the holidays: provisions being shipped from the United States, England, other islands. Guest lists, ever-changing. Tentative, scheduled, and rescheduled arrivals of yachts and private planes. Trunks of fancy dress to be assembled for the festivities which would apparently take place during some local carnival celebration.

"A *dead* woman?" Paul said aloud upon reading the

18

most recent missive faxed from London. Suddenly he had a sinking feeling.

"Do not be concerned about the dead woman. She was apparently murdered on a beach near Indigo Hill. Local matter, nothing to do with us," Lord Farfaine had written. "I will have a treasure hunt this year. Be assured that no pirate treasure is to be found on Boucan, so you will bury something." He'd signed the fax "Farfaine."

When Paul had labored at United National Bank, he had had any number of eager young women willing to keep his business in order. Here in Dallas, his mother's competent social secretary was far too busy to do more than supply him with several yellow lined tablets and a handful of pencils. He could not ask her advice on buried treasure. His mother would probably suggest he plant some gold nuggets, which was a fine idea but not realistic. As a forcibly retired banker, Paul kept an eye on gold prices out of habit.

He wrote on a pad, "Forget dead woman. Bury something." Then he picked up the latest sheet to arrive by fax from Lord Farfaine.

"Here is the plan for housing my guests. The children stay in the big house, and the rest in the bungalows. You need not worry about my mother. She's an old West Indies hand."

Paul looked up from the letter. His mother? Then he wrote on his yellow tablet, "Mother, old hand. West Indies," and hastened to pick up the telephone.

"Margaret? Can you talk? It sounds as though you have people in." Paul was beginning to miss the uncomplicated if penurious life he had led in New York.

"De Vere, Dianne and Charlie Stark, a few others for a pre–New Year's dinner," Margaret said. "Even Poppy consented to join us. It's been years since she deigned to leave her apartment for an ordinary mortal like me. I've been hoping you'd ring. How are the prelims to your great adventure coming along?''

"There's a dead woman," Paul began.

"Dead? In Texas?"

"Boucan," Paul said glumly. "Lord Farfaine said not to worry, nothing to do with us. She was murdered on a beach near Indigo Hill. I wish you were to be on Boucan with me."

"Have Jimmie invite me then," she said lightly. "I'm very good with dead people. But the invitation must come with a pre-paid ticket. My funds are low as usual. I really must see about getting a job myself for the new year."

"There's also Lord Farfaine's mother."

"Good lord, is *she* still alive? She must be a hundred. Let me just ask Poppy." After a moment, Margaret was back on the line. "Alys, the dowager Lady Farfaine, is well into her eighties. Comes from a sugar-planting family that goes back to slave days. Poppy thinks her father was some sort of governor general in that part of the world for a time. Married the old Lord Farfaine during one of her London seasons. Probably very grand, in her own mind at least."

"The job appears to be moving on beyond feeding and clothing the guests, and arranging for beds."

"And soothing wounded egos, mending brief shattered love affairs, and looking out for a suitable bride for yourself," Margaret continued for him.

"This is serious," Paul said. "There is treasure to be buried for a treasure hunt through the palm trees. Since there is no treasure on the island, I must bury it. What would people of Lord Farfaine's sort consider treasure? And where would I bury it?"

He had already considered purloining some trinket

belonging to his mother and passing it off as treasure. Carolyn Sue's worst trash could easily be treasure to most of the world.

"Darling, find some congenial local person and take advice," Margaret said. "Jimmie has run the place there long enough for everyone to know the drill. I'm sure many a false treasure has been buried and dug up over the years to entertain Jimmie's crowd. Well, go on. Tell me who is to be there. I have time. Everyone here is happily eating and drinking."

Paul read off the names on the final guest list as Margaret annotated via long distance. The family: Lord Farfaine and his most recent wife. ("She'd be about Georgina's age," Margaret said. "I wonder if they get on. Probably not.")

The Honorable Anthony Hose-Griffith, the heir, with his wife Fiona. ("Fiona once had her eye on my brother," Margaret said, "who fortunately would have none of it. I should have hated to see her end up the Countess of Brayfield. You've had my opinion of Anthony.") And, finally, Lord Farfaine's mother.

The houseguests occasioned a few sighs from Margaret.

"Ninni Campos is one of those aging Pacific Rim femme fatales," she said. "Surely you've heard of her. Will go anywhere for a good time as long as it's free. Tyrone Pace is the cricketer, world-famous in those circles. From Trinidad or some such place. Quite an eclectic party. Who else?"

"There are some sirs and ladies. A Miss P. Quince, a journalist who will write a little story on Lord Farfaine's festivities for an American magazine."

Margaret had never heard of P. Quince. "I suspect she's a social climber who's wangled an invitation on nearly false pretenses," Margaret said. "But make sure everyone behaves in case she's the real thing. I'll ask Poppy about her.''

"Carlos San Basilio. I have met him," Paul said. ''He once lured away a fetching Swedish model from my side at a cafe in Portofino. I was very young at the time.''

"Dear old Carlos!" Margaret said. "A professional Latin lover is just what any party needs. He's probably after the Honorable Georgina's money. Don't pout over the telephone, Paul. You're ever so much more attractive than he, and he's much older now. He's been romancing and seducing and prospering from it for years and years.''

"The list of guests who will come for a day or two on their yachts or planes is too long to read, but they are quite prominent people," Paul said. "All I must do for them is see that they are transported to the house for the grand fete, and given carnival costumes if they wish them. Lord Farfaine's man on the island has supposedly received all the shipments by now.''

"Then everything is perfectly fine and in order," Margaret said. "I will be thinking of you.''

Later that night, when the guests had gone and Margaret and De Vere were making lazy attempts to remove the glasses and dishes to the kitchen, she said, "I'm concerned about Paul. Jimmie Hose-Griffith and that new wife of his will eat him alive. Not to mention Georgina, who has quite a reputation.''

"Anglo-Caribbean lowlifes." De Vere did not have a high opinion of so-called aristocrats, although he made an exception for Margaret. "Paul will be at ease in that milieu, wouldn't you say? I'd judge he's spent a good part of his life knowing the right people, the right places, the right kinds of cars and wines and tailors and five-star hotels. Knows how to talk to the servants . . ."

"That's the point, partly," Margaret said. "He's going to *be* a servant. And I simply don't trust that family. Jimmie appears the amiable eccentric, but he's as sane and clever as can be. Why choose Paul? He has absolutely no qualifications for the job."

De Vere laughed. "He had no qualifications for that banking job his stepfather found him either. Maybe this Lord Whatnot is thinking of him as a potential mate for the daughter, someone to settle her down." He chuckled. "Put them together on an island with no escape but plenty of warm tropical nights, sunny days, young flesh baking in the sun. Don't worry."

"I shall," Margaret said. "I wish I were going to be there." She shrugged. "Paul said something about a dead woman."

"What?" De Vere nearly dropped the tray of glasses he was carrying into the kitchen.

"Do be careful of the crystal, luv," Margaret said. "Family heirlooms. Did you know you look awfully good tonight?" De Vere had consented to abandon his usual pressed jeans for the evening and wear gray flannel slacks and a black cashmere pullover. He looked quite unlike a police detective, although his expression now was that of a perturbed significant other.

"You look rather fine yourself," he said, "and I don't want to hear about a dead woman, even one several thousand miles away."

"Is Boucan that far from New York? I thought it an easy flight from here."

"Margaret," De Vere said with a definite warning tone, "don't even think about it."

"Sam, I'm just thinking of making a few phone calls. For Paul's sake. To reassure myself."

She knew who she'd call: her brother at Priam's Priory to find out what he'd heard lately of the Hose-Griffith family. Perhaps her former husband, who was marginally in the financial world in London and who probably knew Anthony. Poppy Dill certainly, to find out about this P. Quince and Lord Farfaine's family. Perhaps Poppy would put her onto someone at the paper where her "Social Scene" column appeared to check if the wire services had anything on Boucan, although a local murder did not seem like the stuff of hot international news.

She wondered where Lord Farfaine was spending the holidays.

"Let's leave the rest of the clearing up," Margaret said. "My fairly well-documented maid will be in tomorrow. She takes great care with the crystal."

"My dear Lord Farfaine," Paul wrote, "the arrangements are in place. I leave for Boucan in three days, and will bury something as you have requested."

Paul looked again at the map of the Caribbean he had pinned to the wall. It was one of the few he'd found that even identified Boucan and the slightly larger nearby island that together shared a government.

"I certainly can do this job," Paul said to himself. Then he added to his letter: "I was speaking only recently to Lady Margaret Priam, who now lives in New York, and is an intimate friend. She mentioned being acquainted with you and your son. You will remember her late father, the earl of Brayfield."

Let him take the hint and invite her, and then let Margaret wangle a ticket.

Paul faxed his last letter to the Farfaine flat in London.

"Paul, darlin', you seem to be takin' as much luggage as me when I go to Europe for three months." Carolyn Sue paused at Paul's door.

They were headed for a farewell party for Paul at the Hoopes ranch outside of Dallas, and she was dressed Western today: Thousand-dollar boots with lethally pointed toes, sharply creased jeans, and a jacket of soft beige leather with discreet fringe. Her devoted hair stylist had added some girlish ringlets to her blindingly blond coiffure.

"Ben and I are so pleased you're takin' charge of your life. And your daddy would be proud too." Carolyn Sue tended to become sentimental when speaking of her former husband.

Prince Aldo, far away in Italy, might indeed find it amusing to learn the sort of job Paul had taken on, but Prince Aldo was not really keen on jobs per se. Paul was planning to send him a postcard from Boucan.

"We're leavin' for the ranch in fifteen minutes. They phoned to say the barbecue is ready, and you know, honey, those girls who are comin' jes' to meet you are *real* sweet. And they come from real nice families."

Paul knew her mother meant "rich."

Carolyn Sue hugged her six-foot-plus son. "I sure do wish you'd settle down. It's about time . . ."

"*Principessa*, I will know when the right one appears." Paul was thinking about Lord Farfaine's daughter.

Chapter 3

*D*errick Jackson was also thinking of the Honorable Georgina Hose-Griffith, daughter of Lord Farfaine, as he made his way down the narrow, steep road to Boucan harbor shortly after the start of the new year.

Reports of sightings of Georgina on the island were a fairly common occurrence. In the past month, four or five people had claimed to have seen her: a girl ashore from a yacht who bore a modest resemblance to the long-legged, bold Georgina, with her dark hair and eyes of startling green. Derrick was bound by a solemn promise to Lord Farfaine to investigate all such rumors.

And Boucan was bursting with rumors. The mystery of the unknown dead woman over at Arawak Bay before Christmas had caused a lot of wild talk. Indeed, at first people had said it was Georgina who was dead, and when that proved untrue, they said the woman had come to Boucan with a boyfriend from the big island, twenty miles away across the sea, and less than an hour by a fast boat. People were saying their day at the beach had ended in murder. A lot of nonsense went on over at Arawak Bay that Derrick paid no heed to. No one admitted to seeing strangers arrive. Still, people were still

talking all kinds of rubbish, even though it had happened before Christmas. The police, however, were not
talking, not even the constable Derrick had gone to
school with.

Derrick reached the main street of the town.
"Quaint" was a word applied to Chatham by the few
tourists who managed to find their way to the island,
and by the yachtsmen who put into the so-called marina
for the night and perhaps a lazy day on the island's
uninhabited beaches before they headed off to more
comfortable or glamorous ports.

The local people did have an eye for color, painting
and repainting their small wooden and cement-block
houses, when they could afford the paint, in startling
pinks, blues, yellows, and reds. The adventurous tried
combinations of coral and lavender, the more conservative stuck with white—with touches of flashy color
for the louvered shutters and airy galleries on the story
above the street. Anyone who looked closely, however,
could detect how fragile and poor was the substance of
the buildings behind their shaggy hibiscus bushes, as
though they were dressed in flimsy carnival costumes,
meant to last only a day.

The little red guest house he ran was solid compared
to the town houses, and it was away from Chatham,
right on a beautiful, long, empty beach and surrounded
by palm trees. He'd built it himself, and it was under
the firm management of his sister Alvina, who came in
every day to cook and clean while he made sure it was
kept in good repair.

The problem was filling up the rooms. The one guest
he had presently scarcely paid his expenses. At least
she made few demands and kept to herself. She was
odd, but he had given up trying to understand the white
tourists who bothered to find Boucan. Most of them

went up to the hills for bird-watching, an activity he also failed to understand.

Derrick said polite good mornings to the ample, laughing women from up-country who had known him since he was born and who were bringing their bananas, papayas, mangos, and pigeon peas to the daily market. He pressed back from the street to allow passage of the lumbering green-and-white bus that was headed for the coast road to the small fishing villages.

Derrick reached the rum shop that faced the harbor, and served as the town gathering spot from dawn until well after dark.

"Derrick, my boy!"

"Here come de Captain!"

"What's happenin'?"

Two of the three men at one table out front were laborers who had been out before dawn to cutlass the grass that rapidly overgrew the open drainage trenches along the roads. The third was a town layabout who was the son of Derrick's mother's sister's man and therefore a relation of sorts. Derrick waved. "Morning, morning. You drinkin' your beer so early, Boots?"

The semi-relation beckoned for him to join them, but Derrick shook his head. "I got business in town, Boots. Comin' back just now."

"Lookin' for m'lord's girl, are you? I see she at the club real late last night. I was with those boys from Arawak Bay, they came to town in Fitzie's truck."

"You never saw her," Derrick said blandly, but the possibility of a genuine Georgina sighting was likely. "You don't even know the girl. She never speak to you face-to-face."

"True, but I see she, huggin' up with the Red Man. They dancing and laughing." Boots stuck his chin in the direction of the marina where only two boats were moored. One was a sleek, two-masted schooner that had put in yesterday for provisions before sailing to the Grenadines. The other was a dumpy but serviceable sloop with a tall mast and the mainsail furled. It was painted black with white trim. Derrick recognized it as Rusty Keating's. He flew no quarantine flag, so he had probably cleared customs on Betun, Boucan's sister island.

"He come in yesterday or the evening before," Boots said. "He says he was bringing trunks for Indigo Hill. Man, we going to have bacchanal when m'lord start partying."

It always set the island agog when Lord Farfaine was due to bring in his family and friends like a noisy flock of exotic white birds to settle on the island before migrating onward.

"Red Man find a tourist girl on some island and bring she along is all," Derrick said.

Rusty might have picked up Georgina on St. Thomas or St. Lucia or even across twenty miles of sea on Betun where the interisland planes landed.

"I got to find the Red Man," Derrick said.

"He's on the boat," Boots said helpfully. "I see he come on the deck this morning rubbing his eyes to push away last night's rum and Coke. Then he go down below again. You want me to come?"

"My business," Derrick said shortly, and walked toward the marina, which occupied one side of the harbor. The commercial pier where the local supply boats and the interisland steamer docked was on the other.

Boucan Marina was a simple affair. There was only a fuel pump and a ramshackle shop selling bits of sailing gear, some fishing equipment, and blocks of ice from the town icehouse. Anyone who wanted more went to the shops along Chatham's main street or to the open-air market for fresh provisions. Lord Farfaine wanted to build a competing marina at Arawak Bay for the convenience of his friends. It had engendered some bad feelings around the island.

Derrick walked out on the narrow pier to Keating's boat. It had no glamour, but it was well-cared for. Rusty Keating sailed it all around the Caribbean in calm seas and through near hurricanes with equal ease, carrying occasional paying passengers and smuggling occasional dutiable goods that someone wanted to slip past customs officials. No big thing, but Derrick wondered how close to the law Rusty sailed. He really didn't care to know the details.

Keating did not look especially fearsome when Derrick found him below, lying on a bunk, unshaven and still apparently wearing yesterday's clothes. Derrick looked around. No sign of a woman, Georgina or otherwise. Rusty kept his boat in order. The tiny galley with its propane stove was spotless. Keating had once shown him the LORAN navigation system and the electric anchor winch, the scuba tanks and the diving boat. Derrick was comfortable only in local boats, and he certainly could never be happy living on a thirty-six-foot sloop.

"I know you're there," Rusty said without opening his eyes. "I just don't know who you are." He opened one eye. "Derrick, my man. A welcoming party." Keating's voice had a trace of West Indian lilt. He was, he claimed, native to these parts—a remnant of the English planters who had once held these islands in their grip for the sake of their sugar, spices, and dyewoods. Derrick supposed that it was true.

"Don't stir yourself," Derrick said. "I just looking for Miss Georgina."

Rusty struggled to raise himself up on his elbows. "She's not here. She found a ride to Indigo Hill after the club closed last night. I'm not interested in bringing down the wrath of Lord Farfaine on my head, my friend. He puts a little business my way."

Derrick and Rusty were acquaintances, not really friends. There was too wide a gulf between them, even though the one was at ease as a white man in the local black world, and the other from the island world had spent five years in America working in hotels. Rusty had no home but his boat, but he managed to live pretty well. Derrick had no home but the one among the family houses at the end of St. Joseph's Trace on the hill overlooking Chatham. His life wasn't all that easy.

"What you doing back here so soon?" Derrick asked. "When you drop off the tourist, you said you weren't coming back until end of January."

Rusty yawned and scratched his stomach. "Some trunks and crates for Lord Farfaine were in customs over on Betun. Thought to do a good deed for you, man, bring them across. Some gone up to the house already. You could get the rest tomorrow." Rusty sat up. "I hear talk over on the big island that they never find out who that woman was."

"Woman?" Derrick said cautiously. Rusty always had women hanging about. They seemed to find him glamorous and heroic.

"Man, you got to do something about dead women on the beach," Rusty said. "It's bad for tourism. Is all they're talking about still over on the big island. Come ashore on Boucan and you're dead." He seemed to find that amusing.

"Don't like that kind of talk, Rusty," Derrick said shortly. "Where did you find Georgie?"

"She was here at the marina when I came back last

night. She and her grandmother hitched a ride on a seaplane ahead of the rest. Tante Alys is really something."

Derrick disapproved of the nearly disrespectful reference to Lady Alys, but Rusty didn't notice.

"Georgina and I danced a little and drank a glass or two at the club, and before midnight strikes, I decide I'm going to stick around for the parties. You never know who you're going to meet at Indigo Hill. Maybe I'll pick up a charter from some rich American lady. You running his affairs?"

"I do these things for Lord Farfaine like always," Derrick said evasively. "Seeing to the provisions and such. Keeping a lookout on the big house when he's away. He pays me okay."

"And you have an excuse to keep your eye on pretty Miss Georgie, eh?"

"That is part of my arrangement with him," Derrick said shortly. The distance between Derrick and Georgina was far vaster than between him and Rusty.

"Never mind, my man," Keating said. "She's nothing but trouble. That woman I brought still at your guest house?"

"She's here," Derrick said. "She's no trouble, keeps to herself. I'm getting more business. Some guests in Lord Farfaine's party booked to spend a few days."

"You people have to get more tourists. Can't live on m'lord's pretty birds of paradise."

"I got my plans," Derrick said seriously.

"You too, too serious," Keating said. "Like the tax collector or the constable. Still, it's a serious responsibility to be arranging the big fete."

"M'lord got a boy from America comin' to handle it this year," Derrick said and sounded bitter. "I'm fetching him at the airstrip this evening. M'lord says he's a prince."

"The whole bloody world is full of people calling themselves prince or duke or count. People calling themselves anything they want. Something about these islands make people crazy. I'm thinking of packing it in and getting lost in a big city."

Suddenly Rusty decided it was time to lie back on his bunk.

"You come up to the house, see Mamee Joe while you're here," Derrick said. "She gettin' real old these days."

"I see Mamee when I was here last. And the boy, Coo-Coo. He's looking real grown up."

"Coo-Coo's doing okay," Derrick said. "Daddy still off in America, so I mind him like a son."

"Tell Mamee the Red Man is coming by for a drink of mawby real soon."

"I'll do that," Derrick said. He looked at the disheveled man on the bunk, a noticeable contrast to himself in his ironed shirt and khaki trousers. Keating wasn't much more than forty, forty-five, maybe ten years older than Derrick. He looked twenty years older this morning.

Rusty closed his eyes. "Go 'way, man. I need my sleep."

Chapter 4

"*Ellis, you* getting up? I do not know what is ailing you these days. Everyone gone and you still lying in bed."

Alvina St. Joseph stood at the doorway of the tiny room her son usually shared with a teenage cousin and another boy who was staying at the house for a time to finish school. The others had gone home for the holidays, and Coo-Coo lay on his bed facing the pinkish wall with the louvered window covered by a thin white curtain. It stirred in the morning breeze.

"Cold on my chest," Coo-Coo said faintly. "Fever."

"What a t'ing," his mother said. "You saying you sick once, twice a week now since Christmas." She bent over him and placed her hand on his forehead. It was damp with perspiration.

Alvina was thinking that she ought to be taking him to the clinic to see what was wrong, but she had so little free time. She should have Derrick take him, or one of her sisters, but they had their own jobs and their own children to worry about.

"Let me lie quiet," Coo-Coo said.

His mother shrugged. She had to be on her way to work at Derrick's guest house to make the woman's breakfast, not that she ever wanted much, and then to clean the house. Since her husband had gone to work in Canada three years ago, just when little Dally was born, times were hard. He didn't send money regularly, and she had to take up the slack for Coo-Coo and his little sisters. Derrick paid her some, but there weren't many guests. Sometimes she helped out at Indigo Hill when there were a lot of visitors.

"Some bread and juice on the table," she said. "I'll tell Mamee Joe to come round to see you. She give you something for the fever."

Alvina's husband's grandmother, Mamee Joe, was as old as anybody on the island and wise in the ways of folk medicine. Alvina should have asked her weeks ago to give Coo-Coo something for what seemed to have been ailing him.

"Is *nothing*," Coo-Coo said vehemently, his face still to the wall.

Alvina lost her temper. "Then you get up and get dressed. You cutlass that grass out back before I get home. And I got a jar of pepper sauce Marva want up at the big house. I was having Derrick carry it, but he gone out early. You think you can find the strength to carry it by her?"

"I could," Coo-Coo said hesitantly. Tante Marva had lately become too serious and short-tempered, ever since the day Coo-Coo had rushed in terror to Indigo Hill with the tale of the dead woman on the beach.

Alvina went to the drawing room. She'd swept the linoleum floor and had put a clean cloth on the table up against the wall where they ate. The suite of sofa and chairs that she'd bought with some of the money her husband had sent looked fine, but she wished she could add another room to the house, so the little girls didn't have to sleep with her. Derrick was good about helping out with buying necessities, but he had his own plans.

And now all anybody in town could talk about was these foreigners coming to Indigo Hill for a carnival and spreading money around. Not true. M'lord took care of everything, and nobody spent more than a few pennies on fruit at the market, thinking it was all so quaint. They were nothing but trouble, these white women in their little bikinis and sunglasses trying to get brown like a local, and the men walking about Chatham like they were still the lords of the island.

Coo-Coo could hear his mother muttering to herself as she left the house.

He sat up, feeling a little dizzy. Nothing had been right since he'd seen the picture in the gully, found the gold, seen the dead woman with blood all over her at the bay.

Outside, it was already hot. The chickens scattered as Coo-Coo came down the short flight of wooden steps, then resumed their pecking on the hardened earth where his mother had thrown old rice from yesterday. Hero was stretched out in the shade under the house in the space left by the cement block pillars on which it stood. The dog opened an eye at the sound of Coo-Coo's step, and his tail thumped once. The rooster watched the boy while strutting proudly among the busy hens.

No one was at the cement sink where the washing got done, and there was no sign of Coo-Coo's little sisters, Pet and Dally. They'd been left for the day with a neighbor. The shutters on Mamee Joe's little crooked wooden house were open, but Mamee Joe herself was probably out back, milking her goat or talking to the pigs she kept. Mamee Joe refused to let Derrick build her a better house. "Old like me," she said. "Keep it that way."

Suddenly Coo-Coo remembered the pepper sauce he'd been told to take to Marva up at Indigo Hill. He ran back up to his house, and found a big plastic jar full of reddish sauce on the table.

When he emerged with the jar, he came upon Mamee Joe leaning on the stick she used as a cane. She wore a long dress on her tiny, bent body, and her hair was covered by a cloth folded like a turban.

"Boy, you should be in school," she said.

"Morning, Mamee. No school. Holidays still. I takin' the pepper up to Tante Marva. Ma says so. People come there just now, big fete. Like carnival, with a steel band and dress up."

Mamee Joe snorted. "None of them up there any good except Lady Alys. There's a one. Old like me and almost as smart, I telling you."

"She coming this year?" Coo-Coo asked. He sometimes saw the frail white-haired lady at the big house. Like Miss Georgie and the rest, she was a mysterious creature from a far-off world, but she kept to Indigo Hill and didn't roam about the island the way the rest of Lord Farfaine's visitors did.

"Coming, boy? She already here. She and the girl."

"But no. No plane till this evenin', Derrick says." Betun sometimes seemed as far away as Canada or England or America to Coo-Coo, who had never been off his island.

Mamee Joe chuckled. "But I know, I know, they're here. Fly in like pretty birds. Get along. I got to weed my garden. I could sell my tomatoes for plenty dollars in the market. Got to pull up some cassava for your ma to cook for dinner for Derrick's tourist lady, and pick pigeon peas for we. You have nothing better to do, you could be helping me.''

''I comin' back just now,'' Coo-Coo said untruthfully. He was thrilled that Miss Georgie had arrived out of the blue. ''Just now.''

Mamee Joe chuckled. She knew. She walked slowly toward the back of her house to her little garden growing on the terraced hillside.

Coo-Coo tucked the jar of pepper sauce under his arm and followed St. Joseph's Trace to the main road. He skirted the gully. Some days he peered into the dark depths, but he wouldn't go down there again. He paused at the old sugar mill and looked in. The sacks were still there, and someone had built a fire and drawn broken boxes to sit on. Warily he darted across the dirt floor to the place where he'd hidden his red bundle. It was still there. He hesitated. The image of the beautiful Miss Georgie came to his mind. He quickly untied the bundle and examined the gold, but carefully avoided touching the lock of hair. Two bracelets like local ladies wore, a ring with sparkling stones. A real treasure, and it was his. He put one of the bracelets in his pocket, retied the bundle, and hid it away again. In a second he was running down the track to the main road where he flagged down a passing car for a short ride to the gates of Indigo Hill.

Paul Castrocani was also but a short ride away from Indigo Hill as he settled into an uncomfortable chair in the waiting area of the airport in Betun. He was a mere ten minutes by air from Boucan, but apparently hours away from actually boarding one of the little local planes. The early morning plane out to Boucan had been cancelled. The next one was not until later. How long? No one at the airport seemed to know.

It had been a long two days, since his route had taken him from Dallas to Miami, and, after a long delay, on to Barbados, where he'd had to spend the night.

Lord Farfaine's person in London who handled such matters had inexplicably booked Paul into cabin class, and he had arrived at the Dallas airport minutes too late to entice the young woman at the check-in counter to upgrade him. A distinguished white-haired gentleman ahead of him in line had sweet-talked her into the last available first-class seat to Miami.

Regrettably, Paul's mother had not suggested the possibility of cajoling his stepfather into the use of his private jet for a direct flight to Boucan in perfect comfort.

At the moment, comfort was not noticeably present, and did not appear imminent in the shabby airport where he sat in a sticky plastic chair with his luggage piled beside him. Outside the plate-glass windows of the waiting area, he could see distant low hills covered with trees and the two runways fringed with palms. A couple of small planes sat on the tarmac, and while he watched, a commercial jet from the United States landed. The ground crew lowered the plane's steps—no modern jetways here. Pale tourists with their carry-on bags descended and trudged across the tarmac toward the customs shed.

Paul could smell the difference in the air here in the tropics, and feel the steady heat even inside the airport where the air-conditioning functioned fitfully.

Local people—black, beige, and golden brown—returning home from a life on the mainland, came through the waiting area carrying large packages and luggage crammed with the electronic and fashion bounty of America. The tourists were hustled away by enterprising island guides and taxi drivers to the handful of luxury hotels on the other side of the island. Not many people stayed behind to await the eventual plane to Boucan.

"Our islands can be trying to the inexperienced," a deep voice said. "The rhythm, our sense of time is so different." Paul looked around and faced a well-dressed man of about his age, Afro-Caribbean, with an accent that marked him as a West Indian, but he spoke a careful and elegant English, not the dialect Paul had been hearing all morning around him at the airport.

"Tyrone Pace," the man said, and put out his hand. "We made the same connection in Barbados."

"Paul Castrocani," Paul said, startled. He had read the name on Lord Farfaine's guest list. "You're the cricket player. You're to come to Indigo Hill."

Tyrone laughed. "But what is this? A mind reader?"

"I will be there too," Paul said. "I am working . . . that is, I am handling some of the arrangements for Lord Farfaine."

"Ah. Then you will be working with my old friend Derrick Jackson." He shook his head. "It seems that I am to be the guest this year and Derrick is the servant. But then," he added, "you too are a servant of the same master."

Paul didn't care to be reminded. "Mr. Jackson is to meet my plane in Boucan, if it ever flies."

"You will get on famously with him."

"You're going over today?" Paul was thinking that it was somewhat too early for the guests to arrive at Indigo Hill.

"No, I am stopping here with friends and family before going on to Boucan. I'm waiting on them now. I have been playing cricket for one of the county elevens in England for a couple of years, so I am rather keen on being back home for a few days, and hearing all the gossip. Even as I passed through customs they were telling me about the latest romantic tangles, divorces, new babies, even an unsolved murder on Boucan. It's usually very peaceful, indeed somnolent.''

"I heard about the murder from Lord Farfaine."

"Quite a chap," Pace said. "I met him and Lady Farfaine at a country-house weekend." He had a deep laugh. "He must have thought it would be an amusing gesture to invite one of the locals, albeit a famous one. How do you happen to know Jimmie?" Tyrone Pace looked Paul over and seemed to find him a doubtful choice for a responsible position with Lord Farfaine.

Paul thought for a moment. "I am a prince," he said finally.

Tyrone Pace slapped him on the shoulder. "I am certain you are, old chap. Jolly good."

If Pace was a widely famous sports figure, he probably felt he could be condescending. Paul didn't care to admit that he was unaccustomed to being patronized.

"Would you care to join me and my friends for a few hours?" Pace asked. "You will not find a plane over to the island until this evening."

Paul saw a very small jet land and taxi along the runway.

"I should wait," Paul said. "There is a vague promise of an earlier plane." He watched some people descend from the jet out on the tarmac. One of the women was blond, and Paul thought wistfully of Margaret, back in cold, damp New York, dismantling her Christmas tree and looking for a job.

"As you wish," Tyrone Pace said. "You will have transport eventually, but it will fly on island time, not yours. Ah. I see my friends. Cheerio, until Jimmie's carnival."

Tyrone strode away, graceful and athletic. Some local boys recognized him and stopped him along the way. Tyrone spoke for a moment, and signed a fragment of paper for one of them.

The day wore on, and the shrugs at the check-in desk remained constant. Paul began to get restless. He wiped another line of perspiration from his brow and prayed for the little plane to Boucan to appear. He found a currency-exchange counter and acquired some local money, bought a scenic postcard overburdened with the turquoise sea and graceful palm trees, and sent it off to Margaret and De Vere: *Dear Margaret and Sam, I have almost arrived. It is not what I expected. Paul.*

After a time, he gave up and dozed in the uncomfortable chair with a warm Coca-Cola in his hand, and dreamt of dead women floating in picture-postcard-perfect seas with a line of palm trees in the distance, bending to the trade winds.

Chapter 5

When Derrick left Rusty Keating's boat, he made his way back to the rum shop. The laborers had left Boots leaning on his elbows at the table, staring morosely at the harbor while Jamaican reggae blared out from a radio inside the shop.

If Georgina was at the big house, Marva would see to her. This afternoon, he'd drive up to the north end of the island to the airstrip to fetch this boy, the "prince," who was taking over the arrangements for the parties that Derrick could do just as well. With any luck, the interisland plane would be cancelled, and Derrick could go home. The prince would then have to find his own way to Indigo Hill.

"Where you going now?" Boots asked. He didn't have any work at present, and the day lasted for a long twelve hours that had to be filled somehow.

"I have to leave some provisions at the guest house, then I'm going to Arawak Bay for a bathe in the sea. You want to come?"

Boots shook his head. "Not me. That place is too bad. People don't like it since the woman is dead there. What you hearin', Derrick?" Boots sidled up to him and whispered. "They say them boys over at Arawak Bay trying to keep m'lord from building a jetty for his friends' boats. Causing trouble they are, and maybe it have something to do with that dead woman. Those boys talk rough."

"All talk," Derrick said. "M'lord wants a place for his sailing friends to dock near Indigo Hill."

Boots looked at Derrick. "What you think? M'lord give me some work at Indigo Hill this year? I could handle crates and things. He has plenty of stuff sent over. My funds real short."

Derrick sighed. Everybody's funds were short. The island was not prosperous, although everyone managed to eat and nobody was without some sort of roof over their heads. "Bootsie, I'll do what I can. Maybe you should ask the boy from America he's put in charge."

"Man, I can't talk to those white boys," Boots said. "You're better at it. You're the lucky one. You been to America, you know them."

"It's not luck," Derrick said. "It's hard work and planning that make things happen. Why not ask the Red Man if you can help paint up his boat, pay you a few dollars? He's always working on it."

Boots didn't answer.

"See?" Derrick said. "I give you good suggestions and you too proud to take them."

"It's not that," Boots said uneasily. "I told you I can't talk to those boys. They give trouble to we."

"Bootsie, you got beer on the brain. Red Man's like one of us, lived his whole life in the islands. Listen now. I'm going to start to build on another room on the guest house after Lord Farfaine's fete. I'll take you on to help." Derrick spent a lot of time thinking of his guest house, nice and clean and comfortable. Someday, he'd have air conditioners in every room. Tourists liked that. "I'm going up to Indigo Hill," Derrick said. "Make sure it was Georgina."

"I told you," Boots said gleefully. "I know I see she. Is an omen. She come like a jumby in the night. How she get here? Nobody see she come. Then she's here. Like that other one."

"Don't talk nonsense," Derrick said.

Derrick picked up salt meat and rice for Alvina at one of the shops and flagged down a town taxi. He had the driver wait at the small red roofed house that sat right on the beach surrounded by palms so it was almost hidden from the road.

He carried in his parcels to the big room facing the sea. It served as a lounge and a dining room where the guests could sit at the meals Alvina cooked and enjoy the breezes. Right now, the woman who was his only guest was not there, but Alvina was standing in the middle of the room with a broom.

"Where's herself?" Derrick asked.

"She gone out early," Alvina said. "Ellis make me late today. I didn't see her on the beach, so maybe she went to town. You have my provisions? Mamee Joe sending down some things from the garden, but it's not worth the trouble. The woman doesn't eat much."

"She pays for the room," Derrick said. "These English have their own ways." He did find the woman odd and sad, typing sometimes on a little portable typewriter, taking long walks on the beach by herself, looking out to sea like some lonely captain's wife waiting for the sight of a ship. She was not interested in mingling with the island people, although he did once see her drinking a beer at the rum shop with Boots. Boots could persuade anyone to buy him a beer.

Alvina said slowly, "I haven't seen her for a couple of days. There might have been somebody here one night. Two glasses in the sink, smelling of rum. She doesn't take a drink as a rule.''

"Maybe she find a boyfriend." It seemed unlikely.

"You got to talk to Coo-Coo," Alvina said as he started to leave. "I don't know what's troublin' the boy. Says he have fever, but once he's up and about, he seems just fine."

"I'll do that," Derrick said. Something more to worry about.

The taxi dropped him at the entrance to Indigo Hill. Derrick walked up the back path toward the blue-and-white house. When he reached the building that served as the estate kitchen, he did not meet Marva as he had expected, but rather the Honorable Georgina Hose-Griffith in a bikini, round, dark glasses, and a big straw hat, shelling pigeon peas with Coo-Coo. Derrick's first thought was that she looked as beautiful as ever.

"Hullo, Derrick," Georgina said.

"Morning, Miss Georgina. What you doin' here, Coo-Coo?"

"I need company," Georgina said. "Marva's gone off somewhere about the estate. Very testy this year, she is. Is she having problems with a gentleman friend?"

"Marva's too old for these romantic notions," Derrick said severely.

Georgina laughed. "She's not more than forty, forty-five. Just a young thing." She tossed her head in Coo-Coo's direction. "Like my boyfriend here. And look at Daddy and his romantic notions—he's over sixty. Everybody has notions, my lad."

"I hear you were out with Rusty last night," Derrick said.

"Huh, some evening, riding around to the clubs in

an old truck he borrowed. When's this prince Daddy mentioned arriving?''

"Evening plane, if it's flying today. I'll go out to the airstrip and wait for him.''

"You could ring the control tower from here to learn if it is coming,'' she said. "If it is, I'll drive with you. Daddy says he's lovely, but a prince! What a strange choice for helper. We can take the Range Rover.''

"I'll be back later, then,'' Derrick said. "I'm walking over the hill to Arawak Bay, see some people. Not you, Coo-Coo.''

"Don't care to go anyhow,'' Coo-Coo said.

"Rusty's saying the people at the bay don't like the idea of a jetty,'' Georgina said. "They want to keep the place to themselves. They don't know what's good for them.'' She tossed a handful of peas into the bowl. "Grandmother's here.''

"I heard that Lady Alys had arrived,'' Derrick said. "I hope she enjoys good health.''

"It would take an obeah spell to stop her,'' Georgina said, and did not notice that Coo-Coo spilled a lapful of peapods. "It was such fun getting here. We came by seaplane. Some people I ran into on the big island dropped us off at the bay. Grandmother was a bit shaken by the experience, so she's resting.''

"I found a red one,'' Coo-Coo said, interrupting them. He held up the reddish-brown pigeon pea, a rarity among the usual pale green ones.

"It's a shilling for you, my lad,'' Georgina said. She turned her interest entirely toward Coo-Coo's discovery.

Derrick walked away around to the front of the house along the circular drive. The Caribbean stretched before him, ruffled by a few white-capped waves.

Derrick followed a path past the bungalows and

through the corridor of hibiscus and bougainvillea and broad-leafed banana trees. The path took him down the hill to the beach at Arawak Bay. He headed toward the fishing village at the far end of the beach, then stopped for a moment and looked back. He could see the blue roof of Indigo Hill through the palms, and imagined that Lady Alys, Georgina's grandmother, was at her upstairs window looking down on him.

The old lady knew the island as well as he did, and her sharp eyes missed nothing. Even Derrick, a grown man of thirty, was a little scared of her. That was a quality she shared with Mamee Joe: the power of age and secret wisdom. She'd known him since he was Coo-Coo's age.

Derrick had to laugh. The dowager Lady Farfaine, with those blue eyes and fluffy white hair, swooped down on Boucan in a seaplane and waded ashore while the boys from the fishing village carried her luggage on their heads through the waves.

He waved toward the house, just in case she was looking out.

Chapter 6

It is too dark here, Paul said to himself as the Range Rover lurched along the rough single-lane road away from the Boucan airstrip. Even as they drove away, the little plane he'd arrived on took off again for its final destination, the lights along the runway were shut off, and the so-called control tower went dark.

Half an hour before, the plane with a handful of passengers and a minimal crew had taxied down a runway at the Betun airport, risen into the evening sky, and circled the island. Then it had headed out across the Caribbean as the sun was setting. Paul had looked down and sworn that he could see sharks swimming in the sea not very far beneath him. By the time they had landed on Boucan and offloaded his baggage, night had fallen.

At first, the headlights of the Range Rover showed only dense growth on either side of the road, with the occasional silhouette of a palm tree against a star-spangled sky. Millions of stars, but they shed no light. Now and then land crabs scuttled across the road, and Paul imagined he saw the headlights reflected in their eyes. More than once he heard a crunch as one of them failed to avoid the tires.

He sat in the front seat beside Derrick Jackson, who drove like a man possessed. That was not unexpected. Drivers in Rome were not much different, and traffic in New York had begun to catch up with the rest of the world in that respect. Boucan's terrain in the dark, however, added a chilling new dimension. They left the flat airstrip road and were soon on an even narrower road that twisted upward into the hills and then plunged downward on a series of sharp curves. The unseen sea was off to their left, breaking against steep cliffs that dropped off just beyond the road. Paul could see scattered lights of houses clinging to the hillside. He endured the ride fatalistically: he was speeding into some kind of tropical hell from which he might not emerge unscathed and with his new wardrobe intact.

In the backseat a skinny black boy sat quietly; Paul could feel his eyes staring at the back of his head. Beside him, directly behind Paul, was the woman. The Honorable Georgina, with her dark hair and green eyes, looked entirely unlike any upper-class English girls he'd ever met; they tended, in his experience, to be blue-eyed blondes with rosy cheeks. This one was *bellissima*. He wanted to look at her, but . . . He kept his eyes on the road ahead.

She was certainly bold. She had managed to brush up against him provocatively as he and Jackson loaded his array of fine luggage into the back of the vehicle.

"Prince of exactly what?" she'd asked rather insolently.

"My father," Paul said, "is Prince Aldo Sforzi di Castrocani of Rome. I use my title only when it is of some value. I am sure you understand that, Miss Hose-Griffith."

It seemed to silence her for the duration of the drive, but he sensed that she too was watching him from the backseat. He hoped she wasn't mentally criticizing his travel-worn clothes. He didn't look his best; he was in need of a shave.

Derrick Jackson, neatly starched and pressed and scowling, had nothing to say.

Suddenly they reached sea level. The road now curved gently past a beach. Paul could hear the sound of the waves surging and withdrawing. Finally he saw many lights up ahead.

"Chatham," Derrick Jackson said. There were a few shops and stands still open along the street. Some were lit by kerosene lanterns, and laughing women sold sweets and soft drinks and cigarettes. Groups of men and boys were sitting or standing along the main street.

Paul heard someone call out, "Hey, man. Captain Derrick!"

Derrick waved.

"Stop!" Georgina commanded.

Derrick obeyed, lurching to a sudden stop in front of a brightly lit shop plastered with posters for rum, Guinness, and the local beer. Georgina hopped out of the Range Rover and headed for a well-tanned, red-haired white man who was sitting at one of the tables out front.

"Care for something to drink?" Derrick said without looking at Paul, and then called out, "Boots, bring the man a beer, beastly cold. He's had a long trip."

"I don't think . . ." Paul began. The luscious Georgina was holding a glass while the red-haired man poured a drink from a half-filled bottle.

A wiry, youngish man with a squashed cloth cap ran out of the rum shop with two frosted beer bottles. He peered through the open car window at Paul, and handed him a beer.

Derrick said to Paul, "Drink it, good beer here. You drink the other, Boots. Meet m'lord's new head boy, the prince."

Boots said, "Prince? Like Prince Charles? Pleased to meet you, Charlie."

"No, no," Paul said quickly.

"Is okay," Derrick said softly. "Let it pass. Everybody here have a nickname."

Boots said nervously, "I got to talk to you, Captain."

"Tomorrow," Derrick said. "Everybody have to talk to me. I can give you a little change tomorrow."

"It's not money," Boots said. "I got to tell you. Is something I didn't tell you this morning. I'm hearing things. This dead woman . . ."

Derrick cut him off. "You see too much and hear too much. Don't go listening to them. Coo-Coo, you still there? You're too, too quiet. Somethin' troubling you?"

Paul looked around at the boy in the backseat, and saw that he was staring at the man called Boots, rather as if he had seen a ghost.

Under Derrick's stern look, the boy finally spoke faintly. "Is nothing."

Derrick shook his head and called out to Georgina. "Miss Georgina, we got to be getting to Indigo Hill. Rusty, you leave she alone and let us get on with our business."

Georgina and Rusty strolled over to the vehicle. Georgina had linked arms with him. Boots still hovered near the Rover.

"This is Rusty Keating, Prince," Georgina said. "A famous sailor, a lovely man for a night on the town, and an old friend of the family. Rusty, meet my new prince."

Paul was tiring of the joke. "Paul Castrocani," he said.

"Welcome to Boucan." Rusty Keating seemed a little drunk. "A prince is what we need here, someone to take charge. I'm betting you're good at taking charge. I don't have the stomach for it myself, but you . . ."

Paul was mystified at the slightly sarcastic tone, but before he could respond, a blast of sound came from the rum shop—steel drums, a loud singer. A youth with marvelous dreadlocks came out of the shop moving to the rhythm of the music, his arms spread wide. Raucous shouts from the tables: "See Rasta Man dance! Take she for partner!" A grinning girl in a shiny blouse and a short shirt got up from one of the tables, and the two started dancing. Soon others began to dance. "Carnival comin'! Bacchanal!" Loud hilarity reigned.

By the minute Boucan was becoming less and less what Paul had in mind. He'd rather imagined serene, perfect, and empty beaches, gracious quarters, silent and efficient servants. Sophisticated luxury with a mere hint of primitive, simple living. A glimpse of the locals, perhaps, but not life in their midst.

"Been hearin' more rumors, Derrick," Rusty said, above the music. "If the lads over at Arawak Bay stop Lord Farfaine from building his jetty, they say he'll sell the big house to hotel people from the big island." He swayed a little, leaning on Georgina. "Gone will be the simple life of the island, the freedom to manage affairs its own way. Free enterprise stifled in the government's rush to turn the place into tourist heaven, make sure no more dead women lying on the beach."

Paul listened to his voice. His accent was close to Derrick's.

"Stop that talk," Derrick said sharply.

Rusty laughed and swayed again. "They change the place, old Red Man taking his custom elsewhere. Isn't that so, Georgie?"

Georgina pulled her arm away. "Don't worry, Rusty. I won't have any changes," she said. "I like things here as they are."

"Get in, Miss Georgie," Derrick said. "I don't know a thing, Rusty. These people always gossip. Nothin' better to do."

"Drive on, my good man," Georgina said grandly. "Grandmother and I are happy on Boucan, and that's all that matters.'' She seemed to be addressing the back of Paul's head.

Derrick drove on, passing another long beach outside the town. The road began to wind upward again, and Paul saw lights on the top of the hill toward which they were heading.

''That's it, Prince,'' Georgina said in a throaty voice. ''Indigo Hill. Daddy and his pack of party idiots will be here before you know it. Until then, it's pure peace, just you and me and Grandmother. Lovely.''

''Um, yes.'' Paul found her very bold indeed, and he was not comfortable with that. The Italian part of him preferred to be the one to make advances.

''Marva is staying at the house nights until Lord Farfaine arrives,'' Derrick said. ''Coo-Coo, you in a trance back there?''

''I'm good,'' the boy said in a small voice.

Georgina said, ''Don't worry yourself about me, Derrick. I'm just teasing the prince. And besides, Coo-Coo is my sweetheart of the day, giving me his company and lovely presents.''

''Lord Farfaine reports that you have received all the shipments of food and goods he required,'' Paul said to change all current subjects.

''You'll find everything in order,'' Derrick said. ''Some crates already here.''

''Rusty and the boys already brought up a ton of things,'' Georgina said.

''We will fetch the rest tomorrow,'' Derrick said. ''Coo-Coo, I'm taking you back home after I drop Miss Georgina and the . . . .'' He hesitated. ''The prince.''

''Paul is fine,'' Paul said.

The Range Rover pulled up to the front of a splendid big house. All the windows were lighted: three stories, with a broad verandah, hanging pots of ferns and or-

chids on the ground floor, and little balconies in front
of the louvered windows on the floors above.

As Paul got out of the car, he could hear the rustle of
palm fronds moving in the trade winds. Somewhere on the
edge of his hearing was the sound of distant steel drums.

"I'll carry your bags," Derrick said.

"Of course not. I'll do it," Paul said. Derrick Jackson's resentment toward him was obvious, and made
Paul even less pleased with being here.

A trim, dark woman in a gray dress and white apron
that was almost a uniform appeared on the wide verandah. Behind her came an old lady with white hair,
walking erect with her chin up.

Lord Farfaine's mother, Paul thought immediately,
the old West Indies hand. Georgina's grandmother.

Behind her in the doorway was a very old local woman,
bent over and leaning on a cane, with a wrinkled face and
a fringe of white hair under a calico head scarf.

Georgina said, "Grandmother, this is Prince Paul
Castrocani. Prince . . . Paul, my grandmother, Lady
Farfaine. She's called Lady Alys for simplicity's sake.
There's an excess of Lady Farfaines in the family. Some
of them not our sort at all."

"A pleasure, ma'am," Paul said, and almost bowed.
He hoped it was the right response. It always worked
well with New York society ladies who were inclined
to initial wariness when introduced to a "prince." (But
of course, it always ended up that they knew his mother,
so it turned out all right.)

Lady Alys looked him up and down. "Hmmm.
Where did Jimmie find the likes of you?"

"He was visiting New York . . ." Paul stopped. He'd
met Lord Farfaine at a large and crowded charity
dinner-dance in the autumn.

"New York." The old woman looked disapproving.

"A terrible place. I don't visit any longer. All the homeless and ill. Nothing like that here on Boucan, I can assure you. We take care of our people."

"The prince is a perfect love, Grandmother," Georgina said. "Grand manners and so polite. You'll adore him, even if he is Italian."

Lady Alys's expression said, "We'll see about that."

Derrick said, "I should be taking Mamee Joe home, Lady Alys. And Coo-Coo."

The old woman who had been standing silently behind Lady Alys spoke up. "I can manage fine, boy. Two legs and my cane brought me up the hill, two legs and a cane can take me down."

Coo-Coo spoke at last. "Can I stay for now, Miss Georgie?" The boy was looking at her anxiously.

"Not tonight," Georgina said kindly. "I have things to attend to. Take the Range Rover, Derrick, and bring it back tomorrow. I'm sure you and the princeling will have business. And please let's not stand about out here. The prince and Marva can manage the bags." She turned to Paul and smiled a very winsome smile. "This is Marva. She handles everything at Indigo Hill."

Lady Alys said, "You're to be in the first bungalow. Here, Marva . . ." She waved at Paul's luggage.

The uniformed woman hefted two of Paul's suitcases and departed along a white stone path around the side of the house.

Georgina took her grandmother's arm solicitously and guided her toward the open front door and into the house.

At the door, Lady Alys said, "Come back tomorrow, Eulalia."

The old black woman waved her cane. "If the Lord allows, Miss Alys."

Paul said, "I suppose you and I will confer in the morning about the arrangements, Mr. Jackson."

"Nothing much to confer about," Derrick said. "M'lord's shipments all here, the music is all booked, Marva has the menus, the usual servants are hired. We only have to lay in some extra food and drinks." His face held no expression at all, as though he were holding back a scowl. "You have plenty time to get yourself a nice suntan and chat up Miss Georgie."

Paul was not unaware of an undercurrent of jealousy, which was more than resentment over an interloper taking his job. The Honorable Georgina certainly had a strong hold over the men of the island.

Derrick signaled to the old woman. "Mamee Joe, I not allowing you to walk home in the night."

In spite of her cane, the old woman got into the Range Rover agilely, considering the height of the step up.

"Tomorrow," Derrick said, and started the motor.

"Go along to your bed, my prince." Georgina's mocking voice floated out from the house through the tropical night. Paul saw her standing in the lighted doorway. "The bungalow is along the path, the one with the nicest view of the Caribbean. You won't miss it. The lights are on. Marva will see you settled and send over a meal. Grandmother is off to her rooms." She shut the door. Coo-Coo looked crestfallen.

"Into the Rover, boy," Derrick said. "Quick now."

The old woman peered out at Paul. "You take care, boy. Trouble hovering 'round you. I see it."

"Enough of that, Mamee Joe," Derrick said firmly. He put the vehicle in gear, and the taillights of the Range Rover soon disappeared around a bend in the drive.

Paul picked up his two remaining bags and followed the path to a small blue-and-white bungalow with a light on over the door.

Trouble, Paul thought, is just what I need. Welcome to Boucan.

Chapter 7

*T*ap. *Tap*, tap.

Paul opened his eyes and stared up at the unfamiliar white ceiling.

Tap, tap. Tap.

Paul raised himself on his elbows. The sound must have awakened him.

He knew where he was now. It was dark in the bungalow bedroom he had been shown by a solemn and uncommunicative Marva, who had pointed out the bath, set the louvers on the window ajar, lit a mosquito coil, and lowered a gauzy net around the bed. Minutes later, a maid had brought him a plate of cold chicken and salad. He managed to eat most of it before succumbing to travel weariness, unshowered and unshaven.

Tap.

The sound came from outside, but quite close to the bungalow. He sat up. He could just make out the shape of his suitcases piled near the door on the polished wood floor, with only a square oriental rug near the bed. He had not unpacked except for a few immediate necessities.

Paul squinted at his little travel clock with the illuminated dial. Two o'clock. He could hear the far-off sound of waves washing ashore on a beach. He parted the mosquito net, got out of bed, and walked carefully to the window. He could make out the crowns of the palm trees that grew close to the big house. He could see the dark, massed vegetation that spread out across the grounds of Indigo Hill, and the shapes of the roofs of the unlit bungalows that marched down the hill toward the bay. The scent of some night-blooming flower insinuated itself through the window. He imagined the expanse of the Caribbean lying out there in the darkness, but he could barely distinguish between the water and the land.

He waited, but the tapping sound did not come again.

"Ahh!" His soft exclamation was involuntary.

Far away a sudden bright flame appeared. It moved away through the black night and just as suddenly was extinguished. He strained to hear sounds, any sound, but the island was dead quiet.

Then he heard a powerful engine come to life, the kind of motor that drove the sleek speedboats he knew from the tourist-thronged bays of the Mediterranean. Somewhere out there, a boat headed out to sea, and the sound faded. Silence returned to Boucan.

Paul sat down on the bed. It didn't feel especially hot, but he was suddenly damp with perspiration all over his body. He wondered if he'd contracted a tropical fever in the few hours since his arrival. He turned on the lamp on the table next to the bed and took a glass of water from the decanter Marva had placed there. It tasted warm and flat. Unpleasant.

I won't be able to sleep again, he thought. *I will remain awake until the day comes and then I will feel terrible. I will not be able to think. I will have problems with the unfriendly Derrick Jackson. The beautiful*

Georgina will never see me at my best. I will not make the proper arrangements for Lord Farfaine. I will be forced to retreat to New York, a failure. A disgrace. I should not have accepted this position. And if Margaret were here, she would tell me I am thinking nonsense.

Paul lay back on the pillow, but he left on the comforting little light. He felt another wave of fever pass through him, and he closed his eyes.

Five hours later, Paul opened his eyes to a clear, bright morning, feeling rested and even eager to face the challenges of the inner man and the outer world of his new, albeit temporary, island home.

Outside the bungalow, a woman was scolding someone good-naturedly in unintelligible patois. A man's voice answered her, laughing. Paul heard the roosters crowing in the distance.

The view from his window was spectacular: the blue-green Caribbean with a few colorful fishing boats riding the gentle swells, the palm trees marching down the hillside to a long white beach edging the bay. Paul could see the blue tile roofs of other white bungalows scattered amid the lush planting.

This morning, Paul was certain he was quite capable of handling Derrick Jackson. He would make a stab at handling Miss Georgina, and possibly even the taciturn Marva. Maybe he'd start by asking her to enlighten him on the tapping sound in the night, which had probably been the signal of an exotic tropical woodpecker or the mating sounds of an indigenous animal.

Paul hummed an old Italian pop song he hadn't thought of in years as he went to shower.

Marva finished setting the table for the white boy's breakfast. He hadn't impressed her last evening. Another foreigner who expected to be waited on. Even though he was supposedly an employee, he was staying in a bungalow like one of the guests. At least Lady Alys drank her morning tea in her room, and that was surely her right. Miss Georgina took tea upstairs as well, although she would disrupt everyone in the cookhouse if she felt hungry later.

Marva could hear the thwack of the yardman's cutlass. For a second she could see the blade slicing through the young branches that dared to spoil the symmetry of Lord Farfaine's shrubbery. The house was in readiness for him, although perhaps not for that wife he'd gotten himself a few years ago. Not even English, and nothing but complaints. This Lady Farfaine would like to see her fired, but at least that would never happen. She'd been part of Indigo Hill for too long.

Marva stamped back to her cookhouse with its blue-tiled floor and long wooden worktables. Traditional iron pots blackened by years of use hung on the wall side by side with polished copper pans shipped from abroad by one or another of the Lady Farfaines. When Marva had first come to the big house, Lord Farfaine's first wife Sophie had been mistress here, or as much as anyone could be with Lady Alys about. Marva had painful memories of her departure. The second was a strange woman who had come to Boucan only once. Now this latest one, the worst of all—all the servants thought she'd married m'lord for his money. Marva attacked a tomato for the prince's plate of breakfast eggs, slicing it angrily so that her bracelets clattered noisily.

"Miss Marva, come look." Samson, the yardman, stood at the cookhouse door.

"What you want? I'm a busy woman." She looked around at him. Samson was big and strong, generally cheerful. She'd been to school with his father. "What's ailin' you?"

"Just come, Miss Marva."

She followed him out around the corner of the house. He held back the branches of a hibiscus plant loaded with big red blossoms.

"Look," he said. "This is bad business."

She looked where he pointed. A ragged rectangle of paper had been nailed to the curving trunk of the palm, a picture torn from a magazine of a man and a woman standing on a Caribbean beach with the sea behind them. A typical picture of happy tourists.

The nails had been driven through their faces.

Marva quickly ripped the picture from the trunk and stuffed it into the pocket of her apron.

"Take away those nasty nails," she said. There was a sharp edge to her voice. "M'lord won't want to see his tree defaced. And don't you go running to tell all the boys one t'ing about this foolishness, Samson. I'm going to know if you do. Swear."

"But . . ."

She put up her hand to silence him. "Is nothing. Is some kind of jokiness. Swear to me."

"I swear," he said, not terribly sincerely.

"You break that oath, Samson, the dogs of hell come after you. The crabs bite your feet in the night. Jumbies come and stand by your bed." She put her hands on her hips and glared.

"I swear, Miss Marva." Samson shifted nervously from one foot to the other. "Swear."

Now she believed him. "You finish your work," she said. "Lord, don't I have enough to do without falling over you." This she addressed to Coo-Coo, who was standing on the path staring at the spot among the hibiscus where Samson was prying the nails from the palm tree. "What you doing here so early?"

Coo-Coo said, "Where's Miss Georgie?" His voice was shrill and somewhat frantic.

"She's not up yet," Marva said. "She had her tea sent up. Coo-Coo," she added sharply, "pay me heed. Don't go spreading any tales."

Coo-Coo shook his head, as if to scatter his thoughts to the trade winds so they would be carried far away. "Tante Marva, I see . . ."

"Boy, you didn't see *anything*, you hear?" She was angry. She was looking hard at Coo-Coo, who pulled nervously at his ear and fidgeted under her gaze.

"Go," Marva said. "Go wake that prince of yours. Tell him if he want breakfast, he should come to the dining room now. The girls are too busy with the cleaning to serve him in his bed. I going to the market with Derrick."

Coo-Coo walked slowly along in the shade at the back of the house to the bungalows, sorting out his confused thoughts.

Weeks ago, he'd seen a picture of a woman nailed to the mango tree in the gully, and that same day, he'd seen a dead woman on the beach that no one knew. Now he'd seen another mutilated picture here at Indigo Hill. He fought back the terrible idea that he would see another dead woman.

He shouldn't have taken the bundle, he shouldn't have taken the beautiful gold circle from the bundle. He had set loose a bad spell on this house. His fever rushed back and made him feel weak. If only the danger would not come near Miss Georgie . . .

Coo-Coo could hear the local girls who worked at Indigo Hill when the place was occupied bustling in and out of the house, sweeping the big verandah and washing the windows. They chattered about the coming fete and the arrival of m'lord as though everything were perfectly normal.

Coo-Coo cautiously opened the door of the prince's bungalow. The sitting room, with its nubby white rug and white wicker chairs, was empty. The remains of Paul's evening meal and a vase of magenta bougainvillea were on the low square table in the middle of the room. Coo-Coo heard the shower running, and the sound of someone singing in a language he didn't know.

He peeked into the bedroom: a tousled bed and unopened suitcases near the door. He sat down on the edge of a chair in the sitting room and waited. At least nothing had happened to Miss Georgie in the night. The danger had been close, though. Someone had nailed up that picture. Who? Who wanted to harm a pretty lady like Miss Georgie?

"Well, my good man. It appears to be a fine day."

Coo-Coo stood up. Paul had a big white towel around his waist, and his black hair was damp from the shower.

"TanteMarvawantyounow."

Paul frowned. He could make no sense of the boy's words.

"Breakfast," Coo-Coo said. "You comin' just now?"

"Ah, yes. I'll put on some clothes." He went back into the bedroom, and opened a suitcase. One of his fine new white cotton shirts had acquired a few long-distance wrinkles in spite of being carefully packed by one of his mother's Mexican maids, who certainly knew her business if she continued to work for Carolyn Sue. He called out to the boy. "I'm going to need your help."

"Me, sir?"

"If we're going to work together," Paul said, "you'll

have to call me Paul.'' Of course, there was apparently absolutely no work for Paul to do, but he would keep up the pretense until Lord Farfaine and entourage arrived. ''What's the name they call you?''

''Ellis St. Joseph, age eight and one-half,'' the boy said, ''but is Coo-Coo that everybody calls me. Coo-coo is a kind of cake Mamee Joe make with ochro. Uncle Derrick start calling me that when I was a little boy.''

Aha, Paul thought. The unfriendly Derrick Jackson is the boy's relative. ''Tell me about Miss Georgina.''

Coo-Coo said, ''She . . . she's my friend for a long, long time. She . . . she like a . . .'' The power of description seemed to fail him. Paul knew that adoration had made the boy tongue-tied, and decided to rescue him.

''Tell me, Coo-Coo,'' Paul said, ''is there some bird or animal that makes a tapping noise in the night?'' There was no answer. ''I heard . . .'' Paul came out of the bedroom, dressed and ready for the day. The boy had gone.

Paul heard a ''whish whish'' sound as he followed the white stone path to the front of the house. When he reached the big verandah, he saw a muscular, shirtless man in cutoff jeans swinging a lethal-looking cutlass to trim back some high grass along the path.

Another man up ahead was raking the gravel on the drive.

''Mornin', sir,'' they both said.

''Good morning,'' Paul said.

''Mornin', sir,'' chorused the three girls in gray uniforms who were polishing the already shining broad-planked floor inside the front door, and dusting the dark wood furniture in the drawing room on the left.

''Good morning,'' Paul said.

"You just go in there," one of them said and pointed to the right. "Cleone bring the nice breakfast Miss Marva have for you."

Paul knew they were watching him as he entered a formal dining room that would have been right for England, but looked oddly out of place in the tropics: gilt-framed mirrors, an oval mahogany table, fine wood sideboards and chests, a grandfather clock, and an elaborate chandelier. A single place was set at the end of the table, so that he could look out through the open doors onto the verandah.

After a moment, a maid brought in a tray with slices of papaya and several tiny bananas, scrambled eggs, slices of ham, several tomatoes, and a rack of toast. "You want tea, sir? Or coffee?"

"Coffee, please. Is there some way I can telephone to Mr. Jackson?"

"Derrick here and gone already," she said. "He carry Miss Marva to the market, comin' back just now."

"May I join you?" The Honorable Georgina was standing in the doorway wearing a multicolored jumpsuit with a low-cut halter top, elegant sandals, dangling gold earrings, bracelets, and a necklace.

Paul stood up. She looked sensational.

"No formality, please," Georgina said. "Bring me tea with lemon, Cleone."

The girl hastened away. Georgina sat down next to Paul and leaned her elbows on the table as he made a stab at eating neatly.

"You must tell me *all* about yourself," she said. "An Italian prince is such a fascinating choice for Daddy to have made. Derrick is *quite* distressed, as you may have noticed. I'm sure he's wondering what he did to earn

Daddy's displeasure and be demoted from Man in Charge.''

"I had no idea," Paul said, now having a very good idea about the basis for Derrick's hostility. "It was a spontaneous offer of employment. I'm sorry."

"Not your fault," Georgina said carelessly. "Daddy's always pulling surprises. This is a funny old island. You'd be amazed at what goes on behind our happy façade."

"You refer to the murder?"

The maid brought tea for her and coffee for Paul, and did not linger. Georgina avoided his eyes. "I didn't realize you knew about that episode." She busied herself pouring tea. "Ugly, rough old lemons we have here," she said. "The limes are divine, grow all over the place." She did not wish to talk about murder. "You really don't know Daddy at all? I mean, you don't run in his circles?"

"No," Paul said, unable to imagine the nature of Lord Farfaine's circles. "In fact," he added, "I'm not entirely sure why I'm here. This party he talked about— is there really so much I can do to make it run smoothly?"

Georgina grinned slyly. "Maybe he wants me to associate with a titled lad whose mother is both rich and famous in her way. Daddy and Grandmother don't think Rusty a suitable companion, not a prince for our island." She laughed. "Don't worry, I never do what Daddy expects."

Too bad, Paul thought. Her eyes, he noticed, were truly green, very unusual. Then he remembered once being totally enchanted by the violet eyes of a young woman who called herself an ''actress/model.'' He had been greatly disappointed to discover she wore violet-colored contact lenses. One couldn't be sure of anything nowadays, although Georgina's body appeared not to be enhanced by artificial contrivances.

"And you're not one of Jane's pals, are you?" she said, not looking at him directly.

"Jane?"

"The latest stepmum," Georgina said. "She succeeded the unspeakable Clarissa, who ranks as one of Daddy's biggest surprises. Clarissa wasn't very young or pretty, but apparently she did something well. After Mummy ran off, Daddy had only me and Grandmother, so you really can't blame him." She sounded as though she blamed him entirely. "Anthony and I tried to be polite, but Anthony loathed her. He's so stuffy and proper. Eventually Daddy had to get rid of her." It sounded as though Farfaine had had to put down a troublesome dog. "He replaced her with dear Jane." She spoke the name with distaste.

"I know very little about your family," he said cautiously, and felt a rising discomfort.

"Daddy said you were quite the international figure. I thought you'd know all about us." Her arrogance was rather endearing. She and her family definitely did not move in the lofty Eurotrash circles he had frequented until his stepfather had commanded him to abandon them.

Paul put down the piece of cold toast he was about to taste. "*Signorina*, I am merely an impoverished prince. My mother is the international figure. What I know of your family was merely a mention by a friend, Lady Margaret Priam."

"Her! She must be ancient. I remember her when she was taken up by my brother Anthony."

"She's in New York now," Paul said, "and she's not old at all. Only a few years older than I. Very charming."

Georgina took one sip of her tea and stood up. "And you are very alluring," she said. "Ta." She glided toward the door and stopped. "What on earth . . . ?"

Outside, someone was shrieking.

Paul stood up, and caught a glimpse of the maids running toward the front door. Georgina followed the maids. The cries continued, turning to loud sobs. A babble of voices rose outside the open windows.

When he reached the verandah, he saw people running toward the drive—the maids, the two groundskeepers, and several other men. Georgina was on her knees, her arms around a trembling, sobbing Coo-Coo.

One of the men shouted at Paul, "Down below, sir. Big trouble by the pool. Come!"

Paul frowned, but he followed the man.

Margaret had said it would not be smooth sailing on Boucan.

Chapter 8

Prince Paul Castrocani had seen the dawn of many perfect days in the course of his fairly short life.

Twenty-five years ago, when he had been a toddler living in his father's ancient villa outside of Rome, every day was perfect. Winter mornings at the Hotel Cristallo in Cortina d'Ampezzo with the sun shining on the snowy Dolomites. Greek islands where cascades of white houses on the sides of hills spilled down to the Aegean. Mornings in the harbor at Antibes . . .

This should have been another one of those perfect days. The Caribbean was glorious. A sleek powerboat raced over the waves on the horizon, past a large sailing vessel. A line of brown pelicans flew out to sea. Just a breath of the trade winds stirred the tall palms behind the white pool house.

Perfect, except . . .

In the middle of the pool was a tiny artificial island rising a foot or so above the still, electric-blue water. It was complete with two small palms and a thicket of orange bougainvillea—and the naked body of a woman sprawled facedown, her hand trailing in the water.

Paul kicked off his shoes but didn't stop to remove

his shirt or his really nice off-white linen slacks. He waded in. The woman on the islet did not stir.

"*Signorina* . . . Miss . . . Madame, are you all right?" he called.

The yardman who had led him to the pool shouted, "She dead, man?" His eyes were round with excitement and curiosity, and he was mesmerized by the sight of the body.

"Possibly," Paul called back. He hoped she'd merely taken ill while swimming, but he feared something worse. The body looked peculiar, limp and mottled.

"Who is she?" Georgina had come down from the house. She sounded put out by the intrusion. "I've called the doctor. Grandmother is *extremely* annoyed."

Paul heard her, but didn't answer. He had almost reached the islet.

Georgina called, "It's probably one of those damned nomads from America who go from island to island making themselves at home on private property. Bloody fools."

Paul reached the islet. The water wasn't deep there, only up to his chest, so he could stand and reach out to touch the woman's hand. It was lifeless, and the tips of the fingers were white and wrinkled.

"Bring her in," Georgina demanded. "I won't have her in our pool."

"I don't think I should . . ." Paul began.

"Do what I say," Georgina said. "The girls will send the doctor when he arrives. She sampled too much island rum." Georgina strode away back up the hill. That was fine with Paul. While remaining beautiful, Georgina could be terribly tiresome. This did not bode well for a satisfactory future relationship.

Paul felt for the woman's pulse. There was none. It seemed too late for CPR, and there was in any case barely room for the two of them on the island. He managed to put his arm around her waist and bring the body into the pool. It was a struggle to convey the dead weight through the water to the dry land where Samson waited, wringing his hands nervously.

There was no doubt that she was dead.

Samson reluctantly helped Paul lift her out of the pool and carry her to the pool house, where they placed the body on a chaise. The woman was white, and not too young, with dark hair and a few streaks of gray. Paul covered her with a towel as Derrick burst into the pool house.

"Who's dead? What you been doing to Coo-Coo? He like a crazy person, talking about obeah and dead women. Ah!" He caught sight of the body on the chaise. "What trouble is this? What she doing up here?"

"She is dead, which is trouble for someone," Paul said. "Do know her? Come outside. You . . ." Paul pointed to Samson. "Run and call the police."

Samson was more than eager to depart the scene to carry out Paul's order, and no doubt bring the sensational news to the rest of the household. Paul wished he could follow and change to dry clothes.

"What was she doing in the people's pool here?" Derrick asked as he gazed out toward the horizon where the sky met the Caribbean. "She had a whole big sea out front of the guest house to swim in." He looked very unhappy. "The woman is staying at my guest house for three, four weeks now."

"What do you know of her?" Paul asked. "Someone will have to be notified."

"I never knew her, never saw her before she came here. Look, the doc coming."

A parade of people now walked down the hill toward the pool: a middle-aged, dark-skinned man in a tan short-sleeved safari shirt carrying a medical bag; Georgina; and Lady Alys.

"What is the problem here?" The doctor had a deep voice with an English accent that overlaid the sound of the islands.

He sounds like Tyrone Pace, Paul thought. An island man who has lived abroad.

"Dead woman in there," Derrick said glumly. "She drown in the pool. Is that right, Prince?"

"Paul," he said automatically. "She was on that little island, without clothing. I do not know how she died."

The doctor went into the pool house.

"Do you mean she actually died in *our* pool?" Georgina was outraged.

"Georgina dear, don't be so strident," Lady Alys said. She was wearing a light dress and a large picture hat, as though prepared to attend a garden party at Buckingham Palace. "What a bother. Just when Jimmie's on his way." She did not seem troubled by the body in her pool. An aristocrat of the old school. "I do hope this doesn't mean a lot of unpleasantness. Where is Marva?"

A policeman in white pith helmet, white shirt and shorts, and knee-high black socks approached from the direction of the house accompanied by Marva. Georgina went into the pool house.

"Good morning, Lady Alys," the constable said deferentially. "What is the trouble?" He eyed Paul's wet clothing suspiciously.

"A lady is dead," Paul said. "We presume she drowned in the pool. I brought her ashore from the island, but she was beyond saving."

The doctor emerged from the pool house. "Constable, the woman in there has been dead for some time.

I cannot tell the cause or how long without further examination.''

Georgina joined them. ''She certainly is dead,'' she said. She was considerably more subdued now.

''She was staying at my guest house,'' Derrick said reluctantly. ''Mrs. Smith. Claire Smith.''

''I recognize her,'' Georgina said unexpectedly. ''It's my stepmum.''

''Jane?'' Lady Alys was startled. ''That's impossible!''

''Not Jane, Grandmother. The other one, the unspeakable Clarissa.''

Lady Alys seemed to Paul's eyes to be suppressing a smile. ''I knew that one would come to a bad end. It's taken her seven years, and as always she has managed to cause us the greatest inconvenience. She's actually written me letters over the years, a great deal of nonsense in them. I put a stop to them.''

''Marva remembers her,'' Georgina said. ''Marva, what *is* the matter?''

Marva was staring at Georgina, as though she couldn't believe what she was seeing and hearing. ''Nothing, miss. Nothing at all. Is a shocking thing.''

''Well, don't worry yourself. We didn't really know her,'' Georgina said.

Marva got control of herself. ''It upsets the household.''

The constable said, ''Derrick, why didn't you tell Lady Alys that one of m'lord's wives was on the island?''

Derrick put his hands to his chest, a silent but eloquent gesture of innocence and ignorance. ''Rusty Keating brought her over on his boat from the big island before Christmas. I never met the woman before. I was in America when m'lord married to she, and she didn't say who she was. Alvina never know the lady before.''

He shrugged. "Mamee Joe always knows too, too much, but she never said a word about this woman. And I don't know how she got up here. She was gone from the guest house when Alvina came this morning."

"I knew she'd get back at Daddy somehow," Georgina said.

"She seems to have taken her time," Paul said. Lady Alys looked at him disapprovingly. He knew he should have remained silent rather than arouse her animosity. Besides, he looked damp and unprincely.

Paul thought wistfully of Margaret, back in cold New York City. She was good with dead bodies and the police. He wasn't sure he could handle all of this: Lord Farfaine and his important guests, that damned treasure he still had to bury, and now the police asking questions about murder. Then he caught himself.

No one had said anything about murder. It was simply an unfortunate accident. He should take charge, since the affair seemed beyond Derrick. Rusty Keating said the place needed someone to take charge.

Lady Alys took charge. "Constable, we will be available to answer questions. Marva, see that the servants cooperate. This woman appears to have been unaware that Indigo Hill was occupied. She decided to enjoy a swim where she once fancied herself the lady of the house. She met with an accident."

Good for Lady Alys, Paul thought, and said, "Mr. Jackson and I must attend to some business, so if you will excuse us . . ."

"I will excuse you, Mr. . . ." The constable was very young, but he was not cowed by Paul's airs.

"Prince Paul Castrocani," Paul said. A title couldn't hurt in these circumstances. "I am employed by Lord Farfaine to handle certain matters at Indigo Hill."

"I will excuse you, Prince Paul Castrocani," the

constable said, pronouncing each word with a hint of sarcasm, "and Derrick and Lady Alys and the rest, but I put one question to you. If this lady is swimming in the pool without a stitch, as the saying goes, where are her clothes? Nobody saying they see a naked woman walk up the road from the guest house to Indigo Hill. Nobody see bare bottom walking through the plantation or up the back trail to the house. I see Mamee Joe up by the house just now. She walk up here slow, slow this morning. She didn't say she see a naked woman anyplace about."

"An excellent point," Paul said too heartily. "Someone would have noticed. Good work." The constable seemed convinced that Paul was a deranged foreigner.

"She's hidden her clothes in the bushes," Georgina said impatiently. "Or left them on the island. I suggest she died at Indigo Hill simply to annoy Daddy."

The doctor, hitherto silent, now did say something about murder. "I find indications that this was something other than an accident, Constable. Constable?"

"A search of the estate will be required," the constable said hastily. "Nothing must be touched." The doctor nodded his approval.

"Search all you wish, Constable," Lady Alys said.

Marva said, almost frantically, "Lady Alys, the maids have to get on with their work fixing the bungalows, doing the house. We can't delay, there's enough trouble already. . . ."

"Marva, if you please." Lady Alys's soft but commanding voice silenced her.

The young constable took a breath and said, "Nothing is to be touched, Miss Marva. We'll go fast as we can."

"Jimmie hasn't had much luck with his wives," Lady Alys murmured. "Although people did like Sophie."

"Sophie?" The constable looked confused.

"Georgina's mother," Lady Alys said in a tone of disbelief that anyone would not know. "I must get out of the sun. I never spend time in the sun. So bad for the skin, even with a hat. Get on with your business, Constable."

Lady Alys took Georgina's arm and marched back up the hill. Marva followed with a frown. Paul could see Coo-Coo, and Mamee Joe at the top of the hill, watching the pool house.

"What a t'ing," Derrick said. "She must have fallen in the pool and drowned."

"You don't drown and then crawl out of the water," Paul said. "The doctor said she could have died some hours ago." He remembered the water-wrinkled fingers, the lack of warmth in her body. Yet she hadn't been stiff. He tried to recall conversations with De Vere about dead bodies. Rigor mortis, and then it passed off. How long? He couldn't remember.

"Someone kill her?" Derrick shook his head in disbelief. "Now there's two dead."

"Surely there's no connection between the two deaths," Paul said. He had a sinking feeling that someone was going to come up with one.

"Two women nobody know a thing about to start with show up here out of the blue sky." Derrick was very glum.

"This one had been here as Lady Farfaine, surely. Maybe the other one had been here also."

"I don't know," Derrick said evasively. "Never saw the other they found, and nobody claim she. Man, I got a lot of work to do still. You people coming to the big fete expect everything to be perfect. Go change your clothes, man. We going to town. I don't want to be hanging about Indigo Hill while the police boys get on with it."

Chapter 9

T*he little* town of Chatham was bustling: the street was filled with cars, people, an occasional old horse-drawn cart. Paul wondered if people were already discussing the latest sensation at Indigo Hill, but Derrick was disinclined to pause even though many called out to the "Captain" as the Range Rover made its slow way along the main street.

Derrick turned into a parking area near a pier where a couple of sailing boats were docked.

"Picking up some things from Rusty Keating. It's the black boat," he said as he led Paul along the pier. "We're not lingering. Everybody is going to want to hear about that woman."

They stopped at a black sloop. A jumble of boxes and crates marked for Indigo Hill were piled on the pier near its bow.

Rusty Keating came up from below. "Derrick, why you always coming around before a man gets his sleep?"

"Have to fetch the rest of the boxes," Derrick said. "Is this all?"

Rusty yawned. "That's the lot. Had to repack some

78

that got busted up at customs. No harm done.'' He kicked a makeshift bundle of wire and canvas.

''I suppose you hear already about the dead woman the prince found,'' Derrick said.

''No!'' Rusty's surprise was obviously false. ''What a way to introduce the prince to our island. Another dead one, eh? What did I tell you?''

''You heard then,'' Derrick said. ''Who told you?''

Rusty shrugged. ''Man, I can't sleep for hearing the gossip outside my porthole. Everybody talking. The way they tell it, Tante Alys come at her with a cutlass. What do you think, Prince?''

''Lady Alys may not have liked her, but . . .''

Derrick interrupted. ''You ever see that woman you brought over? The one who used to be m'lord's wife?''

Rusty laughed. ''They said it was her.''

''You never told me,'' Derrick said in a low voice.

''Man, I didn't know that. I see her once years ago, but who could recognize her after all this time?'' Rusty's plea of ignorance was not altogether convincing, but Derrick let it pass. ''Go on, man. Take the crates. I got work to do on my boat.''

''I'm stopping at the guest house,'' Derrick said when they'd put the boxes in the Rover. ''See to my sister. She probably knows about the lady already the way news travels here.''

They turned off the road to a dirt track through the palms to the long, flat beach and a red-roofed house.

''Shallow water way, way out,'' Derrick said. ''Nice beach. People come here on Sundays for a bathe, boats can come in easy, drop them off.''

''What did . . .'' Paul could not think how to call her except for the obvious. ''What did the dead woman do all day?''

''Walk on the beach, take picnics off by herself. Type

on this book she say she writing. She went to Chatham once, twice a week. Post a letter, buy a few things. Alvina! You here?''

''Derrick, what am I hearin'?'' A young, pretty woman came out of the house, looking worried. ''Constable was here asking about Mistress Smith. I said she'd gone out early.'' She looked uncomfortable. ''Could have been yesterday, day before. The food I cooked is still in the fridge. He lock up she room, and tell me she dead.''

''Constable take anything away?''

''He said somebody coming over from the big island.''

''You say anything about those rum glasses?''

Alvina shrugged. ''I already wash up the wares, so he's not interested.''

Paul spoke up. ''Miss, the book she was writing . . .''

''My colleague, the prince,'' Derrick said. ''This is my sister Alvina, Coo-Coo's mother.''

''Good morning,'' Alvina said. ''No book around here. It was nothing but a little pile of paper. It's not here now.''

''She took it with her then when she left?'' Paul asked out loud, expecting no answer, and receiving none.

''Go home now, Ally,'' Derrick said. ''Don't be talking to anyone about this.''

Derrick was silent on the return trip to Indigo Hill. Paul helped Derrick unload the crates and provisions to be put away in a storehouse.

A rum punch was brought to Paul at midday on the little gallery of his bungalow. Miraculously, all his clothes, even those he'd worn into the pool, had been neatly pressed and were hanging in the wardrobe and stacked in the drawers. Later, a maid brought out a tray of club sandwiches and a pitcher of fruit juice that tasted like pineapple mixed with papaya.

Georgina and her grandmother were not in evidence. He caught sight of Miss Marva overseeing the maids removing covers from the furniture on the big verandah, but she looked so grim that he did not care to ask her about the rest of the household.

He couldn't swim in the pool. The white-clad constable was sitting in the shade of the pool house, while two assistants examined the little island.

At the bottom of the hill the gleaming sands of the beach along the bay looked tempting.

Paul gave in to temptation. He found his bathing trunks put away in a drawer and picked up a light nylon jacket.

In fifteen minutes he was on the beach at Arawak Bay, a towel slung over his shoulder and rubber thongs in his hand, so the cool waves could swirl around his bare feet. The sea was calm, with gentle swells washing ashore. He noted one spot where the receding waves appeared to create a strong undertow. He decided to walk farther down the beach where he saw buildings and a collection of boats to ask if there were unseen dangers in the sea he should be aware of.

Several people were visible in the distance: a couple of men painting the bottom of a fishing boat above the high waterline, children playing on the beach. Two or three women stood outside the cement-block houses, and a knot of men sat in the shade of some low trees at the top of the beach.

Paul stopped and squinted. A low, gray boat with a large black outboard motor was pulled up on the beach, its bow just out of the water. It was one of the inflatable craft they called zodiac boats, an expensive item for someone on an island like Boucan. Maybe one of the islanders had become rich in America.

As Paul advanced on the village, the people melted

away. The women returned to their houses, the children kept running about, but took themselves away from the beach and were soon gone. The men painting the boat put down their brushes and walked away. When Paul glanced at the spot where the men had been sitting, they had disappeared.

Paul frowned. Apparently no one was eager to talk to a white stranger. Then it struck him: this must be the beach where that other woman had been found dead.

He stopped to think what Margaret would do. He knew the answer. Margaret would forge ahead.

The village had a single paved street where the usual chickens and goats roamed freely. Off the principal street, unpaved tracks wandered off past two-story houses raised on cement piles that were surrounded by big crotons planted in painted tins. A shop sold drinks on one side and food staples on the other; a square concrete building had a single gasoline pump out in front. There were a number of open sheds where over-turned boats rested on trestles.

Paul approached the only person in sight, a young fellow with oil-covered hands who was changing the tire of a battered, yellow pickup truck in front of a shed piled with boxes, bales of chicken wire, crates, old tires, and oil drums. The youth did not at first notice Paul standing there contemplating the clutter in the shed.

"Hello," Paul said finally. "I am staying at Indigo Hill, and I wonder if it is safe to swim along the beach here."

The youth looked up, startled, then stood, wiping his hands on his dirty jeans.

"Undertows? Steep underwater drop-offs? Sharks?" Paul added.

The youth said finally, "Sharks come by if there's blood in the water. Fish guts, cow carcasses."

"I see," Paul said. "I suppose the people here in the village go up to Indigo Hill from time to time."

"No reason for that," the youth said, "except when Fitzie goes by to sell fish."

"Fine-looking craft on the beach," Paul said. "Who owns it?"

"Don't know, man. People come into the bay all the time, take a swim, and go away." He seemed to imply that his statement meant Paul. He turned back to the tire.

Paul walked back to the water's edge to take a look at the gray zodiac boat. Fifteen feet or so. Nothing to indicate who it belonged to. Paul walked on thoughtfully, turning over with his toe the seaworn shells that had accumulated at the high-tide line and inhaling the smell of drying seaweed.

Halfway back, where the sea rolled in calmly and receded without any sign of dangerous currents sucking away at the sand, he dropped his jacket, towel, and thongs on the beach and waded it. The water was warm, but still mildly shocking to his sun-heated body. It was the perfect escape from a New York winter. He swam out through the clear water, then floated upright to look toward the blue roof of Indigo Hill. A craggy headland that formed one side of the bay was covered with stunted trees that clung to the rocky hillside.

As he floated peacefully on the waves, he thought it would not be a bad life here, if it weren't for these dead women on the one hand, and worrying about fulfilling Lord Farfaine's demands for buried treasure on the other. He hadn't dared mention that task to Derrick. Then there was the matter of impressing Georgina. . . .

At the edge of his hearing he became aware that an engine had come to life. He heard the motor accelerate, and he started to paddle lazily around to see who was taking the zodiac out to sea.

What he saw was the bow of the boat high out of the water hurtling straight at him, very fast and very close. Whoever was at the engine was not visible. Escape by swimming was out of the question. He took a deep gulp of air and dove down, breaststroking underwater as fast as he could through schools of tiny silver fish toward what he hoped was the beach. He felt the vibrations of the engine in the water around him. Suddenly his hands hit sand, and he jerked his head up. He had reached the shallow water, barely two yards from the beach. He stood up, shook the salty water from his eyes, and looked seaward. The gray boat was already far out in the bay, just turning the headland and leaving a high spume of spray behind it.

Paul tried not to stagger as he emerged from the water. The people at the village were probably watching. He strolled back casually to the spot where he had left his belongings, toweled off, and slung the jacket over his shoulder.

The gray boat had long since disappeared by the time he started up the incline toward Indigo Hill.

Derrick appeared at Paul's bungalow around four o'clock.

"You think you can drive here?" he asked. "Left-hand drive, you know. Marva wants me to fetch cases of soft drink. You have a nice swim in the sea?"

"Very pleasant," Paul said. He was beginning to come to terms with the idea that someone had deliberately tried to run him down or at least frighten him. Within hours, he was certain, everyone would know about it.

Derrick took the passenger seat of the Range Rover. "You got to get accustomed," he said. "M'lord might be askin' you to drive him and Miss Georgie and Lady Alys about, now you're heading up the festivities.''

Paul sat in the driver's seat and turned to Derrick. "I did not accept this job with Lord Farfaine knowing that I would be taking it from you.''

"Old man is unpredictable,'' Derrick said. "Anyhow, the old lady is the real boss. You got to remember to look left and right when you turn out, cars coming both ways and the roads are narrow.''

"He only said that you were his man on the island.'' Paul persisted, hoping to reach some rapport with Derrick.

"*His* man?'' Derrick finally laughed at something. "I am that, since I'm a little boy. Fetching, carrying, helping out, clearing up after the people left, calming down the ladies, watching out for Miss Georgie, driving the old lady about.''

Paul couldn't look at his expression because he was watching the oncoming cars tear along the narrow road at him, missing him by inches.

"Watch the lorry, boy,'' Derrick said. "He's not going to give you any space.''

Paul said, "Do you know about the treasure hunt?''

"Treasure? No treasure on Boucan,'' Derrick said.

"You misunderstand. Lord Farfaine instructed me to bury something which his guests will then search for.''

"I hear he did some kind of foolishness like that one time,'' Derrick said, "before I signed on with him. You better ask Miss Georgie. Look now, turn left at that drive. Takes you to the wholesale place, top of the hill.''

After they had loaded up a dozen cases of soft drinks, there was the inevitable stop at the rum shop near the harbor. Rusty Keating was sitting at one of the outdoor tables in conversation with the wiry man called Boots. The other tables were fairly crowded, and Paul could see more people inside. All men except for a tall, ample woman who appeared to be the proprietor. Although there were cups and bottles on the tables and some half-empty bottles of beer, the emphasis seemed to be on talking rather than drinking.

Boots signaled to them to join his table.

"I got to talk to you, Rusty," Derrick said.

"I'm just leaving," Rusty said, and got up. He turned to Paul. "How are you enjoying the place?"

"It's rather . . . very interesting," Paul said. "I've only seen a bit of the town and the road between here and Indigo Hill. The beach at Arawak Bay." He tried to see if Keating reacted. He'd concluded that the one person who might have a boat like that would be Rusty Keating.

Keating said blandly, "You won't have time to see much more, once Lord Farfaine's gang of merry pranksters gets here. When's that, Derrick?"

Derrick shrugged. "M'lord come when he's ready."

"I understood he'd be arriving in a week's time," Paul said.

"Sit down, Charlie." Boots pulled out a chair for Paul. "Have a drink. Forget the old man."

Keating started to stroll away toward the marina.

"Keating," Derrick called after him, "we got some other business to discuss." Rusty didn't stop, and Derrick went after him. Paul saw them conferring as buses lumbered by.

"So what you think?" Boots asked. "Somebody kill this lady up at the big house like they kill the other one over by the beach?"

"No one knows anything. . . ."

"No blood, then? Nobody cut? Rusty's saying she's this white lady staying by Derrick's place, right?"

"Yes," Paul said. "She was found in the pool."

"Pool." Boots was disdainful. "Pool for tourists. Only good place to bathe is the sea." He grinned slyly.

Paul assumed he'd already heard about the incident at Arawak Bay. "I could show you places . . . beaches like paradise, you know? And up in the rainforest, they have plenty birds, all colors. You like birds?"

"Moderately," Paul said.

One of the men sitting at the next table said, "Man not looking for birds. He likes looking at other people's business." The tone was definitely surly, and made Paul uneasy.

"You mind your business," Boots said cheerfully, then turned back to Paul. "We have these sugar mills from the old days. One is on the road to Indigo Hill. And fishing. The boys could take you out for sailfish, red snapper, grouper, kingfish. Catch some big, big barracuda out beyond the reefs. I know all them fishing boys who could take you." Boots seemed like a veritable public relations expert for the island. "We got clubs for dancing. . . ."

"Later perhaps," Paul said. Someone had placed one of those frosted beers in front of him. He drank some and it tasted good. The day was hotter than he thought, even though the sun was starting to sink. Derrick and Rusty had disappeared. At least the keys were still in the Range Rover—Derrick scoffed at the idea that anyone would steal Lord Farfainc's well-known vehicle. He could drive himself back to Indigo Hill alone. Then he stood up and looked down the street to the spot where the Rover was parked.

It too had disappeared. He hoped that Derrick had taken it and would soon return for him.

Paul sat down. Someone had placed a fresh frosty bottle of beer at his place. Boots grinned at him. Today he was wearing a faded orange-and-blue New York Mets cap.

"Don't you worry about them boys," he said. "Derrick come back just now."

Paul was beginning to understand that "just now" could mean anything from a minute to an hour.

Suddenly it started to get dark. Paul looked at his watch: six o'clock. He was expected for dinner with Georgina and Lady Alys at seven.

He felt alone and abandoned, in spite of the fact that several local men had drawn up chairs at the table and were animatedly discussing the dead women, the merits of the jetty, the government's lack of interest in Boucan.

"Mr. . . . um, Boots," he finally said. "I need to be getting back to Indigo Hill."

"I tell you, Derrick come back for you."

"It could be some time, and I must get back." The cold beer in this heat was making him feel light-headed.

"Henry!" Boots shouted, and a heavyset black man came to the door of the rum shop. "My friend Charlie need a lift to Indigo Hill. You could drive him?"

Henry nodded and went back inside. He would no doubt be returning "just now."

It was nearly a quarter of an hour before Henry reappeared. There was still no sign of Derrick and Keating and the Range Rover. It had become quite dark, and he realized uneasily that he was the only white person there. He had a glimmer of the feeling a black person must face each time he enters a room full of whites.

"Come now," Boots said. "You home in a flash."

Henry's ramshackle vehicle was a vintage English car, like something from an old black-and-white movie. However, it sped along the dark roads up toward Indigo Hill without hesitation.

Just outside of the town, they passed by the long beach that bordered the road. Paul saw the Range Rover parked near Derrick's guest house on the beach, almost hidden by the palms.

"There's Derrick," Boots said from the backseat.

"He stopping at his guest house. Look, the police car too. They investigating the woman's things. Man is in big trouble, hiding she, and not saying she's some big lady from Indigo Hill."

"He wasn't hiding her," Paul said sharply. He was annoyed with Derrick for leaving him without warning. As it was, he was barely going to have time to change his clothes before the dinner hour.

"That old sugar mill I tell you about is over there," Boots said. "Derrick and them live up top the hill. Up ahead is m'lord's land starting. He own a whole big piece. They say he could build a hotel easy. Add rooms to the big house. We could have plenty tourists, if they lengthen the airstrip. Now he just rents the house to a few folks from America and England, one month, two, and talking about this jetty over at the bay."

It was a relief to reach Indigo Hill. Boots's chatter would end. Henry at least had been silent, and only spoke when Paul felt his pockets to find some local dollars.

"Naw, man. You pay me next time Derrick leave you on the beach," Henry said.

"Thank you," Paul said. He remembered he had to see about the bank account he could supposedly draw on.

"I going to show you all over the island, Charlie," Boots shouted as Henry pulled away. "I know a place up in the hills . . ."

Then the car was gone, bouncing down the drive into the night.

Chapter 10

*P*aul *was* in his bungalow, having showered and changed into newly pressed white trousers, a white silk shirt, and a pale green linen jacket just in time for seven o'clock.

He dined with Lady Alys and Georgina on freshly caught broiled red snapper and some puzzling but delicious tropical vegetables. Marva, a morose presence, served them.

Georgina wore a white eyelet dress, demure although it only buttoned as far as her thighs, and she was polite and subdued. Lady Alys dominated the conversation, which circled carefully around the dead and former Lady Farfaine.

"Our family always seems to survive disasters," Lady Alys said. "You may go, Marva. That terrible storm last summer didn't touch the house."

"It was the year before, Grandmother," Georgina said.

Lady Alys ignored her. "Jimmie happened to be here. He rang me and told me all about it. I remember another big one when I was a young woman, before I was presented at court. In those days, we were here many months of the year." She looked at Paul. "Things were *quite* different on Boucan then, as you can well imagine. Did I see you returning home in a local's car?''

"Derrick had business," Paul said, "so I found a ride."

"How very enterprising," Lady Alys said grudgingly. "I once knew all of these boys, but the little ones grow up so fast. What was I saying? Boucan, yes. Prince Paul, I do hope you will come to love Boucan as I do, although you should be careful of the local elements. Some rough sorts about, and Jimmie's carnivals always bring out the worst in them. It's in the blood."

"Would you care for more fish?" Georgina interrupted her grandmother with a dazzling smile at Paul. "The food is lovely tonight, don't you think? Marva is a genius, even when she's in a temper."

"Delicious, and the island is charming, ma'am," Paul said.

"Georgina loves Boucan, don't you, dear? She's more like my side of the family. She'll have it one day, since it's mine to give. Once she decides to settle down."

Paul had heard that so often from his mother that he wondered if he and Georgina were destined for each other.

"Only Indigo Hill is yours to give, Grandmother," Georgina said. "And Anthony and Daddy don't like that a bit." She speared the last piece of unknown green vegetable with her fork. "This island, for better or worse, belongs to the people who live here."

"We live here," Lady Alys said sharply. "For nearly two centuries, and we continue to maintain a profitable relationship. Mr. Keating understands that, although his family were merely estate overseers. Prince Paul surely understands what I mean."

"I seem to be getting a sense of the place," Paul said.

"Jimmie's going to keep you very busy, once all those

people arrive," Lady Alys said. "They'll come by the real plane. Not the way Georgina and I did."

"The seas were perfectly calm," Georgina said. "The pilot knows these waters well. It was great fun, and you loved it."

"I did not," Lady Alys said firmly. "Young man, did you meet my . . . daughter-in-law in New York? Jane?"

"No, ma'am," Paul said.

Lady Alys sniffed. "She is even worse than Clarissa, who continues to trouble us to this day. Imagine dying in that tasteless fashion. Nude." At least she had acknowledged the existence—or lack thereof—of her son's dead ex-wife. "I wish Sophie hadn't felt she had to leave Jimmie. She was the perfect wife for him. Our sort, not like these others. Of course, Jimmie has always been so . . . carefree. People sometimes see that as being thoughtless. Isn't that so, Georgina?" Georgina kept her eyes on her plate. It was, after all, her parents Lady Alys was discussing. "Clarissa was *never* happy, here or anywhere," Lady Alys went on. "Look where it got her. Dead. I spoke to the constable, and told him exactly how we felt about her."

Paul wondered if that was wise, given the circumstances of her death, but he kept the thought to himself.

"She was here to spy on Daddy, don't you think?" Georgina said. "She was said to be writing a book."

"A book?" That captured Lady Alys's interest. "The woman was barely literate."

"Someone mentioned it. She was probably going to say awful things about us."

"Georgina dear, there is nothing awful about us," Lady Alys said serenely. "Now that she is dead, we need not worry."

Paul was relieved when dinner ended, and Lady Alys

declared her intention of retiring to watch the telly. Lord Farfaine had installed a satellite dish so that his guests would not be without CNN and bad movies.

"Shall we sit on the verandah with our coffee?" Georgina said. "I was out at the clubs last night with Rusty, and I'm exhausted. Otherwise I'd suggest we go out to them tonight."

"Derrick has not returned the Range Rover," Paul said.

"There are several cars here. He'll turn up eventually."

Paul relaxed in a chair while Georgina sat in a cushioned, hanging banquette that swung gently back and forth. She certainly was beautiful. The Indigo Hill operation indicated that there was, indeed, plenty of money about. Paul's challenge was to capture Georgina's fancy, then decide what to do about it.

Several blasts of a car horn indicated that a vehicle was approaching Indigo Hill.

"What now?" Georgina said, and went to the edge of the verandah. The Range Rover came into view, followed by two other cars. Georgina ran down the steps to the drive.

"It's Daddy!"

No, Paul thought. Lord Farfaine had arrived far too soon. Paul's panic of the previous night returned in full force. He had not yet had an opportunity to bury the treasure. Indeed, he had only a vague understanding of what his responsibilities were here at Indigo Hill. Worst of all, he would have to tell Lord Farfaine that it was he who'd retrieved the naked body of one of his wives from the swimming pool.

Escape. How could he escape? He could only hide in the jungle where the treasure was yet to be buried among those scuttling crabs he'd seen on the road last night.

He could find a plane to take him back to New York. His mother would send the jet.

Then he remembered that New York was in the midst of winter. Everyone who knew how to throw a good party or host an elegant dinner would be flying off to Gstaad and Klosters for the skiing or to Antigua and Jamaica for the sun. He straightened his lapels and went out to greet his new employer.

Lord Farfaine was directing the unloading of luggage from the Range Rover. He was a short, chubby man with a shock of white hair and a toasted complexion, as though he spent his life rather than a mere two months a year under the tropical sun. He accepted Georgina's hug.

"Ah, here's our prince." Lord Farfaine abandoned Georgina to clasp Paul's hand with both of his, soft and nicely manicured. "Found a plane in Antigua the other day that wasn't doing anything. Got the luggage over to it, found some of my people hanging about waiting for their connection, and headed right to the big island. We stayed a day or two doing some last-minute shopping, picked up the rest who were coming over, and caught the last flight here tonight. The other cars will be along shortly." He put a plump arm around Paul's shoulders. "You remember my wife, Janie, what?"

Paul said cautiously, "Lady Farfaine and I have not met."

"Well, here she is, all ready for the fun."

"*Puleese*, Jimmie. I am absolutely *dead*." The current Lady Farfaine was quite as young as he'd imagined, but she looked rather plain, with straight, shoulder-length hair and little makeup.

Paul wondered why, if one had to marry an American, she couldn't at least be a beauty. On the other hand, Paul, who had been well trained by his mother, could see that her clothes were expensive and perfectly tailored. She had a peculiar accent that was not English and not American, but a painfully refined combination of both. He recognized it immediately from a hundred New York charity balls.

"Mother," Lord Farfaine shouted at Lady Alys, "you look superb. Adventures never hurt anyone, what? Good work, old girl."

Jane said, "Georgina, where is that Marva woman?" Jane looked her stepdaughter up and down critically. They appeared to be about the same age. "What a quaint dress, darling. I need a bath and a drink and rest." She turned to Paul. "I'm so glad you're with us, Prince Paul. Jimmie says you'll be splendid." Paul was momentarily taken aback by the direct eye contact, the pink tongue that flicked across her lips, the trace of body language that unexpectedly said, "Come hither, young man."

It occurred to him that Lady Farfaine was about his age, too.

"I'm looking forward . . ." he began. As he wondered if she was Lord Farfaine's version of the American trophy wife that he frequently encountered in New York social circles—a young woman wed to an older rich man—Jane swept away into the house.

The drive turned chaotic, with cars arriving. People began piling out of the cars, Marva came from the verandah to assist, Lady Alys stood at the top of the steps, servants appeared from around back. Paul felt helpless.

Then, like a miraculous apparition, he saw Margaret being helped from a car by, of all people, Tyrone Pace.

"Hello, luv," she said. "Jimmie came through with an invitation *and* a ticket."

"I merely mentioned you in a letter. I didn't ask him."

"I did. I tracked him down at his country estate in

England, and demanded an invitation and transport. Do you mind?''

"No," he said fervently. "I am delighted, but it's too soon. That is, I wasn't expecting him quite yet.''

"Small world, eh?'' Tyrone Pace looked fresh and unwrinkled, as though he had just begun his day. "Lord Farfaine summoned me to the airport tonight. Didn't want to delay the festivities.''

"And I got word only a few days ago.'' Margaret said. "I scarcely had a chance to pack.'' She added in a low voice, "Your competition, Carlos San Basilio, is somewhere out there in this mess. Running to fat, you'll be glad to know.''

"Will someone help me *now*?'' A high-pitched, petulant voice screeched out of the darkness.

"Madame Campos once again relies on the kindness of strangers,'' Margaret murmured. "We picked her up on the big island.''

A petite woman with a pile of very black hair and perfect makeup emerged from a car. She was vaguely Asian in appearance, but not of an immediately recognizable nationality.

"Where are the rest of my luggages?'' she said to the driver who was removing matched leather cases from the trunk. He said something to her, and she responded shrilly, "Not here? But where? I must have them.''

"Madame Campos,'' Margaret said soothingly, "the balance of the luggage is coming in another car. Everything was loaded up at the airstrip.''

"Then take these to my rooms,'' she said to Tyrone.

"He's not . . .'' Paul began.

"Your servant, madame,'' Tyrone said with good grace. "I do not know which rooms . . .''

"Madame Campos is in the third bungalow,'' Paul said quickly, remembering Lord Farfaine's rooms list.

He trusted that the maids had been allowed by the police to prepare the bungalows. He should have seen to that. "Someone will take your bags."

"That is better," Ninni Campos said.

Then Paul caught sight of Coo-Coo, apparently recovered from his fright this morning. "Coo-Coo, find someone to help with these bags, if you please."

"That little bag!" Madame Campos shrieked. "Give it here. The jewelry is always in my hand. Zsa Zsa told me a hundred times . . ." The hand in question had embarrassingly long red nails. "I will require mineral water," she said to the air. "Italian, not French. A good white wine in my room at all times. French, not Californian or German. There is a masseuse? Jimmie promises me perfections in everything."

"And you shall have it, madame," Paul said. He didn't imagine Indigo Hill came stocked with a masseuse, but he wasn't ready to explain that to her. Finally a man from the house hefted Ninni Campos's bags and carried them away.

Margaret said, "You seem to have taken charge of your responsibilities."

Paul sighed. He could see Derrick here, there, everywhere, handling things personally. "I am entirely useless."

"You'll find your rhythm," Margaret said.

"I doubt it. Some rather bad things have been happening."

"Come along, all of you," Lord Farfaine shouted from the verandah. "Drinks and supper when you've freshened up. And it seems we have a mystery at Indigo Hill!"

"Actually," Paul said to Margaret, "it's a dead person found on an island in the swimming pool here."

"Dead?" Margaret looked at Paul quizzically. "Jimmie doesn't seem discomfited. He seems rather pleased."

"Pleased may be the word," Paul said. "It's his second wife. The one you said he was rumored to have tried to kill."

"Ah! So someone did it for him?"

"They only *think* she died suspiciously," Paul said. "The fact is, she's dead, and I had to retrieve her. She had been dead for some time, to judge by the look of her." Paul shuddered, then spoke in a rush. "She had no clothes on, but she couldn't have drowned, since she was out of the water. I hoped it would all be sorted out by the time people arrived."

"Poor darling," Margaret said. "We have a lot to talk about. Murder!"

"We should not interfere with the people in charge," Paul said, without much hope that she would heed him.

"What time do you suppose it is?" She squinted at her watch. "Going on nine. First let me find my room, then we'll talk."

"Ah." Paul frowned. "I don't know what to do with you. You weren't on any of Lord Farfaine's lists." Then he was very pleased with his solution. "I have it! Was Miss P. Quince on your flight over?"

"Carlos, Ninni, Mr. Pace, a Sir Eric someone and his wife, some other English people, Jimmie, Jane, and me. Anthony and his wife are coming from England in a day or two. There were a couple of men from the big island. No P. Quince."

"Then she can't arrive tonight, so you'll take her bungalow. We'll fix everything up tomorrow. It's not the best one in terms of view."

"I have had views in the past," Margaret said, "and shall, I do not doubt, have them again in the future. Anything with a bed will be fine."

Chapter 11

The bungalow assigned to P. Quince was sited behind the others, which had unobstructed views of the Caribbean.

Paul had carried her bags, placed them inside the bedroom door, and hurried to the big house to assist Lord Farfaine in his entertaining. "I cannot imagine what I shall do," he said, "but I feel I must be there. Come around as soon as you can."

Margaret inspected the bedroom. Small but gracious enough, wooden furniture painted blue, a blue patterned coverlet on the bed, and a mosquito net suspended from the ceiling in gathers, ready to be let down. Someone had placed a vase of pinkish flowers with shiny green leaves on the dressing table. She washed her face, combed her hair, and judged from the half-mirror that her clothes didn't look too travel-worn for an appearance at the big house to hear about the sensation of the day.

At the bedroom door, she paused to look around her sitting room. It was lit by a single low-wattage table lamp. Nice flowered curtains and a small oriental rug on broad-planked wood floors. The cushions of the wicker furniture were covered in pastel chintz. She frowned and walked toward one of the chairs, peering at the dark object that absolutely didn't belong in the center of the cushion. At first she thought it might be a species of tropical wildlife, a bat or a lizard. The object came into focus.

"Oh, really," she said aloud. A chicken head with staring eyes. The blood had oozed from the severed neck and was starting to dry. She looked around quickly and listened. Nothing was stirring in the house or outside on the little gallery.

She took lavatory tissue from the bathroom, gathered up the chicken head, and went outside. She could see lights from the bungalows in front of hers and to the side toward the house. On the other side was deep shrubbery that grew up close to the bungalow and stretched on toward a cluster of palms outlined against the starry sky. She tossed the mess as far as she could into the bushes.

Paul wasn't paying much attention as Lord Farfaine held forth in the large square drawing room across the foyer from the dining room. Lady Alys sat in Queen Mother-like dignity in a large armchair while the rest of his guests listened to the master.

Local men in white shirts and dark trousers carried drinks and replenished a buffet table set up at one end of the room. The windows were open to the night, and the distant sound of steel drums drifted in as it had the night before, on Paul's first night on Boucan.

Georgina had changed into a long, red sarong skirt and a halter showing a tanned midriff. Carlos San Basilio—he was beginning to look chunky and older—stood between Georgina and Ninni Campos, who had not changed her dress and was eyeing Georgina's outfit with some resentment. Jane was not yet present, but Tyrone Pace was there with the English guests whom Paul did not yet know, older couples who were of Lord Farfaine's generation.

"Imagine the surprise," Jimmie was saying, "old Clarissa drowning herself in my pool. Didn't even know she remembered where Boucan was."

There was a collective murmur from the guests, a sort of choral tsk-tsk response to his pronouncement.

"She couldn't have been here more than once or twice, never should have married the woman. Mother agrees." Lady Alys nodded.

"Mmmmmm," said the crowd in unison.

It was a strange sort of tropical cocktail party.

"Rum punch, sir?" One of the serving men thrust a tray of drinks in Paul's direction.

"Ah, no. I think not." He spotted Margaret standing just outside the door to the room, looking distracted, and went to her side. "Is something wrong? Has the journey tired you?"

"No," Margaret said slowly. "I had a peaceful day over on the other island, shopping for the clothes I forgot in my rush to meet Jimmie's schedule. It's something else. Something I found in my room." She gestured with a nod of her head that they go into the foyer, away from the others.

"A chicken head!" Paul said when Margaret explained. "I must see about this."

"Don't trouble anyone now," she said. "I don't want to interrupt Jimmie or the party."

Marva opened the door at the end of the hall beyond the staircase to the upper floors. "I know what I will do," Paul said. "Wait here, or go in and have something to eat and drink."

Marva was expressionless as Paul approached her.

"There is a problem," he said severely.

"Sir?"

"Lady Margaret found a chicken head in her bungalow, the one Miss Quince is supposed to occupy. How could this happen at Indigo Hill?"

Marva said grimly, "Some kind of local foolishness. I will send a boy to take it away."

"Lady Margaret threw it away, but she is upset. Doesn't it signify some kind of magic business? Spells?"

"Spells," Marva said slowly. "If you don't believe, no spell is going to hurt you. And it's not the lady's room. Nobody is trying to put a spell on her."

Her logic was good, but Paul said, "It was frightening, for whomever it was intended. I trust it will not occur again. I would not care to have to take up the matter with Lord Farfaine."

Marva almost raised an eyebrow, but said, "Yes, sir."

Paul did not believe for a moment that she was indicating a willingness to take orders from him.

Margaret had been captured by Carlos San Basilio when Paul returned to the gathering. Jimmie had finished his oration, and was now mingling. There seemed to be more people in the room. This time he did take a rum punch as he edged his way toward Margaret. Some faces were definitely unfamiliar, people dressed in casual whites with tanned faces, a variety of accents, some of which sounded Scandinavian. He spotted Rusty Keating, of all people, chatting up Lady Alys like an old friend. She was actually smiling.

"Have you had a chance to speak to Carlos?" Margaret said brightly when Paul joined them.

"We have not met for years," Carlos San Basilio

said. His accent was Spanish, his eyes were dark and dreamy, and jowls were definitely beginning to appear. "How fortunate we will have this opportunity to recall past days. If you will excuse me . . ." He circled the room in the direction of Georgina.

"The housekeeper said the chicken head was a local joke."

"Nonsense. The blood was drying, so it had been placed there some time before I moved in. Surely it was intended for P. Quince, whom someone believed would be in residence. Now tell me why she was so honored. I tried to find out about her in New York, but I didn't have much time. There is a person named Priscilla Quince who's had a couple of articles published in minor magazines, investigative things. She's definitely not on the society beat, according to Poppy. Perhaps someone here is warning her off writing about Lord Farfaine and company. I hope they won't try again."

"We could switch rooms for tonight," Paul said. "As a child I witnessed frequent chicken decapitations at the farms near my father's villa. It would not trouble me to discover a chicken head on the verandah."

"It's not the *thing*," Margaret said. "It's the thought that counts. I'll be all right."

"Where did these people come from?" Paul said suddenly.

"Some yachting people sailed in tonight, and that red-haired fellow brought them," Margaret said. "They all appear to know Jimmie and the rest of the family, and they know how to enjoy themselves ashore."

"Rusty Keating knows everyone, apparently," Paul said.

The crowd was becoming rather boisterous as the rum punches flowed. Paul could hear Ninni Campos's shrill laugh and Jimmie Hose-Griffith's guffaws. He noticed that except for Tyrone, there were no island people there, not even Derrick. Then he wondered if Rusty Keating and Derrick had made peace of sorts after their confrontation about Rusty's bringing the now-dead wife to the island without indicating who she was.

Georgina was arm-in-arm with a blond white man in sandals, a tight T-shirt, and baggy white trousers tied with a drawstring. His muscular definition would be the envy of Paul's fellow exercisers at the Vertical Club in Manhattan.

Paul guided Margaret to the side of the room where the open windows looked out on the verandah. He was not surprised to catch sight of Coo-Coo standing in the shadows. Their eyes met, and Coo-Coo ducked away behind a chair.

Paul felt a sharp poke in his back. Ninni Campos had jabbed one of her lethal fingernails into him to get his attention.

"Who is your family exactly? Jimmie is not making himself clearly to me."

"My father is Prince Aldo Castrocani, madame."

"Excellent." Madame Campos was pleased.

"And his mother is Carolyn Sue Hoopes," Margaret said.

"No! Not my dear friend Carolina!" Now she was delighted, but Paul was quite certain that this woman was no dear friend of his mother's. "What good times we have, Carolina and me."

"Where was that?" Margaret asked.

Ninni Campos spread her arms wide. "Everywhere, darlings. Ah!" She was staring at a man who had just entered the room. He wore a short-sleeved beige jacket and slacks, which were almost the same color as his skin. His short black hair had a touch of gray and he had a luxuriant moustache. "He is official. The police.

I can always tell. You learn the signs when you have lived in a country like mine." She did not indicate which country that might be. She sniffed. "Mixed blood, of course."

The man watched the Indigo Hill revelers, but did not step into the room. Finally Lord Farfaine glimpsed him, and the man raised his hand to indicate that he should follow him into the foyer.

"It is about that wretched dead wife of his," Ninni said. "I know the signs. There will be troubles, but she always brought troubles."

"You knew her?" Margaret asked.

"But naturally. Years ago when she was younger and better looking, she stole a man from me. I do not know how that could happen, but she had large breasts and a gift for intrigue. An adventuress. People paid her money to keep silent. She put a spell on Jimmie. She wanted his money. They all do. Of course she took drugs, and drank like fishies. And she had no sense of style." To judge from her tone of voice, that seemed to be the truly worst sin in Ninni Campos's view. "She was a horrible woman."

"How fascinating, Madame Campos," Margaret said. "I understand she was a writer. Do tell us more."

"A writer! Hah! She was illiterate. I know this as I have attended very fine academies in my country as a girl. But I will not gossip of the dead." Ninni put a finger to her lips, but she was half smiling behind the long red nail.

Chapter 12

"*P*oisoned!"

The word washed like a wave across the assembled guests—not at all surprising, since Jimmie had shouted it out when he returned to the room.

"Nothing to do with us," he boomed. "Happened before we got here. Damned fool woman. Something she et."

The policeman he had been talking to stood at the doorway and gazed impassively at the gathering.

"Where is the boy?" Lord Farfaine's voice rose above the murmurs. "The prince fellow. Aha!" He pointed to Paul. "Copper wants a chat."

Under certain circumstances, Paul was vain enough to enjoy having all eyes on him. On this occasion, he did not care for the sensation of knowing that all were watching him and wondering why he was being summoned to confer with the police.

"Go quietly," Margaret said, "but confess to nothing."

"Margaret, don't . . ." Paul said.

"Silly man, you didn't do it," she said. "Go on. But don't repeat any of Ninni Campos's nonsense. That was merely posthumous revenge for some real or imagined slight in the past. Trust me.''

Paul went, and nearly collided with Jane. Lady Farfaine was making a belated appearance, looking like a different person in a calf-length white silk dress with a sweeping skirt and bare shoulders. Her hair was pinned up, and huge white earrings dangled nearly to her collarbone.

"Scusi," he said, distracted at the sight of her.

Jane said, "The policeman is quite a dish, if one likes older men.'' She looked Paul over. "Or younger ones.''

"My name is Lambeaux,'' the policeman said. "You are a Prince Paul Castrocani?'' He examined Paul doubtfully.

Paul nodded. "My parents . . .''

Lambeaux abruptly brushed aside family history. "I flew over from the big island tonight, on the plane that brought . . .'' He gestured toward the crowded room. "Lord Farfaine and his party. They did not notice me, naturally. Perhaps they did not even see me. I know Lord Farfaine by sight. And Tyrone Pace.'' He sighed. "He is something of a national hero. I would be most extremely distressed to discover that he was responsible for the deaths we are trying to explain.''

"Surely not Mr. Pace. He was not here today when I found the lady's body.''

The policeman smiled a cold smile. "In actual fact, most of the people here could have been on Boucan earlier today or yesterday. It is not such trouble to move from one island to the other and back. Lord Farfaine and many of his guests were on the big island for the last day or two before coming here. The old lady herself arrived by seaplane late one night a few days ago, along with the daughter. Another plane landing in the bay would not seem strange—no stranger than many of Lord Farfaine's antics. Or one of these fast speedboats our young people are enamored of. You have thought of something?''

"No, no," Paul said hastily. "I was considering the possibilities." What he was thinking about, however, was the sound of the powerful engine in the night and the sight of the flaming torch in the distance, after he had been awakened by the tapping sound. He was thinking that the policeman could have heard of his earlier encounter with the zodiac boat in the bay and was watching his reaction.

Paul took a deep breath. "I wonder, sir, why you are talking with me about these matters." He did not feel at ease. He knew well that some countries about the world were quite cavalier about their police methods, able to impose unknown laws, and to deal with matters of crime and punishment in arbitrary ways.

To Paul's surprise, Lambeaux took his arm and walked him out the front door onto the verandah. "You are involved. You carried the unclothed dead woman across the pool to land. Commendable in spirit, but under the circumstances perhaps the body should have been left where it was."

"I did not know that," Paul said. He felt a little guilty, however. It was in obedience to Georgina that he had brought the woman ashore. "She might have been only unconscious, and could have been revived." Paul became slightly defensive. "My actions were entirely natural."

"Yes, yes. Calm yourself," Lambeaux said. "Even the doctor was merely suspicious at first. The poison was confirmed only later. Please take a seat. A gracious house. It is actually the property of Lord Farfaine's mother. Her family has been in these islands for years, although they lived largely in England. How fortunate Lord Farfaine is to have the use of Indigo Hill as though it were his own."

"Lady Alys mentioned something," Paul said cautiously. Rusty Keating had spoken of Lord Farfaine selling out if he couldn't have the jetty he wanted, but it would have to be Lady Alys herself who would make such a decision. She and Georgina didn't seem inclined in that direction.

"These people here are quite foreign to me," Lambeaux said, "in many ways that have little to do with national origins. I assume you are quite at home with them."

"I know the type," Paul said.

"I have little trouble dealing with my fellow citizens," Lambeaux said. "You enjoy mixing with the local people, I understand."

"I do not know them. I only arrived . . ." Paul had to think. "It was only yesterday." It seemed forever.

"But you do know people here now. Derrick Jackson, for one. You were seen at the rum shop with Rusty Keating. He is a frequent visitor, and indeed almost a local. You drove away from Chatham with the fellow they call Boots."

"You forget Henry. And Miss Marva. Samson the yardman." Paul was beginning to wonder if the policeman suspected him of some wicked deed. "I assure you, they are all recent acquaintances. The only person I knew prior to arriving is Lord Farfaine. And Lady Margaret Priam, who arrived unexpectedly today. Certainly she did not poison anyone." Suddenly Margaret seemed like the answer to the prayers of a young prince being interrogated by the police. "I should like to ask her to join us."

The policeman gave him a stern look. "To what end?"

"She is . . . she has . . ." Paul stopped, then said desperately, "She is soon to be married to an American police detective. She has learned a great deal from him." He hoped De Vere—and Margaret—would forgive him for announcing a wedding.

"I do not need a woman's advice," Lambeaux said.

Paul regained his composure. "She has experienced one or two situations where . . . people of this sort were involved in a murder. I would like to have her here. I assure you, she is quite astute. And attractive."

The policeman actually laughed. "Good." Then Lambeaux raised his voice, and his cultured voice was suddenly heavy with the island accent. "Boy, what you doin' hangin' about?"

Paul saw Coo-Coo crouched in a dark corner of the verandah.

"You should be home in bed this hour," the policeman said. "You have no one minding you? What a t'ing to be sneaking around listenin' to big men talk. Come now."

Coo-Coo started hesitantly toward them.

Paul said, "He was the first to discover the woman in the pool. He has been around the house all day. Derrick Jackson is his uncle."

"Derrick's boy, eh? What's troublin' you? Come, I not goin' to lock you up. Don't you want to help the police?"

Paul caught an almost imperceptible head movement by which the policeman seemed to indicate that he should go away for the moment and leave him alone with the boy.

"I'll just see about Margaret," Paul said, and went.

He caught a glimpse of the little boy talking fast into the ear of the policeman.

The party spirit had not been dampened by the news of the poisoning. Margaret was conversing with Lady Alys, or rather she was listening to a monologue that no doubt reviewed the way things used to be on Boucan.

Paul tried to imagine the white-haired Lady Alys or the glamorous Georgina disposing of a hated ex-wife. Or Lord Farfaine in his blue silk shirt, or even the puzzling Jane. Silly Ninni Campos was giggling at something Carlos San Basilio had said. Paul wondered in passing if Carlos was wearing a corset to help hold back the tyranny of age. Tyrone Pace was still talking cricket with Lord Farfaine's English friends, and the now slightly tipsy boating people whooped with laughter at some tale told by Rusty Keating. Somewhere behind the scenes, there were the others: silent Marva, unfriendly Derrick, the ancient Mamee Joe, even the talkative Boots. Why would any of them murder a woman who was barely known to the islanders?

"My apologies, Lady Alys. The policeman wishes to see Lady Margaret."

"Really?" Margaret and Lady Alys spoke together, but Margaret asked a question, and Lady Alys simply sounded disbelieving.

"In my day," Lady Alys said, "the police constables were supervised by experienced officers from home. Very efficient system." She sighed. "How different nowadays."

"What does the policeman expect of me?" Margaret asked as they retreated from Lady Alys.

"I told him you were an expert in upper-class murder."

Margaret sighed. "I did promise De Vere before I

left that I would behave. Did you tell him about my chicken head?''

''There wasn't time. And I didn't mention the boat. Two boats.''

''Boat?''

''I didn't tell you. I heard a powerboat in the very early morning hours last night. The second boat was the one that tried to run me down while I was swimming in the bay today.''

''Oh, Paul,'' Margaret said. Then she added, ''Was it the same boat?'' He shrugged. ''Well, come along, let's 'fess up—the boats, the chicken head, what we know of Miss P. Quince whom someone wants to frighten, and anything else.''

Paul took her arm. He said in a low voice, ''They are curious about why we are speaking to the police.''

''How sensitive you've become,'' Margaret said.

''It takes very little time here to know that everyone hears everything very quickly, and I would not be surprised to learn that the policeman already knows everything.''

Lambeaux was gracious upon meeting Margaret. ''Lady Margaret, what a pleasure. Let us enjoy Lord Farfaine's excellent chairs, imported for his comfort from beyond our modest shores. No doubt without paying the duty.'' He guided Margaret to a large chair with puffy cushions and took a seat beside hers. He sniffed the night air. ''The gardeners planted frangipani to scent our lovely nights. Charming—as are you.''

''You are a flatterer, Mr. Lambeaux,'' Margaret said.

''May I offer congratulations on your coming marriage?''

Margaret opened her mouth and looked at Paul, who said hastily, ''Mr. Lambeaux was eager to meet you when I told him of De Vere and how much you learned about crime from him.''

"Ah," Margaret said. "Thank you, Mr. Lambeaux. We have not settled on a date.''

Lambeaux turned serious. "I have spoken to both Derrick and Rusty Keating, who were most closely associated with the woman during her stay. The constable spoke to the housekeeper at the guest house where she stayed. They can offer nothing. Keating claims that he had no idea she was Lord Farfaine's former wife. I do not entirely believe him. I have heard that she kept to herself, which is apparently true. That she was writing a book, which may or may not be true, since we can find no evidence of it. Lady Alys had no kind words for her, according to the constable. And then there is the problem of her clothes.''

"The constable wondered about them," Paul said. "They were found?''

"Indeed," Lambeaux said. "And where do you think they were?'' He did not wait for an answer. "They were discovered in one of the sheds behind this house, where the provisions are stored. A dress, undergarments, a canvas bag with a few items. Comb, lipstick, notebook and pencils, a bit of local money, and a certain amount of English and American currency. No effort had been made to hide them. They were simply tossed in a corner.''

A serving man appeared. "A drink, madame, sirs?''

"Rum and water," Lambeaux said. Paul and Margaret shook their heads. "How thoughtful of Lord Farfaine to attend to our needs, even during our private conversation.'' He leaned forward. "I wonder, would you have been given household keys as part of your . . . responsibilities?''

"Certainly not," Paul said. "I know nothing about the estate."

"No matter. Security is lax," Lambeaux said disapprovingly.

Lambeaux's drink was presented on a tray—not by the serving man, but by Marva herself.

"Long time, girl," he said. "Plenty waves wash up on beach since we chil'ren in school. What is it? Twenty years now?"

"You don' come across to Boucan, Cecil," she said. "I hear you off in America a long time."

"Here and there, girl. I'll be talking to you in the morning."

Miss Marva very nearly smiled for the first time since Paul had met her, until Lambeaux said, "This t'ing about the woman, and what the boy Coo-Coo tellin' me. Picture nailed to tree up here, then whup—woman dead. Sound like somebody playing a game here."

Marva's smile died. "Don' know anything about it, except what I see," she said. "I tore the picture down, throw it away." She looked grim again. "Nasty business."

"There is also the chicken head," Paul said.

Lambeaux stared at him. "But what is this? You wait now, Marva."

"Lady Margaret is staying tonight in the bungalow assigned to a guest who has not arrived, Miss P. Quince. Margaret was a late addition to the party." Paul was speaking quickly to place everything before Lambeaux at once. "She found a chicken head when she went to freshen up. She enquired about Miss Quince in New York and found that she is not a known society writer, so we were puzzled as to why Lord Farfaine had invited her to write about his party. Also, I heard a powerboat at two or three this morning. It seemed to be leaving the beach below this house—"

"Tell me about this chicken's head, Lady Margaret."

"It had been left on a chair in the sitting room," Margaret said. "I believe it must have been some time before I arrived, since the blood was drying. I threw it away into the bushes."

The policeman made a steeple of his hands and put them to his lips. He was silent for an uncomfortably long time. At last he said, "Coo-Coo tells me a tale of twice finding pictures of women nailed to trees—here and elsewhere. Soon after each discovery, a woman is dead. Now we have a chicken head." He frowned. "We have people here who practice in obeah—local magic— for good and for ill. I must say that those of us who were born and raised here cannot escape a little belief in it, even if we think we have gone beyond such beliefs. The old forces are like an undercurrent to so-called modern life."

"Does someone intend harm to P. Quince?" Paul said. "We are certain it wasn't meant for Margaret."

"Perhaps not," Lambeaux said, "but for Miss P. Quince it is too late. She is already dead."

Marva gasped out loud. Lambeaux watched her nearly stumble as she ran into the house.

Chapter 13

Suddenly it became very quiet on the island of Boucan.

The night breezes dropped away, and the click, click of the palm fronds ceased. The boisterous voices inside the house stopped—one of those moments when no one could find a thing to say. The steel band in the hills was silent, and even the eternal sound of waves washing onto the beach below Indigo Hill seemed to pause.

"Dead?" Margaret and Paul spoke in unison.

The policeman looked from one to the other.

"Neither of you knew . . . mmm, the second Lady Farfaine?" he asked.

"Not I," Paul said.

"I've heard of her, of course," Margaret said.

"Of course," Lambeaux said.

Margaret looked at him. "*She* was P. Quince? How extraordinary! Imagine a former wife of Jimmie's going on to become the author of a few unimportant articles in American publications. She was listed in that book where Poppy's man at the newspaper looked her up. She made her way back here to do what? To even old scores with Jimmie? There was that story about the two of them trying to kill each other, but that's just tired gossip. One of the guests here said she was not terribly nice, so perhaps some old enemy got to her at last. But how would anyone know she was here?''

"If you please, Lady Margaret." Lambeaux interrupted her sharply.

Margaret closed her mouth.

Behind them in the house, the party regained its steam, a noisy prelude to its conclusion. A few of the tanned and blond boat people lurched out onto the verandah. Jimmie's booming farewells rose above the din, and Ninni Campos's shrill laugh pierced the night.

Rusty Keating emerged with his arm around the Honorable Georgina's bare midriff. He brushed his lips against her cheek, caught sight of Paul and Margaret, and raised his hand in a mock salute. Then he bounded off the verandah. Georgina watched him for a second and for another second she turned those amazing green eyes on the three of them in their dim corner of the verandah. Then she reentered the house without a word.

The serving man approached them silently and took the policeman's empty glass, a sign that the evening had come to a close for everyone.

Lambeaux stood up. "I should be going to my bed now."

Margaret said, "You can't leave without telling us why that other Lady Farfaine was here disguised as P. Quince—had been here for some time, lurking about the house that had in effect once been hers, and ended up being poisoned. This does not strike me as a place where the usual poisons would be easy to obtain. And was it self-administered? An accident? Given to her intentionally?''

Lambeaux cocked his head and smoothed his moustache. "You misunderstand, Lady Margaret. The dead former Lady Farfaine was not P. Quince. Miss Quince was someone else entirely.''

"I don't understand at all," Margaret said.

"There are two dead women, Lady Margaret. Lady Farfaine in the pool here, and the woman found on the beach some weeks ago. A woman of color, although quite light-skinned. We have learned that she was P. Quince. Good night." He walked to the steps.

Margaret said quickly, "Wait! What sort of poison was it that killed Lady Farfaine? Was the real P. Quince also poisoned?"

"Miss Quince was slashed on the beach by one of our local cutlasses. As for the other death . . ." He gestured toward the dark grounds of Indigo Hill. "A surprising number of our lovely flora are potentially lethal," he said, "although the locals take care. They know which plants are to be avoided. Foreigners are sometimes not so cautious or well informed. And sometimes knowledge on the one hand and ignorance on the other ends in a tragedy. She very likely died from a toxic plant substance," Lambeaux said. "This is difficult although not impossible to do accidentally. Most adults do not go about chewing on unfamiliar leaves and flowers, especially in a place like Boucan where there are ample fruits and vegetables to satisfy one."

"Poisoned by a plant." Paul considered this. "But how could a murderer induce someone to consume such a thing? It must have been accidental."

"The how and precisely what we do not know, but there are indications that she had been conveyed to the island in the pool well after death," Lambeaux said.

"Indications?" Margaret was listening eagerly.

"These toxic plants cause various types of physical distress before a person succumbs to respiratory or heart failure. There was no sign of that. There is the matter of lividity, the blood settling in parts of the body after death. The discovery of her clothing far from the pool . . . She had been dead for some time before she was discovered on the island.''

Paul brightened. ''Someone brought the body ashore on that boat I heard in the night. But it would be difficult to carry a dead body up the hill from the beach, would it not?''

''Do not be carried away with idle speculation,'' Lambeaux said. ''We will handle it. Enjoy your holiday.''

''But there is a murderer about,'' Margaret said indignantly. ''Even the people staying at Indigo Hill could be suspects. You said it was easy to move from island to island.''

''Do not trouble yourselves further about the affair.'' It was a sharp command made with the assurance that he would be obeyed. Lambeaux could not be blamed for not knowing Margaret's tendency to become involved in murder, even when forbidden to do so. ''In any case, I cannot give answers to your questions,'' Lambeaux said. ''But I suggest, my friends, that you take care what you are offered to eat. The dead lady apparently was not careful enough.''

Lambeaux brushed his moustache again and half smiled as he strolled down the steps toward the drive. Then he called out in a rich island accent, ''No gossipin', chil'ren. Is private between we, right?''

The engine started, and his headlights swept the verandah as he departed.

''What a curious way to conduct a police investigation,'' Margaret said.

''Perhaps Mr. Lambeaux considers this business the affair of foreigners who are to be left free to kill each other off until only the murderer remains. He can then arrest that person, and life on the island can go on as usual.''

"No," Margaret said slowly, "this is not simply a matter of silly tourists dropping down on Boucan and behaving badly. There is a local connection—the spells, the chicken head, the poison, indeed even the weapon in the first death. And there's the connection between the two deaths. P. Quince was invited by Lord Farfaine, and Clarissa was his former wife. Very interesting. I know he looks eccentric and harmless, but if you had heard the stories . . .''

Marva reappeared and Margaret fell silent. "M'lord and the family have retired," Marva said. "The other guests have gone to their bungalows. Is there something more you are wanting?''

"Nothing, thank you," Margaret said. "Marva, is it? How well you take charge of this lovely house.''

"Thank you, madame." Marva looked as though events were becoming more than she could handle. "Breakfast is available in your bungalow if you will say when, and in the house from seven.''

"I would like tea brought at about eight," Margaret said. "I say, did you know the dead Lady Farfaine?'' Margaret asked guilelessly. "Such a terrible thing. That and the other death.''

Marva said vehemently, "I don't know anything about these women, except to hear complaints. The water pressure is not right, but she doesn't know that half the island gets its water from the pump on the street. Indigo Hill has these underground cisterns. That's why she has plenty water all the time. She sees 'creatures' in the rooms, but just geckos and mantises eating up mosquitoes. Toast is always too cold, seasoning too spicy, sun too hot, and never a good morning when every child on Boucan able to speak know enough to say good day.

You learn manners here, learn nothing at all across the water.''

Marva herself seemed stunned by her outburst.

"I do understand," Margaret said soothingly. "I am staying for tonight in P. Quince's bungalow."

"I know," Marva said. "You can find your way?"

"Prince Paul will guide me." Margaret took Paul's arm and made him walk her down the steps of the verandah into the night.

"Are we not to switch bungalows?" Paul whispered.

"Since all possible P. Quinces are deceased, I don't think it's necessary."

"As you wish," Paul said doubtfully. They walked leisurely along the white stone path toward the bungalows. The wall of shrubs pressed in on them and the night scents—Lambeaux's frangipani perhaps—were heavy in the close air of the pathway, which was littered with fallen hibiscus flowers.

"Let me look," Paul said when they reached the door. Around them lights were still on in the other bungalows. Laughter that could only come from Ninni Campos briefly jarred the peaceful night.

"It seems clear," Paul said. "I see the evidence of the chicken blood on the cushion. I'm sure a maid will see to it in the morning."

The table lamp was still on. Margaret headed for the bedroom. "Lovely," she called out. "I've been unpacked and pressed. Jimmie's people know how to extend his hospitality to the limit. Ice in a bucket, bottled water, wine and rum and Coca-Cola. A tin of biscuits. Even a mosquito coil already lighted, and the mosquito net let down. Heaven."

"Lock the door," Paul said.

Margaret gestured at the open louvered windows.

"Not much defense. Security is, as Mr. Lambeaux said, casual."

Both jumped at the knock on the door.

"More treats from the house?" Margaret opened the door carefully.

A vaguely familiar, dark-skinned man held a curved cutlass at least two feet long with a silver blade honed to a lethal sharpness.

Margaret backed away, but Paul said, "Derrick. Have you met Lady Margaret Priam?"

Margaret said quickly, "Of course. You were at the airstrip and around the house. I didn't recognize you immediately."

"It's okay," Derrick said. "I heard . . ." He stopped, then handed her the cutlass. "You keep this under your bed. If anyone comes in, any person you don't know . . ."

"I appreciate your concern," Margaret said, and accepted the cutlass gingerly.

"This is my country," Derrick said. "Nobody here wants headlines all over the world. Bad news when tourists have trouble."

"I am not worried," Margaret said. "But would it not be equally bad for a white visitor to cut down an innocent local who happened to appear at her door?"

"I think you will know when to cut," Derrick said. "I hope you will be comfortable, madame."

The two men left together. Margaret hefted the cutlass and examined its ugly blade. She took it with her into the bedroom and twitched the blade gently across the pinkish flowers in the vase beside her bed. It sliced cleanly through a cluster of blossoms, and petals and shiny leaves fell to the floor. She scooped them up and put them in the wastepaper basket.

How easy, she thought, and how very sharp indeed.

She placed the cutlass on the floor under her bed. She turned out the light and stretched on the bed in a loose, oversized cotton T-shirt, surrounded by the gauzy wall of the mosquito net. Even with the breeze, her skin felt vaguely damp, as though some never-ending tropical heat existed always behind the trade winds.

Tap.

Margaret opened her eyes and listened. It had been a very faint sound, if she had heard anything at all through dreamless sleep. She strained to hear sounds from the sitting room, but she could not hear anyone moving out there.

Then she was certain that she heard a faint sound, as though someone had stepped on a creaking board in the other room.

At least, she thought, I can in no way be mistaken for P. Quince. She realized she was telling herself not to be afraid, but her heart was beating fast.

After a space of time that seemed long but probably was not, Margaret eased herself under the mosquito net and off the bed. She bent down to grasp the wooden handle of the cutlass. A certain comfort there, but she had no idea if she was capable of defending herself with it.

The sitting room was dark as Margaret peered in. She tried to remember if she'd seen any kind of switch for an overhead light near the bedroom door, but no image of one came to mind.

"Who is there?" Margaret called out.

She thought she detected a faint intake of breath, a tiny shuffle.

"I am armed," she said boldly. The cutlass was rather heavy, not to say unwieldy for one unaccustomed to its use.

There was no response. Margaret took a hesitant step

into the sitting room. She could make out the shapes of the furniture, the pale cushions, the light rectangles of the curtains covering the windows.

"Ah!" She spoke involuntarily. She could now see the shape of a person crouching near the chair where she'd found the chicken head.

Neither of them moved, but Margaret's heart was still beating rapidly.

Suddenly, the person sprang at Margaret and she saw only dark clothes, a dark face, a dark head. The person grabbed the wrist of her hand holding the cutlass. She released the big knife, and the blade clattered loudly as it hit the floor.

Then the person shoved Margaret and she stumbled backwards, hitting her head on the polished wooden floor. She lay still for a moment, then struggled to sit upright. In a daze, she seemed to hear a raspy voice muttering in the distance. The intruder halted momentary, then ran into the night.

Margaret stood up and felt the back of her head. An area of pain, but nothing incapacitating. She shook her head to clear it, and stared at the door in amazement. Her attacker had returned and was standing in the doorway.

She snatched up the cutlass. The person did not move.

Margaret hesitated. He seemed much smaller than the man who had knocked her down.

A match flared in the darkness, and in its light, she saw that it wasn't a man or a boy. It was a very old woman with a dark, wizened face topped by a cloth kerchief. She was bent and frail, and she clutched a rough cane in one hand. The match flame died.

"Let's have some light, shall we?" Margaret turned on the table lamp. The old woman did not seem to pose much of a physical danger. "That's better. Please do take a seat." The old woman backed away, watching Margaret with an expression that mingled wariness and fear, but she didn't try to leave.

"I don't believe we've met," Margaret said. "I am Lady Margaret Priam, one of Lord Farfaine's guests."

The woman watched her in silence.

"I'm sorry I didn't put on a robe," Margaret said. "I was rather startled from a sound sleep." Margaret looked down at her large white T-shirt. It was smudged with dirt from her encounter with the intruder. She flicked her hand over her chest, and saw that it was something like charcoal dust. "I wonder if you saw the person who ran out just now?"

The old woman did not answer. Conversation was obviously going to be sticky going.

"Mamee Joe . . ." A small boy burst through the door. "I been lookin' for you up and down the place. What you doin' here?"

"She's paying me a call," Margaret said. She recognized the boy as one she'd seen earlier about the big house. "You are . . . ?"

"Coo-Coo," he said reluctantly. "I takin' Mamee Joe home just now."

"I asked her if she saw someone," Margaret said. "Can't she speak?"

"I can talk all right, missus," the old woman said. "Is you that rise up out of the dark like a jumby and give me bad, bad fright."

"Did neither of you see someone running from my bungalow?" Margaret persisted. She watched the old woman and the boy.

"If I see anybody," Mamee Joe said, "it's only trouble for you." This was not exactly an answer.

"I came along the path from the big house. Nobody

there.'' The boy was hopping from one foot to the other, and Margaret couldn't tell if he were speaking the truth. "Mamee Joe, come now. Derrick is saying you dead in the bush or fall into the sea. Nothin' happening here. Come.''

"Some kind of t'ing happen," Mamee Joe said. Her eyes had not left Margaret. "I look at my Lady Alys and see trouble comin' to Indigo Hill. She tells me she's going to take care of any trouble here. Thinks she knows best, since she was a girl. But she can't see what I do.'' Mamee Joe shook her head. "Is a dark, dark place, Boucan is.''

Suddenly Margaret had the eerie sensation of knowing all at once that a completely different world existed behind the one she knew of servants and creature comforts and the pleasures of a quiet holiday in the tropics.

"You know Lady Alys well then?'' Margaret had found the dignified dowager Lady Farfaine the image of her own frighteningly grand grandmother. Opinionated, still living in a long-vanished world, and deeply conscious of what people thought, what was correct behavior for the world to see. Managing things.

"I work here for years and years.''

"I would still like to know why you came to my bungalow," Margaret said, "and who it was you saw here.''

"Following the footsteps of the trouble, is all,'' the old woman said.

"I was thinking she was lookin' after Miss Georgina, but it could be you," Coo-Coo said mystifyingly. "Come now, Mamee.''

The boy took the old woman's hand and led her away without argument. Margaret followed them out onto the little gallery and watched them descend the two steps.

In a second they had disappeared along the path into the darkness.

Margaret stood for a while on the gallery. There was a flutter of wings in front of the bungalow as a cluster of tiny bats swooped down and away. Lights were on in one distant bungalow, but the others were dark.

Suddenly it began to rain very hard, the drops drumming on the roof and splattering on the leaves of the shrubs. The rain was so heavy, it looked as though a white curtain had been drawn. Then the rain stopped abruptly. It was silent except for the drip of rainwater from the bushes.

The person in her bungalow had appeared to be dark-skinned and male. Derrick? Tyrone Pace? An unknown servant or local man? Yet it might have been an agile woman. It could even have been a white person with a blackened face. She looked down at the dark smudges on her big T-shirt. Charcoal from a disguise? The boy had mentioned Georgina. She shivered. It was surprisingly cool after the rain, and the drip, drip of water from the branches all about her had a soothing effect.

She could make nothing of the visit from the old woman or of Coo-Coo's words. She wondered if they were still out there in the dark, watching her bungalow, or if the intruder waited in the shadows to try again. Perhaps she should seek the protection of the big house or of Paul. She went back inside to contemplate her options, carefully latching the bungalow door behind her, and turning on all the lights in the sitting room. She even found the switch that turned on a light outside on the gallery. Then she closed and latched the windows, which abruptly cut off the circulating breeze, but it made her feel a bit more secure.

She surveyed the room. The intruder had been

crouched near the chair where she'd found the chicken head. She turned over the stained cushion.

Beneath it was a little stack of papers. A jumble of thoughts went through her head: P. Quince the writer dead on a beach, the woman who was not P. Quince but was supposedly writing a book dead at Indigo Hill. Here were papers that someone was probably looking for, but what a silly place to hide them in the first place, and how would the intruder know where to look?

"Of course!" she said aloud. It was suddenly obvious: the intruder was not retrieving the papers, but hiding them—in a place where they were certain to be found when the servants cleaned up. She sighed her relief. Since the intruder had achieved that goal, she decided she didn't need to run off and hide in the big house.

She took the papers with her as she returned to her bed, leaving all the lights on. This time she placed the cutlass on the coverlet beside her, for what good it would do her, and she would endure the lack of circulating air with windows shut and latched.

She leafed through the first pages, some typewritten, some handwritten. "Oh, really," she said and flopped back on her pillow. Here were simple poems, describing the island scenery. Margaret read on. Most of the pages were a sort of daily journal that sounded quite cheerful at the start. The pleasant rooms she'd been directed to, the beautiful sea outside, a determination to avoid Indigo Hill until the time was right. Apparently someone who knew her as the former Lady Farfaine coming soon to Boucan. A meeting was arranged. Financial difficulties would soon be eased. These pages were from the hand of Clarissa, the former Lady Farfaine.

Margaret was growing sleepy, but then was suddenly

wide-awake. *Priscilla sounds like a lovely young woman. I know we can help each other.*

So the former Lady Farfaine had known Priscilla Quince, and quite possibly knew that she'd been killed. The journal went blank for a week around Christmas, and took up again later with comments on the slowly passing days and nights. Now Clarissa was apparently waiting for something else to happen. "Jimmie will be here soon, and matters will be arranged." That was it: the arrival of Jimmie and his guests would settle matters.

The very last entry: *At last I have found an ally when I least expected it.* Margaret counted back. Clarissa had written that two days before her body was discovered.

At the bottom of the stack of papers, she found a letter from the formidable Lady Alys herself, brief and surprisingly cordial, dated two months before: "Dear Clarissa, I do understand your difficulties, but harassing Jimmie with letters will solve nothing. We will be at Indigo Hill after Christmas. I suggest you contact me there, and I will see what can be done."

Margaret pondered the situation. She was surely obliged to hand over to Lambeaux these poor remnants of the woman's life. She sighed, and regretted the lack of a copier. An hour later she had finished copying by hand most of the papers, utilizing Indigo Hill letter paper, pages of her appointment book, and the backs of old envelopes from her handbag. Lambeaux would get everything except Lady Alys's letter—in the name of upper-class solidarity.

Margaret left the light on beside her bed and grasped the handle of the cutlass as she drifted off to sleep again in the hot bedroom.

Chapter 14

*P*aul *was* reluctant to get out of bed with the dawn of this, his second day on Boucan. He could not imagine what disaster, large or small, might occur. At least Margaret was here, and she was capable of handling most things. His take-charge enthusiasm had evaporated. On the other hand, he had an alleged job to do for Lord Farfaine, so he rose at seven and headed for breakfast in the big house.

The maids had cleared away the remains of the previous night's impromptu party. Although there was no one to be seen in the big house, Paul could hear voices from out in the back. The sideboard in the dining room was loaded with chafing dishes of scrambled eggs, ham and sausages, bowls of deep orange slices of papaya, bunches of tiny yellow bananas, chunks of pineapple and melon and sections of orange and grapefruit, and loaves of round, flat, freshly baked bread. There was an urn of coffee and a row of teapots waiting to be filled.

As he poured coffee, Paul wondered what tasks Derrick had for him today. He wished he could safely return to the golden sands of the beach below the house. A swim in the sea was what he needed to set him up for the day. In the old days, when he spent the warm months lounging about the South of France, he was always up early and into the sea. Then there was the summer he'd had a chance to sail around the Greek islands with that beautiful heiress to a shipping fortune. . . .

Paul brought himself back to Boucan. He couldn't behave like a guest. There was the pressing matter of the treasure to attend to, and he needed to sort out his thoughts about Georgina and Rusty, who was entirely unsuitable. In this he was in agreement with Lady Alys. Yet both Keating and Georgina wanted to keep the island as it was, so there was an alliance in which Paul had no part. He had thought about how the body had gotten to the pool, and the connection between P. Quince and the dead Lady Farfaine.

He started first with the easiest matter. He had the beginning of an idea about where to get assistance to bury the treasure. It required a car, but Georgina had said there were several vehicles about the place. He would speak to Derrick or even risk asking Marva.

"Well, well!" Lord Farfaine boomed his way into the empty dining room. Once again he was dressed all in blue to match his bright blue eyes under white, bushy brows. "Here's the prince. Quite a place, don't you think? Been in the family for years. What's the girl got for my breakfast?" He clanked the covers of the chafing dishes as he examined the fare. "Free-range chickens here, lay their eggs any old place. Send the kiddies out to find them. Peahens too, you know. You can see 'em out in back. Big fat ladies. Wanted a peacock, but they make too damned much noise, can't sleep for their shouting."

Lord Farfaine sat down beside Paul with a loaded plate.

"Time's closing in," he said as he attacked his meal

with gusto. "Plenty of work to get through before everyone arrives, expecting a bang-up time. Mother thinks you're going to be fine. Janie does too." He paused with his fork halfway to his mouth. "What do you think of old Georgie? Hell of a girl, what?"

"Georgina is quite . . ." Paul didn't know quite what to say.

"Ho! Got you speechless, has she?"

"We haven't had much time . . ." Paul started again and stopped.

"What do you think of this Clarissa business? That's the ex-wife. Nasty. Very nasty." He leaned toward Paul. "The policeman didn't want to come right out and say it, but the old girl was murdered, take my word for it."

"Who . . . That is, why do you think that?"

Lord Farfaine put down his fork. "I'm not a fool, my boy. They don't send over the top CID copper for nothing. They'd like to have something on me, kick us off Boucan. It's probably a government plot," he said gloomily. "I think old Clarissa was hanging about with some locals and crossed somebody. That's the way she was, always rubbing people the wrong way."

"They're saying she kept to herself," Paul began.

Lord Farfaine dismissed that. "That's just the story. Somebody probably strangled her to shut her up. Don't know why I married her, except she was a good-looking woman, seven, eight, ten years ago. My first wife had run off, not that I didn't give her reason. Mother was a brick. The children and all. Sophie's some sort of Austrian countess now. I spent a few years as a lonely old bachelor, so I married Clarissa. Figured out pretty damned quick I couldn't stand the sight of her. Then I met Janie. Likes my money, but devoted. Yes, absolutely devoted. She's young. Not so cosy with Georgie as I'd like. Thought they'd be chums."

Paul thought that an extraordinary misperception of the characters of both women, especially if Jane had nothing but complaints about Indigo Hill. What he said was, "A terrible thing, though, to have your second wife murdered out of the blue, and here of all places."

"Have to confess," Lord Farfaine said. "I didn't let on to the police fellow, but I had a letter from Clarissa back before Christmas. She needed money. She didn't come right out and say it, but blackmail was implied. Pay up or you'll regret it, that sort of thing."

"Did you pay?"

"Sent her a bit," he said shamefacedly. "I have plenty. I didn't know what she was talking about, but you can't have that, y'know. Bad for business, bad for the reputation if blackmail rumors get about." He seemed unaware that blackmail was a classic motive for murder.

"Was she here to demand more?" Paul asked. The members of this strange family seemed compelled to share their secrets with Paul, so why not allow them every opportunity?

"Didn't have a chance to, did she?" Lord Farfaine said, then added, "Leave it to me to tell the police about Clarissa's letter." It was an order.

"Indeed, I will say nothing," Paul said.

"Mother never liked Clarissa. Georgie didn't either. My son Anthony couldn't bring himself to speak to her. I had a call from Anthony, by the way. He has to stay in London to settle some business matters, so he won't be joining us." Lord Farfaine's blue eyes twinkled. "Of course, the pressing business only got mentioned when I told him about Clarissa being dead. Smart lad. He didn't want to get mixed up in murder. Very conservative, not at all like me."

Lord Farfaine devoted himself to breakfast, which

gave Paul a chance to formulate a careful question about work that needed to be done, and another about drawing on an account at the bank in Chatham. Instead he surprised himself by asking, "This Miss Quince who is to write about your fete. When will she be arriving?"

"What? Oh, her." Lord Farfaine shook his head. "She won't be coming after all. I invited her as a favor to . . . an associate. Now I learn she has to be elsewhere. Probably just as well with people leaving obeah spells in her bungalow."

"You know about that?"

Lord Farfaine looked momentarily disdainful. "My house, you know. It's my business to know what goes on. Mother told me. She's up on all that native stuff. Old hand in these parts."

"I wonder who Miss Quince's associate might have been?" Paul asked, surprising himself with his boldness.

Lord Farfaine played with his food in a most unaristocratic fashion, then said, "Marva, the housekeeper. She knew the young woman from some visit to Boucan, is what she said. Needed a leg up in her profession, didn't think it would hurt. Marva told me the other day she had a change in plans. Should have told you."

"No harm done," Paul said, somewhat mystified. Marva? Did Lambeaux know this? It was too complicated to think about.

"About the treasure hunt," Lord Farfaine said. "As soon as you can, you give me the details of where it's planted. You've got to point them in the right direction, don't you know, or the damned fools will fall into the sea."

"I am dealing with that problem . . . that project today."

"Good work!" Lord Farfaine said heartily. He stood up. "I'm off to roust Janie out of her bed if she's not up yet. Can't waste a beautiful day. Only have two months.''

"The bank," Paul said hastily. "You mentioned an account."

"Need money, do you?" Lord Farfaine reached into his pocket and brought out a wad of bills. He handed Paul a handful of English ten-pound notes. "Should be plenty for today, with the exchange rate here." Then he was gone.

Paul dawdled in the dining room for a time, but no one else appeared. He made his way cautiously through the door at the end of the hall where he'd seen Marva the previous night. The door led to a passageway with rooms lined in cabinets filled with china and glassware. The passageway ended in a screened gallery lush with hanging plants and mismatched chairs and tables: a comfortable room for the servants. Outside a covered arbor led to a white building with a wall of crimson poinsettias from ground to roof.

Marva was outside directing Derrick and Samson in carrying sacks of rice and baskets of produce. Paul caught a glimpse of sheds, their doors wide open, behind the poinsettias. In one of them, Clarissa's clothes had been found by the police. The ubiquitous Coo-Coo struggled to carry a stalk of reddish bananas that was almost as tall as he. A battered, yellow pickup truck was parked a distance away. A shirtless man in the back of the truck held up big, silvery fish with gutted bellies by the gills for Marva's approval before he plopped them onto the hanging scale. Paul was certain that it was the same truck he'd seen yesterday in the village by the bay.

Something hovered on the edge of his consciousness about his visit to the village. The empty street, the truck, the boy in the shed.

Inside the cookhouse, a woman was alternately singing and scolding an unseen person. A maid flew out, bearing a silver tray with a teapot, cup and covered dish, and headed along the path toward the bungalows.

Then Paul was discovered watching the scene, and all movement stopped.

"Please, don't let me interrupt," Paul said. "I need a word with Derrick."

Derrick put down the sack he was carrying and joined him. The others watched for a moment, and then went on with their tasks, all except Coo-Coo, who rested the banana stalk against a shed and kept his eyes on them.

"Do you need my assistance in anything this morning?" Paul asked, although he was certain what the answer would be.

"Me?" Derrick looked surprised, as though he couldn't imagine any further assistance that Paul could provide beyond his useless presence the previous day. "Is all in hand for the present moment. You go off and enjoy yourself."

"I shall need the use of a car," Paul said. "Is this possible? Not the Range Rover," he added hastily. "Georgina said there were several, and I thought you would know . . ."

"M'lord keeps a Jaguar, but . . . it's not here just now. Miss Georgie has a little sports car, but it has a mechanical problem. There's the old Toyota we use to run about when we don't need plenty of room. But it would be best if you found one of the taxi boys or Henry to drive you about."

"I prefer to drive myself," Paul said. He wanted to be free to find a spot for the treasure without having to explain to a driver.

"Take the red one, then," Derrick said reluctantly. "Petrol is low, but the station is right in town past the market. Keys in the ignition.'' Derrick turned away and then looked back. ''Your lady friend good today?''

''Lady Margaret? I haven't seen her,'' Paul said. ''Wait. Is something wrong? The cutlass . . . Were you expecting trouble?''

''I wasn't expecting anyt'ing in particular,'' Derrick said. ''Hey, boy. Put the banana in the shed.'' Coo-Coo obeyed. ''That boy. Mind's all over the place.''

''Samson, you carry the fish to the freezer house,'' Marva called out. She glared at Paul, quite unfairly, he thought. He was behaving himself. She handed money to the fish seller, who jumped from the back of the battered truck and got into the cab. Then he picked up a big white conch shell with a shiny pink interior. ''And don't be blowing that t'ing until you away from the house, Fitzie,'' Marva said. ''You'll wake the people.''

The fish seller grinned, backed up, and drove away down a steep back road Paul hadn't been aware of. A few moments later, he heard a distant blast of sound, a sort of deep wail that went from low to high. He understood: the man was blowing on the conch to signal his coming to the ladies in the houses tucked away on the back roads. The island's life was going on around him, unseen by those who enjoyed the luxuries of Indigo Hill.

Paul walked back through the big, silent house and out onto the verandah. The police must have finished at the pool, since a few guests were sitting around it.

The fleshy man in flowered shirt, white shorts, and dark glasses stretched out on a chaise was Carlos San Basilio. He was languidly giving orders to a serving man without raising his head. On the opposite side of the pool, the two English couples were drinking their tea at a table shaded by a big blue umbrella. They viewed the Caribbean rather than Carlos.

''In my day, we did not go out in the sun, early or

late.'' Lady Alys's voice was languidly cultured and vaguely disapproving.

Paul saw that she had taken up residence on a large wicker sofa at the end of the verandah, with teacup, a pile of newspapers and magazines, and a box of letter paper on a low table in front of her. Facedown on the sofa beside her was a mystery novel. Agatha Christie. Lady Alys was wearing a pink blouse and a white skirt, sensible sandals and—Paul surprised himself by noticing—proper pale hose although it was already hot, even with the steady trade winds.

"Matters were handled very differently," she said, and sounded as though the errors of this modern age were Paul's direct responsibility.

"Those days must have been interesting times, ma'am," Paul said. He was resigned to hearing more family confidences. "My grandfather and my father often spoke of times that were quite different from what we know today."

What he remembered his grandfather saying about the old days in Italy was that Mussolini had execrable taste in architecture. Paul's father merely bemoaned the fact that Roman *la dolce vita* as Fellini imagined it had disappeared and had been replaced by tour buses from Germany.

"The only one who remembers how it was is Eulalia."

"Ma'am?"

"Mamee Joe, they call her now. I have known her since I was a girl. She was my maid. You get close to your maid when you're a young girl alone on an island like Boucan for months at a time. My father ran the Indigo Hill plantation then, and had to be here half the year, but there were very few people of our sort. It was lovely when he was acting governor general over on the big island. Parties and handsome boys from home . . .''

Lady Alys's eyelids fluttered. Paul thought she might have dropped into a doze. Then she said, "In those days, it was possible to find devoted servants." She looked away from Paul and past the hanging plants toward the estate grounds. "Sometimes Jimmie talks about selling, but it's still my house, my island. Jimmie has some odd ideas. It's always been necessary to keep him in line."

Paul was about to make his excuses and find Margaret.

"I am not pleased that matters have taken a bad turn," Lady Alys said. "I did not care for that woman, although she was once my daughter-in-law. She should not have come here. I can't imagine why she did. In any case, she was ripe for murder."

"You are certain she was murdered then?" Paul asked.

"My dear young man, if you had known her, you would have no doubt." Lady Alys smiled complacently. "She's gone now."

"And the other murder?" Paul asked.

"The other?" Lady Alys frowned, and patted her snowy well-coiffed hair. "Do you refer to that native woman who was killed some weeks ago? She had nothing to do with us," Lady Alys said firmly. She appeared not to know that the other was scheduled to be a guest at Indigo Hill, invited by Lord Farfaine at the housekeeper's request. "I must get on with my correspondence. The mails out of Boucan are so terribly slow." A trace of a smile appeared. "And so many of my friends are of an age that a delayed letter might not reach them in this life."

Paul took that as a dismissal. "And I must see to my . . . my business here."

"Wear a hat," Lady Alys said. "My mother insisted that we always wear hats."

Margaret opened the door to her bungalow almost as soon as Paul knocked.

"I hoped you'd come 'round early," she said in a rush. "You truly won't believe what happened to me last night. I must look a fright."

"Are you all right?" Paul thought she looked especially attractive.

"Someone was here last night. Dressed in black, a man, possibly a woman. He knocked me down and ran away."

"Margaret!"

"And after the intruder, a strange old local woman came in. Happily, I didn't slice her up with that cutlass. Then Coo-Coo came and took her away. Mamee Joe, he called her. I have no idea why she was here, and she wouldn't tell me who the intruder was, if she knew. I had the sense that she was watching over me."

Paul said, "I don't like this. I wonder if it would be possible to resign at once. We could fly to Lyford Cay. My mother knows everyone with a decent house there, and it's quite as sunny and tropical as Boucan."

"Retreat is not yet in order," Margaret said. "Don't you want to get to the bottom of this? Someone attacked me, someone attacked you, and there are all these dead women about."

"Do we have to become involved?"

"We are already," Margaret said. "Look." She handed him the bundle of papers she'd discovered the night before. "I thought at first that the intruder was looking for these—Clarissa's feeble poetry and disconnected ramblings. She obviously knew P. Quince, she was here when the woman was killed and knew about it. She had an ally, and she was practically encouraged by Lady Alys to come to Boucan. There was a letter . . .''

"That can't be right,'' Paul said. "Lady Alys just told me that she couldn't imagine why Clarissa had come here."

Margaret shrugged. "It's sufficiently ambiguous that Clarissa might have willfully misunderstood."

"Especially if Lord Farfaine seemed amenable to blackmail.'' Paul told her about his comment at breakfast.

"It's all too odd,'' Margaret said. "I realized after the intruder had gone that he had been hiding them under the cushion, not taking them, so they certainly would be found by the maids, and brought to someone's attention—and connecting everything up, the chicken head, the dead Lady Farfaine, P. Quince who should have stayed here and who, like Clarissa, arrived early."

"Two women here at the same time, and both of them are dead,'' Paul said, "and connected in several ways. Marva the housekeeper asked Lord Farfaine to invite P. Quince. I have this from m'lord himself."

"Goodness, I must sort this out,'' Margaret said. "All I have is the fact that both women were writing things, there was some obeah business around the time they each died, but now we have Marva. This Rusty Keating who brought Clarissa to the island . . .''

"Please let Lambeaux handle it,'' Paul said desperately. "I do not like the looks of Keating. Come with me to find a place to bury the treasure. Lady Alys states that we will wear hats."

Margaret said, "She is probably right. Many perils lurk among the palm trees."

Chapter 15

"*It is* not the most elegant of vehicles," Paul said as he backed the old red Toyota from its space at the back of the house and drove it around to the main driveway in front of Indigo Hill.

"Serviceable," Margaret said. She had a broad-brimmed cotton hat on her lap. "I only hope no one wants a lift somewhere."

Someone did. Tyrone Pace, all in white, signaled to them from the verandah steps. Margaret determined that the tall, athletic Pace did not resemble the figure she had seen in her bungalow.

"Good morning, Lady Margaret, Prince. Are you headed into the town?" He peered in through the car window.

"Yes," Paul said, resigned to an unwanted passenger. "I have an errand related to Lord Farfaine's festivities."

"Perhaps Lady Margaret would then be willing to do a favor for Madame Campos." He smiled briefly. "And for me. She continues to cling to the illusion that I am here as her personal servant." He took a scrap of paper from his shirt pocket. "Madame Campos is in need of

142

nail varnish. Since the women among my fellow citizens are fond of nail varnish, I am sure you will locate some. There is a general store and pharmacist, I recall, past the bus station. I am not so certain you will find the particular color she desires." He handed Margaret the paper.

"Mmm. I judge this brand is not to be found outside of Paris or New York," she said. "Let me try for very red, and hope that if I am wrong, it will not lessen your tip."

Tyrone laughed. "Thank you. I would prefer to spend my time at Arawak Bay watching the boys play cricket on the beach. I hope only that there are no more bodies in the pool—or in the bushes on the beach." Pace looked thoughtful. "Our islands are so beautiful that it is hard for foreigners to realize that the people are not carefree gods and goddesses playing in paradise. Life is not easy."

"I am coming to understand that," Paul said.

"This woman on the beach some weeks ago. They were speculating on the big island that she was a local girl who met with misfortune, but I do not think that can be so. Perhaps she was born here but emigrated as a child. Our local girls don't go off in boats with men carrying cutlasses—and most especially not leaving anyone to report them gone missing, and no one to claim them if they are found dead. It is not easy to remain invisible here. Your business is everyone's business."

"True," Paul said. "Everyone knows everything."

"If no one knew her on Boucan or on the other island, she was not from here."

Paul and Margaret looked at each other. If Pace knew the identity of the woman on the beach, he was not admitting it.

"If she came from elsewhere," Margaret said carefully, "she must have handed in a landing card at the airport. Or if she came by boat, she would be cleared by immigration at the port."

"There are many unofficial ways of arriving," Tyrone said. "And leaving. I prefer to have the authorities sort it out. I do not wish my holiday to be troubled by murder." He paused. "Two murders." Tyrone strolled off.

Paul put the car in gear. "Who the woman on the beach was is no longer the issue. The questions now are how she got there, and why she died."

"The same questions apply to Clarissa in the pool," Margaret said. "At least we have an idea of *why* they were here."

"We do?"

"They both wanted something from Jimmie. Wait!" Paul applied the brake.

"Your dream woman makes my simple but expensive denim outfit look positively primitive. But she does not look her cordial self this morning," Margaret said, looking toward the house.

Georgina stormed down the steps wearing a big, sheer green shirt and a long, off-white crocheted skirt that showed the outline of her long and shapely legs. She wore a stack of bracelets halfway up her arm, and a belt made of heavy gold links. Her dark hair had been braided into elaborate corn rows in the local style with bright beads at the ends of the braids.

"I want a lift to the marina," she said. "There's no free car." The Honorable Georgina was clearly very annoyed. She got into the backseat. "Oh, get moving before before we have a carload to deal with."

Paul moved. It was not exactly like driving the incredibly expensive Ferrari his mother had permitted him to drive around New York City until the expense of keeping a permanent guard to watch it could not be justified. He turned onto the main road.

"Mind the lorry, Prince. They take no prisoners."

Margaret made an attempt at soothing Georgina's ill temper. "I didn't have a chance to speak to you last night," she said.

"I had to see that the servants took care of the guests. Janie is simply terrible about that. Grandmother regularly bemoans her lack of breeding, but really expects that from Americans. Daddy gets so caught up in socializing." She paused. "But don't let his manner fool you. He's very shrewd about business. Much shrewder than my brother, although Anthony thinks he's got the world by the tail."

Margaret said, "Exactly what business is Jimmie into these days? My brother heard he'd gotten out of chemicals or computers." Her brother had actually said that Jimmie had allegedly taken some bad licks in the stock market recently.

Georgina's answer was evasive, to say the least. "I saw your brother a while back in London. He seems to be engaged to a barmaid. She's an odd choice for an earl."

"Yes," Margaret said. "But she loves Priam's Priory, all that estate business I'm no good at. I don't suppose your father actively farms the Indigo Hill lands."

"We lease out most of our lands to local farmers," Georgina said. "The government prefers it. Plantation days are over." She seemed to have gotten over her temper.

"But you've been coming here for years and years."

"It seems more like home than England," Georgina said. "Sometimes just Grandmother and I come here for a few weeks."

"I suppose you grew up knowing about the customs and such," Margaret said disingenuously. "Things like obeah . . . isn't that the local magic business I've read about?"

"That ghastly Ninni Campos—do you think she's had her eyes fixed?" Once again, Georgina responded with an entirely different subject. "She claims to have been a chum of Clarissa's. I wonder if she knew Clarissa was hiding out here all along. I can't imagine why Daddy invited her, unless she has something on him he'd rather not have broadcast. He does get into situations, even now that he's married to Jane." She spoke the name with distaste. "He's always been that way."

When Georgina finally paused for breath, Margaret said, "What takes you to the town so early?"

Georgina was silent for a moment, then said, "I'm breakfasting with those divine people from Sweden. Did you get a look at Gunnar? Imagine sailing all the way from there to here. It makes Rusty's adventures seem mild. Sound your horn, Prince. It's one of the boys who works at Indigo Hill, and he knows this car. They are offended if you don't acknowledge them."

Paul sounded the horn, and wished Georgina would call him Paul.

"Stop," Georgina commanded. "That woman up ahead wants a lift. She lives at Arawak Bay, and sells souse outside the club after dances. Pig's head and trotters stewed with lime and cucumber and pepper, served up cold."

Paul stopped. The woman was middle-aged, plainly dressed, and carrying a big, empty woven bag for her purchases.

"Mornin', mornin'," the woman said. "Happy to hear you come home, Miss Georgie."

"Hullo, Pearl. These are some of Daddy's friends."

"You tell m'lord to get on with building that jetty at the bay and never mind those boys talkin' against it. We could get good business out of it. Little houses on the beach for the tourists, snackette and souvenirs. Those boys saying it's ex-ploi-ta-tion." She sucked her teeth in disgust. "You can't make a good living from fish pull from the sea with no big freezer house like you have up at Indigo Hill."

"Now, Pearl, you can't have everything," Georgina said.

"Spoil the natural beauty they say. Those boys don't know anyt'ing about natural beauty. All they know is driving fast boats, smoking and drinking, and finding trouble. Somebody put them up to it, tellin' them they better off to keep the bay like it is. You tell me if dead woman on the beach doesn't spoil natural beauty."

"That was simply awful," Georgina said soothingly.

"That girl not one of we. Nothin' to do with we," Pearl said sharply. "Lookin' at the boys like some bold, bold hussy."

"Really?" Margaret said. "You saw her? Did you tell the police?"

Pearl said, "You could drop me at the crossroads up ahead. Those boys tell me to mind my business, so I mind it. Don't need to talk to police. I raise my chil'ren, send them to America so they can make something of themselves. I don't need to tell about some light-skinned girl I see in one of those boys' sheds. Boats come in and you don't know who gets off. This is the place."

Paul stopped at the crossroads. As they pulled away, Pearl could be seen crossing the road.

"What about that?" Margaret said. "She saw the dead woman."

"Margaret," Georgina said, "she didn't see anyone. People here make up fantastic stories all the time.

They're like poets. No one saw this woman. If she were really there, no one could keep it a secret.''

They reached the fringes of Chatham, and the road began to clog with cars driven in a somewhat haphazard manner.

"Drop me there," Georgina said. "Oh, don't look for a place to stop. Just stop. They'll wait."

Paul stopped where he was, causing a minor backup while Georgina got out. She waved gaily to the line of cars behind them waiting to move, and they responded with cheerful greetings and short blasts of their horns.

"Everyone," said Margaret, "knows and loves Georgina."

The car lurched forward as Georgina swung off toward the concrete pier where quite a few sailing boats were docked, sails furled and national flags of various sorts flying from the masts. Blond men and women were on deck performing housekeeping chores and chatting back and forth between boats.

"Colorful," Margaret said. "I wonder if it's the amazing Gunnar she's seeing or Rusty Keating."

"One will surely lead to the other, if that's what interests her," Paul said crossly.

"She is not interested in you, then?"

"I have been at a disadvantage," Paul said. "She won't even call me by name. I must locate that petrol station. Ah, there it is, and there's the bank. I need Caribbean dollars." He was pleased that he had managed to slip into the one available parking space just as another car pulled out.

"I wonder where I can find Ninni's nail varnish," Margaret said as she observed the row of small and unpromising shops.

"Would you mind going to the bank while I stay

about here?'' Paul said. ''I am looking for a particular person.''

''I shall probably have a·long wait on a queue,'' she said, ''to judge from the activity.'' A number of people were coming and going through the glass doors of the concrete building.

While Margaret took Lord Farfaine's British pounds and ventured into the bank, Paul stood in the sun and leaned against the old red car. The space in front of the rum shop was occupied by several loungers, but he did not see Boots among them. He hesitated to approach them and ask. He felt highly conspicuous: No one else was wearing a peach-colored cotton designer shirt and tan slacks from Neiman's and brown buffalo-leather moccasins. No one had as much money in his pocket, or an air ticket to fly away from Boucan at will.

A woman thrust a basket of brown, fuzzy egg-shaped fruit at him. ''Sapodilla, sir? Just pick this morning.'' Paul shook his head and sidestepped a man pulling a makeshift wagon bearing a crate of noisy white chickens. Boots was nowhere to be seen.

A big lorry loaded with crates of Coca-Cola rumbled to a stop in front of the rum shop, blocking it from Paul's view. He decided he had no choice but to stroll over, since there was no other place he knew of to look for Boots.

When he reached the shop, the lorry pulled away, and he saw Mr. Lambeaux sitting at a table.

''Prince Paul,'' he said. ''You will join me?''

''For a moment,'' Paul said. ''Lady Margaret is in the bank. I can watch for her from here.'' He sat down.

''Will you take something?'' Lambeaux said. ''It is too early in the day for me for rum or beer, but you perhaps . . .''

''I think,'' Paul said, ''that I would risk becoming

more of a menace on your roads than I am now. But thank you.''

"I am observing the arrival of quite a grand vessel,'' Lambeaux said. Paul looked out toward the water and saw a very large, handsome motor yacht approaching the harbor.

"She will not be able to dock at the marina, but will anchor in the deeper water,'' Lambeaux said. "One of Lord Farfaine's friends, perhaps?''

"To tell the truth,'' Paul said, "I am supposedly in charge of his affairs, but I do not know about anything that is happening.''

"Life is quite different here, even from the big island,'' Lambeaux said. "Ah, there is your Lady Margaret.''

She spotted Paul and Lambeaux almost at once.

"Lovely in the bank. Real air-conditioning to pacify those waiting on line,'' Margaret said.

"You are enjoying your visit?'' Lambeaux asked. He appeared to be quite taken with Margaret, who was, Paul had to admit, a good-looking woman.

"I would enjoy it more if I knew whodunit,'' Margaret said.

Lambeaux looked puzzled for a moment, then smiled. "The murders. So would I, but you should not feel uneasy, good lady. You are not involved in these unfortunate events. They are a local matter. I understand. I grew up on Boucan, you know. People like Marva are very old friends. I went off to a larger world.'' He gazed at the yacht. "Marva could have come too, but she chose to stay. Twenty years of devotion to Lord Farfaine's family. I'm sure he treats her well. The old lady is not, I think, so kind.'' He shook his head. "Marva is not the person I remember. I must ask her questions today, and I do not look forward to it.''

"Do you think she knows something of the murders?'' Margaret asked cautiously.

"I think,'' Lambeaux said, "everyone here knows something.'' He was looking hard at Margaret. "We usually do not have a large number of murders, unlike what I understand is the rule in New York City.'' He turned to Paul. "Or Dallas. I do not know the situation in Rome.''

Paul wondered how he knew what cities Paul called home.

"Fortunately, I have quite a few forensic resources to help solve the ones that do occur,'' Lambeaux said. "The big island is more advanced than Boucan.''

Margaret leaned back in her chair. As he had still given no indication of his rank, she went for a substantial title. "Superintendent,'' she said, and ignored his deprecating hand gesture, "I know something.'' He nodded, as though he was expecting that. "Let me tell you about last night.''

She told him about the intruder, although she did not mention Mamee Joe and Coo-Coo. She told him about the papers. "I believe they were being placed under the cushion, rather than being removed,'' she said.

"Where are these papers?'' he asked rather brusquely. He seemed to have forgotten his solicitous concern about Margaret. He did not dwell on whether she had been damaged by the intruder.

"I took the chance that we might encounter you,'' Margaret said. "Here they are.'' She pulled the bundle of papers from her bag.

He riffled through the pages and then stuffed them in his pocket. "Did you look at them?'' he asked.

"A glance through,'' Margaret said innocently.

"Poems and deep thoughts, not to my taste. Perhaps you can make something of them. It appears Clarissa was aware of P. Quince."

"I had reason to believe that several people were so aware. You have no idea who this intruder was? A local? A guest?"

"Whoever it was had dirty hands," Margaret said. "Something like charcoal dust ended up on my sleeping garment when he pushed me to the ground."

Lambeaux pondered this. "Many households here still use charcoal fires for cooking. Not everyone on Boucan can afford gas cookers."

"A clue, then," Margaret said. She leaned forward on her elbows. "What else do you have to tell us about the dead Lady Farfaine and the dead P. Quince?"

Paul listened uneasily. He watched the traffic move past the rum shop and recognized the doctor who had come to Indigo Hill to see about the dead woman. And that surely was the young constable who had been at the house, now patrolling Chatham's main street, and the yellow pickup truck from Arawak Bay, driven by the man who had sold fish to Marva. A small, cozy world, with few places to hide.

"Lady Margaret," Lambeaux was saying, "I must beg you not to ask too many questions or seek out any answers."

Paul suddenly had an answer, or rather, the beginning of a question.

Lambeaux stood up. "What a beautiful craft." He gazed out to the harbor where the yacht had anchored. "I could almost wish that it was taking you away, Lady Margaret, out of harm's way."

Chapter 16

"I do not believe that Mr. Lambeaux has told us anything about what he knows or suspects," Margaret said. "I wonder about that obeah business he mentioned. Perhaps he thinks someone else is in danger of dying."

"Not us!" Paul was alarmed.

"I shouldn't think so," Margaret said, "unless we happen to uncover something we shouldn't."

Paul relaxed for a moment. Then he said, "You said Lady Alys had written encouraging Clarissa to come to Boucan. What will Lambeaux think of that? Should you have given him the papers?"

"I chose not to give him Lady Alys's letter. It would simply raise unpleasant questions, but I did spend a good deal of time copying them out, so we could reread them at leisure. Now let's be off."

"Where?"

"To uncover something we shouldn't," she said impatiently.

"Please, Margaret . . . I don't want to uncover anything, and I need to find Boots."

"What is a Boots?"

"A local person. You told me back in New York to take advice about the treasure. I am doing so."

"Mmm." Margaret was gazing out toward the marina and harbor beyond. "I say, that *is* a fabulous yacht. Something like Robert Maxwell or Onassis would have condescended to call home. Of course, they're both dead, and only the Saudis and the Bruneis have that kind of money. Are they here for Jimmie's fete?"

"Then they are too early," Paul said grimly. "The people coming on yachts aren't due until the end of the week."

"Cheer up," Margaret said. "This really is quite a charming place. Here, take your local dollars." She handed him a fat wad of bills. "Just look at all these bustling people and . . ." She looked again toward the marina. ". . . the picturesque scene before us." She spied a country woman with a huge basket on her head. "What's that woman got? Mangos! Don't go away!" Margaret dashed away and quickly disappeared into the crowd. Paul caught one glimpse of her blond head as she pursued the woman with the mangos, but now several fair-haired persons were in evidence in their casual yachting clothes, mingling with the locals.

"Hey, man. What's happenin'?" Boots had arrived. He was unshaven, and his clothes did not look entirely up to the standards set by someone like Derrick. "Out all night, Charlie," he said with a grin. "Taking these boat people out to the clubs." He waved toward the marina. "Rusty leave them to their own devices. He find some woman or whatever. They were on the loose with nobody to mind them, so old Bootsie take charge. You want me to show you some things now? Beaches, the plantations . . . anything you like."

"I do need your services," Paul began. "A business proposition. Could we find a place out of the sun to talk away from here?'' He did not wish to have Lambeaux find him hanging about the rum shop with Boots.

''Across the road,'' Boots said. ''What you have in mind?'' He seemed excited by the prospect of business. He grasped Paul's arm and maneuvered him through the slow-moving traffic, as voices called out to him. Everyone appeared to know Boots even better than Georgina. ''Sit.'' He indicated the low seawall shaded by a couple of sheds that faced the harbor.

The seawall dropped sharply twenty feet to the water, where the sea bumped gently against the gray stone and concrete. Paul looked down. Even here in the harbor, the water was clear.

''So what's the plan, Charlie? Nobody here to listen.''

''I have to bury some treasure,'' Paul began. ''I thought you might be able to assist me.''

Boots's expression conveyed a mixture of puzzlement and wariness, as though he might be dealing with a madman from across the sea masquerading as a prince, or perhaps merely a foreigner whose words failed to convey any recognizable meaning.

''No treasure on Boucan,'' Boots said finally. ''Government say, 'Our island's beauty is our greatest treasure.' You see the signs posted? Trying to tell we not to worry about not havin' money or work. You talking about some kind of treasure like that?''

''No, no,'' Paul said hastily. ''It's for Lord Farfaine.''

That seemed to explain everything to Boots: the island's own madman was entirely understandable.

''In a week's time, when all the guests are here and the big fete takes place . . .''

''All of we join in, m'lord fixes it so the steelband boys play and we could dress up in carnival costumes if we like, plenty to drink, eat. We get some tips even. Old man's okay.''

Paul ignored Boots's digression. ''There is to be a treasure hunt. I am to bury something in a place that is not too difficult to reach, and perhaps provide some clues to set the searchers in the right direction. I think perhaps this has been done before. . . . ''

Boots frowned, as though checking back through the island's social history. ''Once, twice a few years back maybe,'' he said.

''I would have to find a place near a road or a well-marked path. Nothing too difficult.'' He could not imagine sending Madame Campos off into the middle of the jungle.

''Man, just plant it up there on Indigo Hill.''

''Too obvious,'' Paul said firmly. ''I would pay you for your assistance in locating the right spot.''

''I'm not goin' to ax you how much,'' Boots said. ''I am goin' to trust you to do right.'' He stood up. ''I got one, two places in mind. Let we go.''

''I can't leave without my friend, Lady Margaret,'' Paul said. He searched the opposite of the busy road, but did not see her. Perhaps she was searching for Ninni Campos's nail varnish.

''Is she a good-looking lady with yellow hair?''

''Margaret is blond,'' Paul said, ''and she's quite attractive. I last saw her going toward the market.''

Boots shook his head. ''She went to the marina. I see she just now. Headin' for the Red Man's boat.''

''Indeed?'' Paul stood up and searched the pier for Margaret. ''Why would she look for a red man?''

''It's what we call Rusty Keating, Charlie. All the girls like Rusty. Big sailing boat, goes where he likes, plenty of money. I know him a long, long time. Sometime I do these little jobs for the Red Man. Private business, you know." He looked at Paul out of the corner of his eye. "M'lord's girl have an eye on him, too."

Paul thought of Georgina swinging along on her long legs toward the marina—perhaps to visit Rusty Keating, and perhaps to be interrupted by an unwelcome visit from Lady Margaret Priam.

"There's Margaret," Paul said. He waved to her as she strolled along the pier in no apparent hurry, stopping twice to say a word to people who looked like those at Lord Farfaine's gathering the night before. She finally saw Paul, and waved back.

They converged at the point where the pier met the land.

"I found the thing for Ninni," Margaret said. "She will complain loudly, but the shops here are not exactly the Galeries Lafayette. And I've got us some lovely mangos. Marva probably has tons at the house, but it was fun to bargain for them. And the marina is . . . fascinating." She put out her hand to Boots who took it briefly and gingerly. "Hullo, I'm Margaret Priam."

"This is Boots," Paul said.

"Is only what they call me," Boots said. "I have these cowboy boots once. Clifford Phipps is the name."

"Ah," Margaret said. "Probably not related to the Phippses I know."

"Boots is going to help suggest a place where I might bury the treasure," Paul said. "I must get gasoline for the car."

"Why don't Mr. Phipps and I have a nice cold drink while you're getting filled up," Margaret said. "It's terribly hot, and Rusty didn't offer me a thing." She smiled blandly. "He had a guest, so I didn't linger. Come along, Mr. Phipps . . . Boots. Do you think they'll give me lots of ice in my Coca-Cola?"

"If I say to," Boots said.

As they parted, Paul heard Margaret say to Boots, "You're surely the one to tell me all about the interesting plants on Boucan."

Paul decided to proceed without undue speed, while Margaret extracted useful information from Boots. He wondered if Boots would make a connection between Margaret's wide-eyed questions and the fact that poison was involved in the former Lady Farfaine's death. Everybody must know that by now.

There were two cars ahead of him as he waited to be served at the single gas pump. Out the open window, he watched a small launch coming toward the pier from the big yacht anchored offshore. As he watched, a sleek gray boat with an outboard motor sped away from the marina and headed out to sea. It was like the boat that had tried to run him down, but this one looked full of carefree, blond Scandinavians from the docked sailing craft.

The traffic on the main road thinned as housewives finished their shopping and workers reached their places of business. Paul had fixed his eyes on a car parked in the shade near the gas pump.

Paul finally pulled up to the pump, and said to the man pumping gas, "That car."

"What car, sir?"

"The Jaguar over there."

A dark green Jaguar was parked at the side of the gas station in the shade.

"Somebody make a deal with the boss to leave it," the man said. "We got the lights on all night, car stays in sight, and the constable can keep an eye on it." He chuckled. "But you couldn't get away with stealing m'lord's car. Everybody know it. Only one on the island."

"It has been here all night then?"

The man shrugged. "Could have been here an hour or a week."

"Thank you so much," Paul said. He pulled out of the gas station and eased onto the road. Boots and Margaret got into the car at the rum shop.

"Lovely cold drink," Margaret said, "and Boots knows an awful lot about everything on Boucan. He tells me there's an interesting old sugar mill just up the road."

"Excellent," Paul said. "Boots, there must be many back roads through the center of the island that could take you anyplace. I saw the fish seller take a back road from Indigo Hill. Steep. Would it go around to Arawak Bay?"

Boots said, "How you think Fitzie and those boys get into town? They're not swimming here. There's plenty of roads to all the villages. Tourists stick to the main road. The others are for we." He suddenly went quiet, as though he'd said too much. Paul glanced over at Margaret. She wore a faint smile, as though she understood what Paul had asked and what Boots had told them.

"I had a chat with Rusty Keating," Margaret said. "His guest was down below. I heard her voice, before she knew I was on deck chatting up Rusty—before he efficiently got rid of me."

"Lord Farfaine's Jaguar has been left at the gasoline station," Paul said casually.

"Ah," Margaret said. "That explains it. It didn't quite sound like Georgina. I didn't realize that Jane was so . . . so . . . adventurous. We do have a good deal to discuss when we get back to the house."

"Stop here!" Boots said. "Up ahead is a little track off the road. End of St. Joseph's Trace is up there, by the bougainvillea you could see over the bush. Turn in. It's a rough road, but people drive up.''

Paul followed the rutted track up the hill until he reached a flat spot beside an abandoned-looking round stone building.

"The old sugar mill," Boots said. "In the old days, it have big blades turned by the wind. There's always a breeze here off the ocean.''

Now that they were high on a hill, they could see the thick vegetation that covered the island, and the distant, sparkling sea. They could even catch a glimpse of Chatham's colorful houses on the hills above the main street.

''Mamee Joe, Derrick, all of them, live up there at the top of the trace," Boots said. "Fifteen minutes that way to walk to the big house. There's one or two paths through the plantation. Easy. So what you think?''

"Let's look inside," Margaret said. She gazed at the vine-covered building. "Is it safe?''

"Couple of stones fall down one time in a big storm. The works department check it out. It's okay. Come.'' He pointed to the round doorway.

As they entered, Paul and Margaret were greeted by a skittish brown-and-white goat, which looked at them with startled eyes and stumbled out of the mill into the bush.

''Picturesque," Margaret said. She looked up. The roof was mostly gone. "Someone's had a fire here," she said, and pointed with her toe at a circle of stones with a heap of ashes in the center and some pointed, blackened sticks lying on the ground.

"Someone barbequeing fish or meat," Boots said. "The farmers from the plantation lands come in, and little boys who want to play like Caribs or Arawaks.''

"What do you think, Paul? Could this be a place

where pirates buried their treasure?'' Margaret strolled around the round, empty space.

Then she bent down and peered into a wide chink in the stone wall. "Boots, any spiders or snakes about?"

"Nothing dangerous," Boots said, and Margaret put her hand into the opening. "Except scorpions . . ."

She withdrew her hand quickly. She was holding a little red cloth bundle. "What do you suppose this is?" She weighed it in her hand.

"Some old t'ing one of the boys leave," Boots said nervously. "Put it back, right? I don't want somebody troublin' me about stealing."

"It can't hurt to look," Margaret said. The bundle was loosely tied with a piece of strong white cord. Margaret had no difficulty untying the knot. The bundle fell open, and Paul peered over Margaret's shoulder at the objects lying on the red cloth in her hand: a lock of hair, a gold bangle bracelet with rough gold nuggets at each end of the circle, a delicate gold ring with pavé diamonds forming a pattern.

Margaret and Paul examined the ring.

"It has to be a 'Q' or an 'O'," she said softly. "Quince."

Paul frowned. "It may be just a pattern and not an initial at all. But the bracelet . . ." He closed his eyes. Carolyn Sue Dennis Castrocani Hoopes had been a good teacher to her son with respect to noticing women and what they wore. "Margaret," he said, "ask me about it later."

"Put it back," Boots said. "Is valuable stuff. If somebody see we drive up here and the things are missing, everybody going to think I took it."

"But Boots, if we could find it, someone else could too. You say people do come in here."

"Boy brings a girlfriend, farmers take a rest out of

the sun. They're not looking for a t'ing stuffed in a hole in the wall.''

''Put it back, Margaret,'' Paul said firmly.

''But . . .''

He said slowly in Italian, ''We will return.''

''Of course,'' Margaret said. ''You are clever.'' She retied the bundle, approximating the original knot as best she could. ''You're right, Boots. Back it goes, but . . .'' she added warningly, ''if it goes missing, we *will* know who took it.''

Boots threw up his hands. ''Not me. Lock of hair in there, you see it? Has a spell on it. I'm not going to touch anything like that. You want to look at the beach now? It's a better place to hide that treasure thing. Nice sand, nice palm trees . . .'' He was nervous now to the point of being unnerved. ''This is a nasty place. The beach is better.''

''We will look at the beach another day,'' Margaret said. ''Paul and I must return to Indigo Hill. I did not realize how late is was.''

Boots had edged to the mill's open doorway. ''Good, tomorrow. I'll be at the same place, Charlie. Help you some more.''

The three of them emerged from the mill.

''I'll settle up with you for today,'' Paul said. He counted out some bills, the amount of which appeared to please Boots. ''We can drop you anywhere you wish.''

''I'm going back to town then, see what's happenin'. I don't need a ride.''

''Mamee Joe lives up there, you say?'' Margaret said.

''Just up so, past the gully. You see the top of the big mango?'' He grinned. He was his usual self, now that he was out of the old mill, and waved as he started down the track.

"What do we do now?" Paul asked. "Take the things we found now that Boots is gone?"

"I wonder," Margaret said. "On the one hand, let us assume that the initial is a 'Q'—not common and therefore conceivably a ring belonging to Miss Quince. Let us assume in that case that someone connected with P. Quince put the objects there. It could well be the murderer. If that person returns and finds them missing, what will be the reaction?" She answered her own question. "Find the person who took them, and that person is in jeopardy. If we leave them in place, the murderer has no reason to think that anyone knows about them."

"P. Quince died several weeks ago," Paul said. "Do we assume that the objects have been here undisturbed since that time? If we leave the bundle, we can perhaps contrive a reason for the murderer to feel compelled to retrieve it."

"Paul darling, you are terribly clever," Margaret said. "We'll do just that."

Paul said slowly, "There is one problem. The bracelet."

"Unusual, with those rough gold nuggets instead of the typical smooth bead. I've even seen some with faces or animals. . . . "

"Margaret," Paul said seriously, "Georgina wears a bracelet exactly like it. She had it on yesterday, and she was wearing it today."

"Oh, dear," Margaret said. "And you can get to Arawak Bay by car. What if it wasn't Jane on Rusty's boat, and the Jaguar had been damaged on one of the back roads and is being repaired? . . . And what if Georgina knew that her former stepmother was staying on the island, prepared to pursue blackmail for some unspecified sin? Or to work with this P. Quince to produce some scandalous piece about the family rather than a social puff piece about Lord Farfaine's fete? It's almost Georgina's personal island to hear her talk. What scandals, then, that would justify murder? Surely Lady Alys's activities are beyond reproach. Anthony? Jimmie?'' She stopped. ''Marva has been there for years. Perhaps plantation days are not necessarily over.''

''What are you thinking now,'' Paul asked suspiciously.

''I'd really like to talk to Mamee Joe and the little boy who sees obeah signs right before a woman is found dead.'' She looked up at the sugar mill. ''A boy who lives just up the hill, and probably enjoys playing in a place like this. Someone who is also very fond of the Honorable Georgina Hose-Griffith.''

She looked out at the splendid view for a moment in silence.

''The intruder in my bungalow could have been a woman,'' she said. ''A white woman with charcoal to darken her face.''

Chapter 17

"*D*o we drive to see Mamee Joe?" Margaret said. "Or do we walk?"

Paul frowned at the way St. Joseph's Trace quickly dwindled to a steep footpath. "We walk," he said. "We leave the car with the goat."

The resident goat had returned and grazed peacefully outside the mill.

Paul and Margaret started out toward the cluster of houses at the top of the hill. The tangled brush on either side was oppressively close. Little air stirred here. Margaret peered down a steep hillside into a dark gully where a huge tree grew.

"The mango tree Boots mentioned," she said. "You can see the fruit on the top branches. You can almost feel the place holding on to its secrets."

At the end of the track they found themselves on a broad, flattened area on the top of the hill, crowded with small, neat, pastel-colored cement-block houses set on piles of blocks so there was open space beneath them.

"There's Coo-Coo," Margaret said. He was standing in one of the houses behind a half-door reached by a short flight of wooden steps. "Hullo. We took a look at the old sugar mill and decided to continue on up the hill."

A frayed-looking brown dog that had been asleep under Coo-Coo's house raised its head at the sound of her voice, but apparently decided it was not worth the effort to defend his terrority against strangers.

"Derrick's gone," Coo-Coo said. "I stayin' home because of fever."

"We came looking for Mamee Joe, not Derrick," Margaret said. "Is she here?" Coo-Coo momentarily looked as though he were ready to retreat into the house. His eyes flicked to his right, in the direction of a tiny unpainted wooden house with a very steep roof and a crooked wooden louvered window covered with a thin yellow curtain.

"Perhaps we could go 'round and speak to her in a moment," Margaret said, "after we've had a chat." She tapped her wrist, and Paul nodded.

"Coo-Coo, my friend," Paul said, "Lady Margaret and I need to ask you a question. No big thing." Paul was rather proud that he'd picked up a local phrase, but he seemed to have alarmed Coo-Coo considerably.

"I wonder," Margaret said, "if someone special— someone like Miss Georgina—ever gave you a beautiful gift, and told you to hide it away carefully but to tell no one."

The terror on Coo-Coo's face sent a pang through Margaret. She had not intended to frighten the child. He slammed the upper half of the Dutch door shut.

"Oh, dear. What have I done?"

"Can't rest with chattering all about the place." Mamee Joe was standing at the open window of the wooden house. "Who's that?" She peered at them.

"What you comin' here for, miss? You belong at Indigo Hill. This is St. Joseph's Trace."

"You belong here," Margaret said, "yet you come to the big house. Indeed, you come into my bungalow."

Mamee Joe's scowl became a suppressed smile, and she chuckled. "Come to the back, I let you in my place."

Paul and Margaret made their way around the corner of the wooden house. On the other side was a patch of bright flowers and on the hillside, a terraced vegetable garden. Mamee Joe had opened the door at the top of three wooden steps, and stood aside as Margaret and Paul entered her unimaginably tiny house. The kitchen had a blackened stove and a sink with a drainboard piled with washed pots and dishes. The floor of the kitchen was covered with worn linoleum, and there was a small, square table and a single chair pushed up against the wall. At the end of a narrow hallway was another tiny room with a leatherette sofa and a matching chair. The walls everywhere were covered with framed photos of young people in graduation gowns, bridal gowns, tuxedos with frilly shirts, babies in lace and in winter clothes and bonnets that suggested to Margaret that some of Mamee Joe's descendants had emigrated to colder lands. Some photos were so yellowed that they must have been taken decades before.

"Sit in the drawing room," Mamee Joe commanded.

They went and sat side by side on the sofa. A little breeze came through the window. A large red vase was filled with an abundant arrangement of plastic flowers, and there was also a very large television set, probably acquired for Mamee Joe by one or several of the children, grandchildren, and great-grandchildren whose photos looked down on the two aliens from Indigo Hill.

Finally Mamee Joe appeared, walking slowly, and balancing a tray with two glasses, a pitcher filled with a brownish cloudy liquid, and a bowl of ice.

"Is real ginger beer," she said. "Some still make it the way we did in the old days." She poured a glass for Margaret and Paul and watched them sip. "Now, what you doin' coming around to frighten the boy? I hear you. He's having a real bad time."

Margaret took a deep breath. She felt as though she were about to ask stupid and possibly offensive questions about someone's religion. "I want to ask about obeah," she said. "About the things that Coo-Coo has been finding. Do you know about them?"

Mamee Joe's eyes were on Margaret, but she didn't answer.

"I am certain," Margaret said, "that there is a connection between these . . . these pictures Coo-Coo saw and told the policeman about and the dead women." She took a deep breath. "I believe that the chicken head I found in my room was also meant to suggest death. But I don't believe that it referred to the lady who was to stay there, Miss Quince, since she was long since dead."

Mamee Joe nodded, but it was not clear whether she was agreeing with Margaret.

"Perhaps it refers to me," Margaret said after a long, uncomfortable silence during which Paul took tiny sips of ginger beer to keep himself occupied while Margaret traveled a road she had discovered on her own.

"It is more likely that it was meant to refer to some other woman here on Boucan," Margaret said finally. "But there is something wrong about these spells, isn't there?" Now she strove to will Mamee Joe to meet her eye. The contest was a draw. Mamee Joe did look at Margaret, but quickly looked away.

"Magic spells—by whatever name they are called—are not expected to succeed in a matter of minutes or hours," Margaret said. "I know that from folk magic back in England. Yet a little boy finds an object and he immediately sees the result—a dead woman. These are false signs, aren't they, not true spells at all."

Mamee Joe sighed deeply. "Some kind of bad trouble around the place. I feel it. The boy tell me just now about finding a picture with nails in the gully right before they find the girl on the beach. Then he see Marva taking away a picture at the big house somebody nailed to a tree. Now he find another lady dead. I already tell Miss Alys it's not right. She say she's handling everything, I shouldn't think about it. But I do."

"Then I am correct. Is that why you came to my bungalow on hearing about the chicken head?"

"Marva tell me. I looking to see if you dead in your bed. I see somebody run out. Can't say who . . ." Mamee Joe said, then added, "I know all there is to know, but I know when to keep still. Nothing to do with we."

Margaret thought the old woman must at least suspect who it was, but for her own reasons, she would not tell.

Paul recognized the refrain. Nothing to do with we: the woman on the beach, the woman in the pool.

He spoke up, "It does. It has something to do with the people at Indigo Hill and the people of Boucan."

Mamee Joe nodded. "Is like everything from before and from now mixed up together. Like Miss Alys always talking about the way things were, always thinking about keeping the family's good name like the old days. I tell she times have changed, this is now, and we two old women who just get to watch."

"Tell us about Marva," Margaret said suddenly.

"How did she know P. Quince? And is Marva some kind of relation of yours?"

Mamee Joe's response was a genuinely mirthful cackle. "Girl, everybody related to Mamee Joe. I can't remember how many chil'ren I have, how many they have, how many cousin, uncle, tante there is on Boucan. Off in America, Canada, England. They come back home sometimes, sometimes they send money. Marva the daughter of my husband's baby brother. She have forty years now. Pretty girl when she was young, have plenty of men chasing she. This Lambeaux who used to live here. He liked her plenty. But she find another man who is real good to her, a rich man. He give her gold jewelry, nice clothes. Take her to Venezuela on holiday, up to Barbados, all around. Lambeaux go off someplace to study, end up big police fellow on Betun."

"Does Marva have any children?" Margaret asked.

Mamee Joe looked at her slyly. "She have a child once, but she sent it away to cousins in America, and stayed at Indigo Hill. She's a good woman, missus. She's not killing people and playing with obeah spells."

"Do you know who the father was? Was he a white man?" Margaret asked.

"Could be," Mamee Joe said evasively. "I don't pay heed to these girls' business. It happen more than twenty years ago. You take more ginger beer, sir? Good local stuff." She appeared to be closing down that area of discussion.

"No, no thank you," Paul said hastily.

"Did Marva keep in touch with her child?" Margaret asked. "Or did she visit here?"

Mamee Joe looked away. "What is keep in touch? Ask for money? Marva been doing all right without keeping in touch." She got up from her chair slowly.

"People have too much discontent here, looking at all the things they can't have. Want money to buy big cars, big boats, all kind of foolishness. They see the Red Man who's like one of we having everything, and they have a craving."

"Yes," Margaret said, "Rusty Keating. Is he from here or another island?"

Mamee Joe shrugged. "Daddy and grandaddy worked around on the sugar, coconut plantations here, other islands. Maybe his grandaddy before that. Red Man always come by to see me when he sails in. Bring me nice present at Christmastime this year. Scarf for my head with sparkles and all. I tell him I too old for fancy dress, but I'm keeping it. Wear it for m'lord's carnival." She grinned a nearly toothless grin. "Still like to dance, you know. Jump up in the street with the steel band."

Paul and Margaret followed her along the narrow hallway.

At the door, Margaret said, "I've learned that there are some plants and the like which are dangerous if eaten. Boots was telling me some things. . . ."

"Everybody knows," Mamee Joe said. "Derrick tell me the lady die at the house by poison. We have plenty of such things, but the lady eat food cooked by Alvina at the guest house. How she going to eat something bad?"

"How indeed," Margaret said. "Unless someone who knew about such things saw to it that she did."

"Margaret," Paul said almost pleadingly.

Mamee Joe looked at them both sharply. "Missus, we people don't poison white folks."

"No, no," Margaret said hastily. "I didn't mean that. I am curious about these plants."

Mamee Joe hobbled down the steps and took her cane

from beside the door. "Come now. See those cassava growin'?" She pointed the cane at a row of tall, spindly plants seven or eight feet high with a crown of leaves at top. "Roots are cassava. Bitter cassava could kill you fast if you grate it, don't cook it. Sweet is all right, but some can't tell difference between bitter and sweet. I know which is good. Castor oil seeds, they could make you sick. Fire plant. Oleander—look at it there." She pointed at a tall, bushy shrub with pinkish flowers. "Leaves, flowers—everything bad. Even the smoke if it burning. Lantana, crown of thorns . . . We got plenty such plants. But good ones too. Over there, that's a monkey tail, plenty of bougainvillea all about, all colors, and hibiscus . . ."

"Fascinating," Margaret said. She was thinking hard. "We must be going. Thank you for the lovely ginger beer. Boucan is a delightful place."

Mamee Joe said, "Delightful? They have people who don't know about delightful, want Boucan to change. We have people who want it to stay the same. Both are going to do anything to get their way. Good day, sir, missus."

The sun beat down on them as they started along the trace back to the sugar mill and the car.

"Georgina's bracelet, false obeah, Marva and her child," Margaret said aloud. "People who want the island to change, people who don't. Marva having Jimmie invite a so-called writer, who ends up dead."

"Who might have been Marva's daughter," Paul said. "This is terrible. Who is the father then?"

"I wonder," Margaret said. "We also have Jimmie's ex-wife who might have been a blackmailer, who felt encouraged to come here, and who ends up dead. A secret cache of gold jewelry that probably belonged to P. Quince who was also encouraged to come here. A gold bracelet on Georgina's fair wrist that is similar to the hidden treasure. Plants that kill. Did you look at Mamee Joe's oleander bush, by the way?''

''No,'' Paul said.

''Somebody cut some branches, not too long ago. One can see the cuts.''

''I cannot fit it all together,'' Paul said. ''And I cannot believe that Georgina is capable of killing someone, even her former stepmother.''

''It seems to me that the magic signs were intended to make events seem connected to local people, but I don't believe they were the work of a local person. They take obeah quite seriously—that is, a serious attempt to manipulate events. I doubt locals would treat the symbols so cavalierly.''

Chapter 18

The shade had moved since Margaret and Paul had gone up the hill. The red car was now no doubt as hot as an oven.

"What's this?" Margaret said suddenly. Coo-Coo was peeking from the round door opening of the sugar mill. "You talk to him. I may seem too alarming. I think he wants to tell us about the red bundle and perhaps his lovely gift to his passion, Georgina."

"Is that possible?" Paul murmured aside to Margaret, who nodded. "Hot today, isn't it, Coo-Coo?" Paul said lightly. "Let's all go inside the mill and cool off."

"Ifounditinthegully," Coo-Coo said in a rush.

"You found what in the gully?" Paul asked.

Coo-Coo nodded. "The treasure."

"And you hid it away here," Margaret said, although she had planned to keep silent. "That's all right," she added quickly. "It should be in a safe place. And you shared your treasure with Miss Georgina."

"I gave a bracelet to Miss Georgie," Coo-Coo said guiltily. "Tante Marva ask Miss Georgie where she find it, but she didn't say it came from me. Then I see that Tante Marva have one like it."

Paul looked relieved that Georgina had not ripped the bracelet from P. Quince's wrist. Unless, of course, it was she who had put the things in the gully in the first place.

"Does anyone else know the bundle is here?" Margaret asked.

Coo-Coo shook his head.

"Then we will leave it here," Paul said, remembering what he and Margaret had agreed. "You should tell nobody at all about it—not Derrick or Mamee Joe or your mother or Miss Marva. Or Miss Georgie. Promise?"

Coo-Coo hesitated.

"Not the policeman either," Margaret said slowly. She remembered the meeting between Lambeaux and Marva, and what Mamee Joe had said. From the look on Marva's face, there was something more, going back to the old days when Marva was a pretty young girl.

"Right," Paul said, but he frowned. Paul did not like hiding things from the police.

"We need your help, Coo-Coo," Margaret said. "We need to find out who is doing terrible things to ladies who come to Boucan. Do you understand?"

Coo-Coo nodded.

"Nobody's doing spells," Margaret said. "It's a trick. Somebody bad is putting obeah signs about, but they are not real. Don't you worry about that any more."

"True?" Coo-Coo suddenly looked as though the weight of the weeks of worry had flown away.

"Absolutely true," Margaret said.

"I won't tell anybody about the bundle," Coo-Coo said. "I promise. Three times I promise."

"Good," Margaret said. "And it will be over soon."

She smiled at the boy. "You shouldn't have these worries. You should be having a good time. . . . "

"Carnival comin'," Coo-Coo said happily. "Week's time, all the boys comin' out on the street with the steel band. Dress up in costumes and come up by Indigo Hill."

"What fun," Margaret said. "Coo-Coo, don't go off alone for a time. Not until after the carnival."

"Then school start again," he said glumly. "I don't like school. I want a boat like they do at Arawak Bay. Go out to sea, ride all around the island." He looked longingly across at the chink in the wall where his treasure was hidden. "I could buy a boat with gold."

Margaret said, "Not quite enough, I think."

"Are they big, fast boats they fill up with air?" Paul asked suddenly, "or the wooden ones I've seen them painting on the beach?"

"Fishermen use wooden boats, pirogues," Coo-Coo said disdainfully. "The boys have zodiacs, go fast like a hurricane. They keep them away in the sheds when they're not using them."

Paul and Margaret looked at each other. "I saw one at Arawak Bay," Paul said. "No, I saw two—there was a different one at Chatham harbor."

"And you likely heard one in the night," Margaret said. "We don't know that it was one of the other two. Coo-Coo, tell me about that." She pointed to the circle of stones where a fire had once been lighted.

"Somebody cook up something," he said. "But it wasn't long time. Stones weren't here before."

Margaret picked up one of the charred sticks.

"Do you know what kind of stick this is?"

Coo-Coo shrugged. "Any old kind of tree."

Margaret frowned, then looked at the dirt floor. A few limp leaves near the makeshift fire, scattered dried

leaves blown in by the trade winds, a pile of dried coconut fronds stacked against the wall. "Come along
then. Is your mother at Derrick's guest house now?"

"She went down this morning," Coo-Coo said.
"Told me to stay home."

"I think we'll stop to see her," Margaret said. "Do
you want to come with us?"

"I could," Coo-Coo said.

"Then run open the car doors to take out the heat.
Good work." As Coo-Coo ran to the car, Margaret
said, "Paul, I think we take the bundle with us. Coo-
Coo might be in some danger if it becomes known that
he took it from the gully. Goodness knows, it may be
difficult for Boots to keep silent about its existence.
And here, take this stick. Put it away carefully in the
boot of the car."

She bent down and picked up a couple of the leaves
near the makeshift fireplace and tucked them in her bag.
While she was leaving, Paul extracted the red cloth
bundle from the crack in the wall and stuffed it into his
trouser pocket. He looked at the stick—thin, a foot or
so long, and charred on the end. When he got to the
car, Coo-Coo was pointing out the sights of the island
and did not notice Paul putting the stick in the car trunk.

They bumped down the trace to Derrick's guest
house.

"What you doin' away from the house?" Alvina
sounded annoyed when Coo-Coo went in ahead of them.

"I came with m'lord's friends," Margaret and Paul
heard him say.

"Good morning. So sorry to intrude," Margaret said
as she and Paul followed Coo-Coo.

"Morning. I'm not busy," Alvina said. She nodded
to Paul and looked Margaret over. "The lady who was

staying here is dead. He knows,'' she said, looking at Paul.

"We both know," Margaret said, and looked around the pleasant and comfortable room. Big plants, nice bentwood furniture, bright cloths on the round dining tables. Derrick knew how to take care of his guests.

"Nearly scared the life out of Ellis when he find her in the pool yesterday."

"Only yesterday," Margaret murmured, and remembered the last entry in Clarissa's journal.

"Someone came to visit her," Margaret said. "Was it two days ago, rather than one day?"

Alvina looked uncomfortable. "I told Derrick and the policeman that I thought someone had been here the day before they find her, but I'm thinking now it was two nights ago. I didn't see her day before yesterday but I thought she had gone out. I only see she the day before that." Alvina shrugged. "But I don't know for sure."

"Did she ever visit you up at St. Joseph's Trace?"

"Once I bring her up to take a look at the view by the sugar mill. I say she should come by us for Christmas dinner, because she started moping around real bad, and I'm sorry she's alone for the holidays. But no, she won't come."

"That must have been about the time the woman was killed on the beach," Paul said.

Coo-Coo looked briefly frightened.

"What you askin' me?" Alvina asked suspiciously. "You think she cut that woman?"

"No, no," Paul said hastily.

"I'm finished here," Alvina said abruptly. "Ellis, we going up home now. You got to mind that fever."

"I good now, ma," Coo-Coo said. He met Margaret's eye and grinned. "Feeling real good."

"Then help me lock up. People coming to stay soon for m'lord's fete," she said to Margaret and Paul. "Make a few tips. The dead lady promise me a big tip by the time she leave, but . . ." Alvina shrugged. "She leave too soon."

Alvina refused a ride, to Paul's relief. He did not think the old red car could manage St. Joseph's Trace a second time.

Paul and Margaret stood outside and looked down the long beach.

"I am convinced she died two days before she was found," Margaret said. "Somebody had the body somewhere for a long time before it reached the pool."

"How could that be?" Paul asked. "A body in the tropics . . ."

Margaret smiled. "Think about it. There is an answer. We'll talk about it over lunch, if we can avoid the others. I don't want to share my thoughts with Ninni Campos or anyone else."

Chapter 19

"*We will* take our lunch at Prince Paul's bungalow, Marva," Margaret said when they returned to Indigo Hill and sought out the housekeeper at the cookhouse.

"Yes, madame," Marva said. "What is it you wish?"

"What are my choices?" Margaret asked.

Marva smiled faintly. "Anything. M'lord sees that the larder is well stocked."

"I understand from Paul that provisions have been brought in from everywhere, and stored for the fete."

"That is correct," Marva said, and was distinctly disinclined to say more.

"You decide on lunch," Margaret said. "Local foods would be delightful, I'm sure. What lovely bracelets you have."

Marva started to speak, and then chose not to.

"I've never seen anything like the gold one, with the nuggets on the ends."

"It comes from Venezuela," Marva said reluctantly, "long time ago."

"I see," Margaret said. "Prince Paul would like to

have a look at the sheds where the trunks and such are stored for Lord Farfaine's big party.''

Paul looked momentarily surprised and then nodded vigorously.

''And I'm curious about which shed the dead woman's clothes were found in,'' Margaret said guilelessly. ''It's so exciting. . . .''

''I don't know,'' Marva said. ''Police don't confide in me. Sheds are over there. Red Man put the trunks someplace. Is not my business.'' She departed abruptly for the safety of her cookhouse.

''I know the shed,'' Paul said.

''Let's take a look at it,'' Margaret said, then added softly, ''and the freezer house the woman mentioned this morning. But not until we're sure nobody will see us snooping.''

''Of course!'' Paul said. ''A place to store a body.''

''Hush,'' Margaret said. ''Costume shed first.''

In the farthest shed, they found trunks and boxes marked ''Indigo Hill.''

''Nothing to see,'' Margaret said as she poked around a bit. She was disappointed.

''There is,'' Paul said. ''Take a look at this bale of items.'' He kicked the big, sloppy bundle bound up in wire and canvas. ''We brought it up from the marina yesterday. It didn't mean anything at the time.''

''It means something now?''

''After lunch, we're going to Arawak Bay. We'll take the car on the back roads. I'll ask the yardman how to get there. I have an idea that might answer the question about how the body got to Indigo Hill's pool. The Jaguar's back, by the way. I saw it when I parked the Toyota. It must have passed us while we were at the mill or at the guest house.''

''Then Jane must be back. Possibly Georgina too.''

They walked around to the front of the big house where they could look down on the pool. Indigo Hill looked so elegant, so civilized, so like a travel agent's dream. It was quiet, and the breeze scarcely stirred the tall trees in the distance and the palms around the house. A gloriously colored hummingbird hovered above a bright yellow blossom and then whirred away. The sea was a smooth expanse of every imaginable blue, and a majestic row of puffy white cumulus clouds sailed along the horizon.

"Jane is taking the sun by the pool," Margaret said, "while Carlos sits beside her, no doubt recounting his amazing exploits around the world."

"I wonder if they are for gentle ladies' ears," Paul said. "And is Georgina there?" He scanned the group around the pool.

"Not seen. I asked for her at the other boats at the marina. Some had seen her briefly, but no one knew where she had gone."

"Should we worry? Women here seem to have problems about dying. She hasn't really had a chance to get to know me."

Margaret said, "Don't worry. Since we have half an hour at least until lunch appears, shall we trail down to the pool to see what people have to offer? I'm dying to see if Jane lets on that I was at Rusty's boat. Our Jimmie has hooked up with a seriously unsuitable woman even for him."

"Lady Alys finds her so," Paul said.

It was a somewhat awkward group pretending good fellowship around the pool. Carlos and Jane; Tyrone still dressed all in white; Lord Farfaine's English friends and a couple of the transoceanic blondes, Ninni, looking glamorous; Jimmie at his mother's feet. Even Rusty

Keating was there on Lady Alys's other side. Only Georgina was absent.

"Here is our prince," Ninni Campos trilled. "I am swimming for two minutes in the pool, and then you will talk to me about Carolina." She donned a frilly bathing cap and stepped carefully into the pool, keeping her head high above the blue water.

"Been busy, have you?" Lord Farfaine boomed. "Everybody was up and about early."

Margaret looked quickly at Jane, who made an effort to look cordial and innocent.

"Come sit here with Mother," Lord Farfaine said. "She's quite taken with you. You too, Margaret."

"What have you done with Georgina?" Lady Alys said. "They say she drove off with you."

"We left her in town," Margaret said. "She had some shopping to do."

"No shopping on Boucan," Jane said languidly. "All trash. Jimmie brings everything in, except proper water pressure."

"Janie, dear . . ." Lord Farfaine said warningly. "We're going to look at the costume things tonight. Always a treat."

Jane stood up. Paul noted that she had quite a good figure in her maillot-style bathing suit. "And I can choose the best before the others pick them over at the Friday night barbecue. Paul will see to opening up the trunks for me."

"Now, Janie," Lord Farfaine said, "Prince Paul is looking after Georgie and Lady Margaret. He may have other plans."

"He's working for you," Jane said with an icy look at Margaret. "That's the only plan he need have."

Suddenly Paul felt a rush of dislike for her that had something to do with her general offensiveness and something to do with the fact that he was indeed a servant here.

"Old Derrick is fixing up snorkeling out at the reef this afternoon after luncheon. Got a wonderful reef out beyond Arawak Bay. World-class." Jimmie beamed happily.

"What fun," Margaret said. "I'm sorry Paul and I can't join you." She looked around at the group. "I didn't sleep well, and Paul does have some tasks for Lord Farfaine, he tells me." She stood up.

"I'll walk up to the house with you," Rusty said. "I have to get back to my boat. I'm bringing the diving boat around to the bay to carry Jane out to the reef." He grinned a rather charming grin at Margaret. "Lord Farfaine has kindly given me the use of the Jag for a couple of days." He half bowed to Lady Alys. "Always a pleasure to see you, Tante."

Margaret tried to read the old lady's expression. The pursed lips could have meant disapproval of his familiarity. The pale, aged hands clenching the arms of the wicker chair could have been conveying her sense of his unsuitability as a companion for Georgina.

Margaret, Paul, and Rusty walked up the hill toward the house.

"No one seems troubled that a dead woman was discovered in that pool only yesterday," Margaret said. Ninni Campos was still paddling about.

"They don't think too much," Rusty said, "and very little troubles them if their comforts are in place. However, they are taking care to avoid the little island."

"How did you happen to meet the former Lady Farfaine?" Margaret asked.

"I found her hanging about on the big island, eager to get a cheap ride over. Even the interisland steamer was more than she wanted to pay. I had to come over to Boucan anyhow, so I brought her. Free. Nice enough woman. She was meeting a friend.''

"How extraordinary. Just a chance meeting then?''

"Actually not. Someone told her to look for me. I'm easy to find.''

"Who was that?''

Rusty laughed. "We didn't discuss it.''

"You had no idea that she was once Lord Farfaine's wife?''

"I didn't say that, did I?'' Rusty tipped an imaginary hat and strolled off around to the back of the house where the cars were parked.

"This is a most peculiar place,'' Margaret said. "Murderers roam about freely, and yet it does look like paradise.''

"What do you mean?'' Paul said.

"I mean, that's how I feel. I wonder what Marva has given us to eat? I asked for local foods.''

"Margaret! Are you asking to be poisoned?''

She laughed. "I hardly think that will be the outcome of lunch. This time.''

"Delicious,'' Margaret said, spooning up a thick, spicy soup made of pureed greens and okra, with chunks of crabmeat. Cleone, the maid, had brought them the callaloo soup, stewed chicken, fluffy rice with flecks of green pepper and orange grated carrots, small boiled green bananas, and slices of an unfamiliar white root vegetable. "A bit hearty for the climate, but I did ask for local food,'' she said, then gasped suddenly at the fire of the yellowish-red pepper sauce she's spooned on the chicken. "I suppose this is cassava.'' She poked the white root vegetable with her fork. "I trust it's not the poisonous bitter kind Mamee Joe mentioned.''

Paul put down his fork. "Did not Lambeaux advise us to be careful of what we ate?"

"Don't worry," Margaret said. "I think cooked cassava would not damage one."

"But you see how easy it could be to give a person something deadly to eat," Paul said.

"I have an idea about that," Margaret said. "Shall we make a list? You start from the beginning, then me." She fished a notepad from her bag, along with her copies of Clarissa's papers.

Paul leaned back in the comfortable reclining chair on the gallery and closed his eyes. "Lord Farfaine told me about the first murder a day or two after Christmas, when I was in Dallas. At about the same time, I received from him the list of Indigo Hill guests, including Miss P. Quince."

"Thus," Margaret said, "he did not then make a public connection between the dead woman and one of his expected guests. Go on."

"There is not too much I can say about my first hours. So much was happening. I met Tyrone Pace at the airport on the big island. Derrick met me at the airstrip. Ah! The fellows in town called Derrick 'Captain.' My brief experience here indicates that nicknames have some reason. Boots calls me Charlie."

Margaret nodded. "As in Prince Charles. Quite reasonable. Perhaps Derrick, unknown to us, is a skillful boatman."

"He seems more prosperous than most of his countrymen. He could perhaps afford one of those zodiac boats."

"Excellent," Margaret said. "I hope you understand that those big inflatable zodiacs are used by drug smugglers and others who need to get about quickly. You can sink them in an instant to hide the evidence."

"Smuggling occurred to me," Paul admitted, "but Boucan seems like such an out-of-the-way place. If there is smuggling going on, it would be more like a cottage industry than a major undertaking. And where would these drugs come from? Do people grow opium poppies, or marijuana to a commercial degree?"

"A good point," Margaret said. "Go on."

"On my first morning, Georgina joined me at breakfast. I believe she was wearing a bracelet like the one we found. She and Rusty appear to be . . . acquaintances of long standing, and it appears that the two of them, along with Lady Alys, feel that Boucan should remain fixed in time."

"I can see Lady Alys's point of view and even Georgina's, but Rusty? Why would he care?"

"It would interfere somehow with the way he leads his life?"

"He has a boat he keeps for skindiving," Margaret said. "The inflatable kind. Could he be involved in smuggling of whatever?"

Paul said, "I wouldn't doubt it. But does it have anything to do with murder? I mean to say, what damage could a fairly eccentric ex-Lady Farfaine and a small-time journalist do to him? In a place like this, surely everyone has an idea of what goes on, even if they prefer not to know precisely."

All at once, voices could be heard as a number of people came along the path toward the bungalows.

"Lunch must be finished. They're off to snorkel," Margaret said.

"Another task I should be handling," Paul said, "except that I would not know where to begin. Why am I here?"

"To mind Georgina," Margaret said, "and it is not your fault that you cannot control her actions. Perhaps

Jimmie was hoping for magic between you and it didn't happen.''

"Magic?"

"An unfortunate choice of words," Margaret said.

Derrick led the procession, with Ninni Campos and Carlos following. Then at a distance came Jane and Jimmie, the English couples, two Scandinavians, and Tyrone Pace.

Paul and Margaret stood at the gallery railing and watched the party make its way down toward Arawak Bay, where two pirogues rode at anchor, waiting for their passengers. Far out in the bay, a speedboat was heading for shore, no doubt Rusty Keating, to join the party.

"Look," Margaret said. She pointed toward the beach. "Your wandering Georgina has reappeared. That's she, isn't it, in Rusty's boat?"

"At least she's not out somewhere chewing a stick that could kill her," Paul said.

"Very true," Margaret said. "We haven't even considered how Clarissa was poisoned, but Georgina will live to see many days on Boucan. Now we can nip around and have a look at the freezer house. We'll tell Marva some tale about . . . about something."

"No!"

"Just a cursory examination," Margaret said. "Then we're off to the Arawak Bay village for a look around. And then, my dear, we plan your treasure hunt."

"I will have to tell Lord Farfaine where it's hidden," Paul said.

"All the better. And we'll let slip to a chosen few hints of red cloth bundles with gold jewelry in close connection with the buried treasure, and see what happens."

Chapter 20

The house seemed dead in the midday sun. The kitchen was closed, and Marva and the servants were nowhere in sight. They must have rushed through lunch and the washing up.

"Rest time for everyone while the children are playing in the sea," Margaret said. She looked up at the back of the big white house. All the windows on the upper floors had drawn curtains. "Lady Alys must be above, since I didn't see her venturing out to the reef. Now, which is the freezer house?"

"There," Paul said. "Behind the poinsettias. That's where they were taking the fish."

Margaret strolled casually in the direction of the building, stopping to admire the wall of red flowers. "Come on," she hissed. "Quietly and innocently."

They slipped out of sight behind the bushes.

The freezer house wasn't locked. There was simply a heavy bar in a notch keeping it shut. Paul lifted the bar, and the door swung outward. A rush of chilled air greeted them as they stepped inside.

"Hold the door," Margaret said. "Nice and cool though it is, I wouldn't want to be trapped inside. Let me just look about.'' The area where she stood was empty except for some cases of rather good wine in racks affixed to the wall. Although it was difficult to tell, since they had just come in from the heat, apparently the outer room was the right temperature for the Bordeaux and Merlots. She didn't imagine Jimmie would allow his wine to be spoiled by heat or cold. The concrete floor was swept clean, and she could hear the hum of a motor—the refrigerating unit operating beyond a set of heavy doors that probably guarded the actual freezer room. These, however, were firmly locked with sturdy padlocks.

''Unless one had the keys,'' Margaret said, ''one couldn't leave a body in the freezer proper, but this room is cool enough to keep a body for a time. Do you suppose she was dumped on the floor?''

Paul said, ''More likely, a trunk containing Clarissa's body was put inside the door.''

''Brilliant,'' Margaret said. ''Are you suggesting Rusty Keating?''

''Yes. I know he brought her over from the big island, but to get the body here . . .''

''The boys at Arawak Bay?''

''They have the necessary vehicle,'' Paul said. ''Derrick has the use of the Range Rover. Georgina would need assistance, as would Marva. Let us go.''

They drove the stuffy Toyota with burning seats down a terrifyingly steep hill behind the house, passing small terraced garden patches and little houses shaded by palms. At the foot of the hill, they turned left on a narrow but fairly well-kept road.

''Samson said to keep on this road until the crossroads, take a left there and continue on. It will take us into the village,'' Paul said. ''I am not certain what to expect.''

Margaret said, "We ask for Pearl. We behave like ignorant yet innocent tourists. We boldly refer to your brush with the boat as the result of you not paying attention. And then we paddle our toes in the surf. The people from Indigo Hill are out at the reef, which can't be far away, else Ninni would not consent to join them, nor Jane, I should think."

The car bounced as they hit a bad patch of road. It was fairly flat here, with stately rows of palms on either side. A laborer was burning a pile of coconut shells, sending up a stream of smoke. He stood with one hand on a long rake and watched them pass. Three large brown cows tethered to trees grazed in a field. Suddenly the car came upon a frail shack plastered with the usual beer advertisements at the roadside. Two old men sat out in front, and each raised a hand in greeting as they passed.

"Old Indigo Hill retainers out to pasture?" Margaret said. "They seem to recognize the car. Look! There's the crossroads where you turn."

The road now became sandy. Indeed, the closer they approached to the village, the more like a beach mixed with pebbles it became. The palms leaned in over the road and on the inland side, a stream meandered through the palms on its way to the sea. A boy on a bicycle approached them and inspected them curiously as they passed. Now they could catch glimpses of the sparkling sea between the palms and beyond the sea-grapes, and scattered houses set well back on the other side of the sandy road. Up ahead, a line of sheds, built to face the beach, appeared. The tarred road of the village's main street began abruptly. Paul drove slowly toward the shed where he'd seen the truck.

"Here," Paul said. "Act terribly British. I will act terribly Italian."

"Ah, *buona sera!*" He got out of the car. "Good day again!" The youth was squatting down on the floor of the shed, examining a dismantled outboard motor. He looked up at Paul's voice.

"Hullo, hullo," Margaret said. "I say, would it be too terribly awful to leave our car here while we took a swim? Lovely!"

"Not too terribly British," Paul said quietly. He was trying to look over the boxes and crates piled in the back of the shed without seeming to.

"Is a free country," the youth finally said.

"Lovely!" Margaret said again, almost too heartily. "What an interesting place you have. What's this for?" She pointed her toe at a bale of chicken wire.

"Fish pots," the youth said, eyeing Paul as he strolled around the open shed, edging closer to the back. "Is private property, man."

"*Scusi,*" Paul said. "Excuse me. When I was on the beach yesterday, I was very stupid. I did not attend to where I was swimming and almost collided with a boat. I shall have to be more careful, ha ha. Do you know who it was that I almost hit?"

The youth looked at him suspiciously. "I didn't see anyt'ing," he said. "I got my work."

"The truck with the damaged tire. I have seen it in Chatham, so I know you did a good job."

Paul wondered if he were overdoing the amiable idiot act, since the youth got up and approached him.

"Sea's right out there. I keep an eye on your car, nobody trouble it. Look, you could go right between the sheds and you on the beach. People from Indigo Hill gone out to the reef to snorkel. I saw them go out with Red Man and the others." He sounded as though Paul and Margaret should have stayed safely with the herd, rather than nosing around the village.

"Is Pearl about?" Margaret asked. "I met her near Chatham this morning."

"Miss Pearl go about too much," the youth said.

"She said she was hoping the new jetty would be put in, although some folks don't care for the idea."

"And Miss Pearl talk too much." The youth decided to ignore them and went back to inspecting the pieces of the motor.

Margaret and Paul walked between the sheds and found themselves on the beach. The palms leaned out over the sand, and the waves breaking on the beach were again modest and inviting. Farther up the beach, a group of boys were spread out on the sand, one wielded a flat cricket bat. The person bowling was Tyrone Pace.

"What did you see?" Margaret asked.

"I saw at least one deflated zodiac boat," Paul said. "It's stored in the shed. And I saw the trunk."

"*The* trunk?"

"One like those in the shed at Indigo Hill, with a label marked 'Indigo Hill.' Not just a shipping crate, but a real trunk. I half-remembered it from yesterday."

"Surely if it was used to store Clarissa's body, they would have disposed of it, although it is probably rather too nice to burn up or toss into the sea. Perhaps the people here had no idea . . ."

"For the moment, at least, we keep silent, I think," Paul said. "We don't know if they see us as a danger or not."

"Come along, then," Margaret said. "As long as we're here, we ought to enjoy the sea."

Some yards out from the beach, Paul and Margaret treaded water.

"What if," Paul said slowly, "Lord Farfaine is the mind behind the smuggling—drugs or whatever.

Wouldn't that be a scandal if it were revealed? The trusted big man of the island involved in something obviously illegal, bringing shame upon the family. He's well known here and in England, I take it. Plus an illegitimate child, even one two decades ago, the mother being the housekeeper at his estate.''

"Not politically correct," Margaret said.

"If Clarissa knew all about this, and P. Quince knew, and they had joined forces for some kind of mutual revenge or blackmail . . . Margaret, are you listening?''

"Yes," she said. "I am listening closely. Let's go back to Indigo Hill. I think I've got it now."

The village was empty in the afternoon sun when they returned to the car. Even the youth in the shed had gone. Paul turned the key, and the motor turned once and died. He tried again.

"We may have to trek across the beach," Margaret said. "It's not far."

"No," Paul said slowly. He was gazing out through the windscreen at the road through the village. "But we are not alone." A battered yellow pickup pulled up behind them, and the space in front of the red car was rapidly filling with men and boys from the village, some of them carrying cutlasses. They did not look welcoming.

"I do not believe that being very Italian and very British will provide a simple solution this time," Paul said.

"What will?" Margaret said.

An older man walked to Paul's window. Paul recognized him as the fish seller, the man with the yellow pickup truck. Fitzie.

"What you people want here? There's nothing to see." Fitzie sounded belligerent.

"We came for a swim," Margaret said, "on your lovely beach."

"Plenty of other beaches." The men were close to the car now, some peering in the windows. "You got to be careful here. It have dangers for them who come prying into people's business.

"We were trying to leave," Paul said, "but there is a problem with the car." He glanced over at Margaret. It seemed foolhardy at this moment to get out and walk away across the beach. The intentions of the crowd—not really a mob—were not clear. On the other hand, the car was excessively hot, since it was now standing in the full sun.

"Problem with the car," the man repeated. "How could that happen? You would think m'lord up at the big house with his big freezer house and plans for jetty and such could keep some old car runnin'."

"Jimmie is not entirely beloved, I see," Margaret murmured. "What shall we do? No one knows where we are." She was determined not to be nervous, but this was, after all, the place where P. Quince had met her death.

The crowd had nearly surrounded the car now.

Suddenly, Margaret had an idea. "I say." She leaned across Paul to the man at his window. "I wonder if someone could go along the beach and ask Tyrone Pace to join us. He's the cricketer."

"I know who he is. Where you think you're going to find he?"

"He's bowling for the little boys. Our good friend," Margaret said. "Ah! There he is!"

Pace was strolling in their direction, surrounded by a gang of boys. The crowd of men fell back as Margaret stepped out of the car.

"Lady Margaret." Pace bowed slightly. "What is happening?"

"We are having trouble with our car," Margaret said, "and these gentlemen are determining how best to help us. You must recognize Mr. Pace," she said to the nearest person.

"Yes, ma'am," the man said. "We know he. From the big island." The crowd moved back.

"Let us see what we can do, my good man," Tyrone said. "Lady Margaret, you stay in the shade. Paul, if you will allow someone to try the engine . . . Who's the mechanic here?"

Pace's star power seemed to be working. The youth who had been repairing the motor took Paul's place in the driver's seat, turned the engine, then got out to raise the hood.

Tyrone Pace joined Paul and Margaret in the shade. "I brought the boys for a Coca-Cola, and I find you besieged by my countrymen."

"It was a misunderstanding," Margaret said. "But you seem to have calmed them down."

"A pleasure to be of service," Pace said. "After all, you did me a favor in the matter of the nail varnish."

"Can we offer you a lift back to the house?" she said. "The car has been miraculously brought back to life."

"I will see you on your way, but I shall stay behind to discuss the finer points of my sport with the lads here." Pace stopped. "It is not always the case at Arawak Bay, is it? Being miraculously brought back to life."

Chapter 21

"This is an answer to one question," Margaret said. They sat in her bungalow with the charred stick and a handful of drying leaves on the low table before them. "I shall have to ask someone, to be certain, of course, but I assume these things are from the oleander bush near Mamee Joe's house. Someone built a fire, using the oleander sticks, and then for good measure roasted something on it using the longer stick. 'Have a lovely picnic, Clarissa,' and then she is dead. Maybe there was a little extra force applied, just to be sure."

"It sounds highly speculative," Paul said.

"Perhaps she was fed the bad kind of cassava for good measure. In any event, it was another attempt at giving the death a local flavor. As it were."

"Then someone conveyed the body in an Indigo Hill trunk—from Rusty Keating's boat—placed it in the freezer house for a time, and tossed her clothes in another shed. On my first night here, someone put the body on the island in the pool, perhaps thirty-six hours after she died. The trunk got sent off to the village at Arawak Bay, where the boys are accustomed to keeping their business to themselves, and the contents of the trunk were bundled up with canvas and chicken wire, so that Derrick and I could carry it up here with the remaining crates.''

''Succinctly put,'' Margaret said. ''I have an idea of who and why, but we have to be certain. I'm not sure I could explain my reasoning to Mr. Lambeaux, who doesn't seem to be haunting us in any case. So,'' she added briskly, ''we will now get on with your problem of the treasure.''

''The sugar mill will be the place,'' Paul said. ''I have thought some about this. It will begin at dawn on Saturday. We cannot have these people roaming about the island in the dark. In any event, the barbecue is Friday and the grand carnival party is Saturday evening. That will last until the next morning, I understand, so Saturday morning is the only time.''

''That is the day after tomorrow,'' Margaret said.

''Everything happens too soon,'' Paul said. ''We must have treasure maps. And clues.'' He added rather shamefacedly, ''I brought with me a sort of necklace thing that belongs to my mother. She's never worn it. She told me she loathes aquamarines and can't imagine why she ever bought it.''

''But if we plan with care,'' Margaret said, ''we will hide not only Carolyn Sue's necklace, but also the incriminating red bundle, and make certain the murderer understands the importance of getting to the mill ahead of the others.''

''Lambeaux will be there to apprehend the person.''

''Perhaps,'' Margaret said.

''Wait,'' Paul said. ''How will the murderer know?''

''We'll leave a special clue or two.''

Cleone the maid was suddenly at the bungalow door. ''Sir, madame, people have arrived and m'lord's not back from the reef. Lady Alys shut up in she room with a sick headache and Marva's gone to Chatham.'' She spoke in a rush. ''We don't know what to do. . . . ''

''What sort of people, Cleone?'' Paul asked.

''Visiting from some boat. Ten, twenty. Lookin' for m'lord.''

''Too soon,'' Paul groaned.

Margaret said, ''Find the other servants, and put all kinds of drinks and fruit juice and ice in the drawing room, the way you did last night. And see that there is some at the pool house. Send one of the men down to the beach to see if someone can get word to Lord Farfaine at the reef. Can you handle that?''

Cleone nodded.

''You'll have to be quick. Prince Paul and I are coming right now.'' Margaret turned to Paul. ''You are about to assume your rightful role. They must be from that yacht in the harbor, so one of them at least is very rich.''

A large dark-haired man with heavy brows stood at the top of the verandah steps while a flock of tanned, casually but elegantly dressed men and women milled about the drive.

''What a relief,'' Margaret said. ''I know him.'' She called out, ''Aziz, what a pleasure!''

''Margaret, is that you? This is a welcome surprise.'' The big man had a slight accent and a gigantic diamond ring.

Margaret called out gaily to the others, ''Drinks in the house, ladies and gentlemen, and around the pool!''

Cleone and the other maids were suddenly everywhere. People began to move. Several called out Margaret's name. One even greeted Paul.

Margaret took Paul's arm and brought him to the verandah. ''Aziz, may I present Prince Paul Castrocani? You surely know his mother, Carolyn Sue Hoopes. Paul, this is Prince Aziz. I recognized your yacht this morning." She hoped it was a lucky guess. It was.

"We arrived earlier than planned," the prince said. "I do know your mother," he said to Paul. "A fine woman. I know your stepfather as well." He smiled deprecatingly. "We people with an interest in oil cannot avoid knowing each other."

"My mother has spoken of you, Your Highness," Paul said, untruthfully but politely.

"Where shall we sit?" Margaret said. "Cleone, bring His Highness a drink. Fruit juice, Aziz?"

"Excellent. I prefer to sit on this charming gallery. A house from the old days, is it not?" He seemed to be excusing Indigo Hill's simplicity compared with what he was no doubt accustomed to.

"Paul, run down to the pool and see that everyone is being taken care of, and then join us," Margaret said.

As he headed toward the pool, he heard Margaret saying, "Jimmie is off with some of his guests, but will be here shortly. Now you must tell me what you've been up to. It must be three years since we last met. Ibiza, was it not?"

"And later that year, in Gstaad. The snow was not good."

"I remember . . ."

Paul sighed with relief. Cleone had rounded up a couple of the serving men, who were dispensing drinks from the pool house. He recognized several people, hangers-on of the very rich with whom he had crossed paths in his glory days, when his mother had paid the bills without question.

"Is this your place, Paolo?" A good-looking man of Paul's age put his arm around his shoulder. He was, like Paul, part Italian, and had been successfully sup-

ported for a number of years by a series of older women
who enjoyed his company.

"Not yet, Mimmo. It belongs to a Lord Farfaine."
In a manner of speaking, it did.

"I have it!" Mimmo said. "The beautiful Georgina,
am I correct? The daughter. I see, I see."

Paul didn't argue the point. Anything was possible.

"You must meet my good friend, Mrs. Robinson.
Sadie! *Cara*, meet Prince Paul."

A middle-aged woman, heavily made up and decked
out in top-of-the-line resort wear, simpered at the intro-
duction and took Mimmo's arm possessively. Paul res-
olutely refused to speculate on their relationship.

"I am expected to rejoin His Highness," Paul said,
"if you will excuse me."

"Old Aziz is extremely . . . generous with his hospitality," Mimmo said. "But he is worth billions, so it
is only fair that he share some with us."

At the top of the incline, Paul looked back at the
pool. This crowd had no qualms about making full use
of the pool. Very likely they were unaware that a body
had been found on the little island, since two slim,
blond young women were happily sitting on its edge
under the miniature palms, dangling their feet in the
water.

Everyone seemed to be well taken care of, but such
people simply drifted through life at the top, expecting
to be taken care of. Paul had much to thank Margaret
for.

She and Prince Aziz were engaged in light banter in
a corner of the verandah. As Paul approached, he saw
the prince hold out an empty glass without taking his
eyes from Margaret. Instantly, a maid with a pitcher of
fruit juice appeared and refilled the glass.

Paul and Margaret's hosting responsibilities were

lifted with the breathless arrival of Lord Farfaine, in advance of the rest of his party.

"Well, well, Aziz old chap. People looking after you?"

"Margaret has been most gracious," Aziz said. "I thought for a moment that it was she you had married."

"Ha, ha. Nothing wrong with old Margaret," Lord Farfaine said, "but wait till you meet Janie."

From his tone, Margaret thought he was implying that perhaps Margaret was a bit too old for him.

Jane now emerged from the house. She must have gone in through the back way and done a whirlwind change, since she was now dressed in a colorful flowing caftan, appropriately accessorized, with her hair pulled back in a sleek bun.

"Here's Janie now," Lord Farfaine said. "Come meet Prince Aziz."

Jane glided forth with an expression of welcoming cordiality. She knew how to behave before mountains of money.

Margaret and Paul made a move to depart.

"Good work, my boy," Jimmie said. "Knew you'd come up aces for me." He turned to fawn again over the prince.

Margaret took Paul's arm and steered him back toward the bungalows. On the way, they encountered Ninni Campos racing toward the house while fumbling to pin up tendrils of hair and tucking them into her high-piled coiffeur.

"I know His Highness for years and years," she said breathlessly as she passed them. "And all his wives," she called back over her shoulder. "You would not believe their jewels."

Paul said, "I cannot imagine what treasure I could bury that would interest a man like Prince Aziz."

"Don't worry," Margaret said. "His participation is highly unlikely. He will appear briefly for the festivities on Saturday night, and his yacht, loaded with exhausted guests, will depart with the dawn the next day."

To their surprise, Georgina was waiting for them on the gallery of Margaret's bungalow. She hadn't changed, and was still wearing a damp denim shirt over a wet bathing suit. At least she wasn't wearing Coo-Coo's bracelet. The fewer who knew she had it, the better.

"Hullo," she said. She sounded very subdued. "I hoped you'd be back soon."

"Prince Aziz and party arrived at the big house," Margaret said. "We were seeing to them until Jimmie returned."

Georgina wrinkled her nose. "I don't care how rich he is, I don't like the way he looks at me."

"Middle Eastern men have a different view of women," Margaret said. "And of course you are a very beautiful woman."

"Indeed," Paul said fervently.

Georgina almost grinned at him. "Thank you for your support." She turned to Margaret. "I have to talk to you."

"About Jane? And Rusty?"

"That . . ." She waved them away. "Jane's impossible. I spoke with Mr. Lambeaux." She walked to the railing and stared out at the least desirable view with her back to them. Margaret thought she might be crying. "Lambeaux thinks . . . thinks that Daddy is somehow responsible for both deaths."

"That's impossible," Paul said. "The first happened several weeks ago. Your father wasn't here."

Georgina didn't respond.

"Do you mean that he could have been here?" Margaret asked.

"Immigration on the big island has a record from just before Christmas. I was in England and we were all to meet at our country place for the holidays. Daddy was out of town, and we thought he was in France."

Margaret flopped down in a chair. "That was about the time that Clarissa arrived. Something is quite wrong. Has Mr. Lambeaux spoken to your father about this?"

Georgina nodded. "Daddy denied being here. He swore he'd been in France, and he could prove it. If he'd been on Boucan, everyone would have known it. He can't be invisible here, even if he came over by seaplane as Grandmother and I did. And if he wanted to kill somebody, he would never have done it here." Georgina put her hands to her face. "This is so awful. It will simply kill Grandmother. She's so proud—her family and all going back here forever."

Paul went to Georgina and put his arm around her. He led her to a chair and knelt at her side. "Don't worry, *carissima*. Margaret has an idea of who did the murders, and I do not believe she thinks it was your father."

"Did Jimmie spend his childhood here?" Margaret asked.

"Not at all. My grandfather didn't care for the tropics or for running the estate. It's from Grandmother's family, you know. She used to visit, but Grandfather stayed in England and Daddy was at school. When he grew up and married Mummy, he broke the Farfaine landed-gentry tradition and went into business and made lots of money. It was only when Anthony was seven or eight and I was a baby that we started to come here regularly."

Margaret noticed that Paul had taken Georgina's hand, and continued to hold it.

"Did Lambeaux mention anything about P. Quince's background?" Margaret asked carefully. "You do know she was the dead woman on the beach."

"He told me that. He said they were looking into her history."

"Ah. Good." At least Georgina apparently did not know that P. Quince might well be her half-sister. Time enough for that later. "Was Jane with you at your country place while you were awaiting your father's arrival for the holidays? Or was she also in France?"

"Actually, she was in New York. She arrived after Daddy did. Why do you ask?"

"She is also 'J. Hose-Griffith.' I wonder how Immigration listed the person who was here in its records."

"Of course!" Georgina brightened considerably. "It could have been her. I can't imagine why." She made a face. "Rusty, I suppose."

Margaret said, "And he was around the big island at that time. Indeed, some unspecified person told your other stepmother, Clarissa, to seek him out. Georgina, you must not repeat a word of this to anyone. For Jimmie's sake, and for your own safety. And in the meantime, I trust Jimmie will keep denying everything."

"She won't say a word," Paul said. Surprisingly, Georgina did not bristle at being instructed by Paul.

"Where is Marva, do you suppose?" Margaret said. "I really must speak to her."

"I caught sight of her in Chatham much earlier," Georgina said. "Hasn't she come back yet?"

"She wasn't here when Prince Aziz arrived," Margaret said. "Cleone came and found us to take charge. Well, we'll find her soon enough."

As it turned out, they didn't.

Georgina went off a much happier young woman to

change and be cordial to Prince Aziz. Margaret and Paul drafted some clues for the treasure hunt, none especially satisfactory. Late in the afternoon, Cleone reappeared. Lord Farfaine wished to see them at once.

"Haven't had an easy day of it," Lord Farfaine said. They were again on the verandah of the big house while the servants cleared up after the departed Prince Aziz and his group. "Had to talk to the police fellow, making some wild accusations. I've sent out word to see if anyone can locate Marva. No one knows what's become of her. Don't know how to handle it, what with the people here. Mother's good at dealing with crises, but she's not feeling well. Not young, you know, even if she's accustomed to the climate."

"I suggest you have Derrick bring his sister Alvina up to the house," Margaret said. "Have her take charge of the kitchen for the moment. Keep searching for Marva, of course, but . . ."

"Gone, you think?" Jimmie peered at Margaret anxiously. "What would she do that for?"

Margaret said softly, "I think she talked to the policeman today as well. I think he expressed his suspicions of you, and I don't think she wished to face you. Because of Miss Quince."

Lord Farfaine was silent. He suddenly seemed much older and sad. "I've been a damned fool all my life, only thing I know how to do right is make money and throw a good party. Marva wouldn't take money from me, unless she was being paid for a job so she could send her earnings off to the girl. Stayed on to work here. A job for life, I told her. It took a while to convince Mother. Could have been my child. Marva only hinted."

"Did you once give her gold bracelets, with rough gold nuggets on the ends of the circle?"

Lord Farfaine frowned. "Something like that. She picked 'em out. Four of 'em."

"She only wears two now," Margaret said. "She probably gave the others to her daughter."

"Never noticed really. Thing was over years and years ago. Twenty-two years. Lost Sophie over it. Well, that and other things."

"The other two are here on Boucan again," Margaret said. "Georgina has one, although she doesn't know its source. The other one . . ."

Paul spoke for the first time. "The other one will be discovered during the treasure hunt."

Lord Farfaine sat upright. "I say, not the best of taste . . ."

"Nevertheless," Margaret said. "It will catch us a murderer."

Even if it happens to be you, she thought.

Chapter 22

*M*arva *did* not return.

Because of the two deaths, many questions were asked and many people looked for her about the island for a day. Finally an answer came from one of the Scandinavians, who sailed back into Boucan harbor after a day at sea. He had taken a local woman across to the big island. She had said that a family member had died, and she needed to get there. Had he done wrong to take her? She knew his friend Rusty Keating. She said she had worked at Indigo Hill for years, and indeed, one of the crew recognized her from a party there.

"Surely Marva did not murder anyone," Paul said when Margaret told him, after she had been informed by a serious and taciturn Lambeaux.

"Mr. Lambeaux implied that at the very least, she knew who did," Margaret said. Lambeaux had also not taken kindly to her suggestion that it could have been Jane Hose-Griffith rather than Jimmie that Immigration had admitted before Christmas. He had nodded brusquely, and departed before she could mention her idea the oleander fire at the mill. Lambeaux was not interested in a woman's touch.

"Perhaps Marva's own loss and the possibility of Jimmie's involvement were too much for her at last." She paused. "Or perhaps she did know too much about everything. I doubt that she is still on the big island. More likely, she has flown off to another where she won't easily be found."

"The household does not appear to be disconcerted by her absence," Paul said. "Georgina and I had a perfectly fine lunch on my gallery."

Alvina had taken Marva's place in the estate kitchen, with Cleone as her lieutenant, since she knew the customs and arrangements at Indigo Hill. Meals did appear on schedule, for an increasing number of strange faces. With Alvina's elevation to the big house, the party guests staying at Derrick's guest house were brought to Indigo Hill to dine. People who were arriving on yachts tended to drop by for drinks and conversation at all hours.

Derrick was busy overseeing the comfort of Lord Farfaine's guests, but since everything was well organized in advance, Paul still had little to do, except to see to Georgina's comfort. That was just as well, since Margaret wondered if the source of the murders knew Georgina had been conferring with the police.

"I hope," Margaret said, "you will have time to attend to your treasure-burying duties."

"I wonder if we should cancel that hunt," Paul said. "Lord Farfaine seems distracted."

Margaret had seen Jimmie trailing about the grounds, always dressed in blue, and always with a hearty greeting for a guest, but as soon as he was alone, he seemed to slip into a bemused thoughtfulness.

Lady Alys kept entirely to her rooms, with only Mamee Joe in attendance.

"Mamee Joe saying Lady Alys bearin' great pain,"

Coo-Coo had explained. "Mamee say she felt it in the night, so she come to sit with she."

The pain of old ladies did not mean much to a boy of eight, and besides, Coo-Coo had been elevated to a position of importance, fetching and carrying for his mother.

The rest of the people in residence at Indigo Hill seemed to prefer to be waited upon. Jane spent hours lounging beside the pool, the lady of the house, greeting new arrivals, often with Rusty Keating at her side, enjoying the endless rum punches offered by the serving men. Ninni Campos had latched firmly onto Carlos San Basilio, who was growing increasingly morose as Georgina's attachment to Paul became evident. Margaret wondered if Carlos was beginning to doubt his legendary touch with the ladies.

Finally, Margaret managed to pry Paul from Georgina's side long enough to explain the plan for the treasure hunt to Lord Farfaine.

"Old sugar mill. Excellent. Can't lose themselves too badly getting there. Early morning on Saturday. That's tomorrow. Fine, fine. Marva will give them breakfast before they start out. . . . Ah, well. The new woman will . . ." He wandered off.

"We will bury it this evening," Margaret said. "Coo-Coo will guide us. That way we can see the route they'll have to take, and make sure the red bundle is hidden where only the murderer can find it, early tomorrow before the others start out."

"Mmm." As they stood on the verandah, Paul's eyes were on the pool down the hill. Georgina was talking with the extraordinarily well-muscled Gunnar. "I'll be back just now," he said, and headed toward the pool.

Margaret pouted momentarily. The urgency of finding a murderer seemed to have eluded Paul. True, she hadn't shared her feeling that Georgina was not in the most secure position, but that would probably drive him to never let her out of his sight.

There was a telephone in the entrance hall of the big house, Margaret knew, and she wondered how difficult it would be to put a call through to New York. Where would De Vere be at this hour of the afternoon? Then she stopped herself. If she rang him, she would want to talk about the murders, immediately after she heard his voice. She had promised him not to get involved. . . .

She returned to her bungalow. In one of her emptied suitcases, she had locked the charred stick and dry leaves from the mill and the red bundle with the bracelet, the ring, and the snip of hair. She also had the backup treasure from Paul's mother's boundless supply of discarded necklaces.

She and Paul had contrived simple maps of the island, with Indigo Hill, Arawak Bay, the sugar mill, the beach near Derrick's guest house, and Chatham marked. The seekers would be sent to search first the grounds of Indigo Hill, where Coo-Coo would have hidden notes. All said the same thing: Sweet. The clue was so simple that she did not imagine many would misunderstand. Just to be sure, she would see that the guests in residence knew pretty much all about it in advance. The person she was after would, she hoped, leave before the rest. The plan was for her and Paul to be stationed unseen near the mill, with Boots in support at the foot of St. Joseph's Trace. Paul refused to allow them to do more than see who the person was.

All the same, all would be settled the day after tomorrow.

Margaret opened the red bundle and looked at the

gold bracelet. She slipped it around her wrist, combed her hair, and set out for the pool.

"Hullo, Jane. Lovely day. Will you be joining us tomorrow morning for the treasure hunt?"

Jane was stretched out facedown on a lounger beside the pool and barely acknowledged Margaret's presence. Rusty, in a chair beside her, signaled for another rum punch, and said, "Be a sport, Janie."

"It's a wonderful treasure," Margaret said. "Gold." She shook her wrist gently, but no one noticed.

"It's just more of Jimmie's nonsense," Jane said and turned over to look at Margaret.

"Perhaps I can persuade Ninni and Carlos," Margaret said.

"They'll never see Indigo Hill again in their lifetimes," Jane murmured.

Ninni was doubtful. "I do not care for rummaging through the bushes, but if Jimmie insists, and if Carlos will take me through the jungles."

"The treasure is lovely old gold," Margaret said. "A real treasure."

"Will there be photographers?" Ninni asked. "Jimmie said the society writer would be here. It will make a difference in what I wear. And will Prince Aziz be there?"

"I cannot predict His Highness's movement," Margaret said. "Tyrone, surely you will hunt treasure."

"I will do whatever is on the program," Tyrone Pace said.

"Then Pace will accompany me," Ninni said. "He will take care that no damage is done to me. The nail varnish is quite excellent," she added. "I did not believe he would find exactly what I wanted."

Tyrone grinned at Margaret, and strolled off whistling a calypso tune.

Everyone was preoccupied with the sun and the pool, although Paul and Gunnar at the other side were focused entirely on Georgina. Only Georgina appeared at first to notice P. Quince's bracelet. She seemed about to speak, then changed her mind.

Suddenly Paul's eyes lighted on Margaret's wrist. "Oh, Margaret . . ." he began.

"Bait," she said. "Hush."

"We will go to the beach now," Gunnar said, and pulled Georgina to her feet.

"A grand idea," Paul said quickly. "I'll show you the way."

"We have business in an hour," Margaret said.

"I will be back," Paul said.

"Lady Alys askin' to see you." Cleone met Margaret on the path up to the big house.

"Then she's well enough to have visitors?"

Cleone sniffed. "She's not really ailin', I think. She's just tired of the people, live ones and dead ones."

"The dead ones don't trouble you?" Margaret asked.

"Me? It have nothing to do with we. Is you people that have to worry."

Lady Alys's rooms were on the side of the house that looked down on Arawak Bay and the roofs of the cookhouse and sheds.

Margaret entered the pale blue sitting room. Tall windows opened onto balconies. There was a scent of English lavender about the place. The door to the bedroom was closed.

After a moment, Mamee Joe opened the bedroom door and limped slowly across the sitting room toward Margaret.

"Morning, miss. My lady wishin' to speak with you." She sat in a chair beside one of the windows.

Margaret went into the bedroom. Lady Alys sat in a

fine antique armchair beside her floor-to-ceiling window that allowed access to the balcony. She wore a light robe, and her hair was beautifully arranged.

"I hope you are feeling better," Margaret said.

"I am feeling quite fine, thank you," she said. "These affairs tire me more than they did. In the old days, I was the center of attention. People often came from the Antilles islands to visit. These people . . ." She dismissed them with a wave of her hand. "I saw you and that young man, the prince, prying around the storage sheds."

"Paul felt that with his responsibilities here, he should know the lay of the land."

"The two of you overreach your place here," Lady Alys said. "You do not need to know anything. I know everything necessary for the running of my house." Their eyes met for a moment and then Lady Alys looked away. "I do not care for upsets," she said. "I do not care for actions that reflect badly on my family and our very long and distinguished history in the islands. How came you to cause trouble at the Arawak Bay village?"

Margaret was astonished. "We caused no trouble," she said. "We certainly had no idea that our presence would give rise to such hostility. How did you know?"

"I know everything that goes on," Lady Alys said. "I wish for you and that young man to mind your own business, not mine. I will take care of that as I always have." She was silent. She was staring at the gold bracelet Margaret had forgotten to remove.

"You became acquainted with Marva before she left?" Lady Alys asked. "She had bracelets like that."

"Yes," Margaret lied.

"She was told to leave immediately."

"Then you sent her away," Margaret said.

Lady Alys looked at her sharply. "I should have done

it years ago, but Jimmie had made a promise. She was the cause of all this unpleasantness.''

"Murder is rather more than unpleasantness," Margaret said. There seemed little left to say, so she went to the door.

"I will not tolerate impertinence, young woman. And be kind enough to inform the Italian boy that I do not think he is suitable for Georgina. Prince," she added with a disdainful sniff for the upstart title. The only good prince was an English prince, at least in the old days.

Margaret looked back from the doorway. "I think that is one matter that neither you nor I can control."

"Thanks to our little adventure at Arawak Bay," Margaret said, "you are not esteemed by Lady Alys. It may also have something to do with the fact that your father is not a pretender to an acceptable throne."

Paul said, "Georgina has informed me that her grandmother is a woman with strong convictions. I hope this attitude does not hamper our relationship." He sighed. "At least Gunnar has gone to his boat. There are only Rusty and Carlos remaining at the pool. Carlos is out of the running, and Jane's interest in Rusty, unlikely though it is, has diminished Georgina's interest in him."

"Did you tell Georgina where you were off to?"

"Party business. She is quite understanding."

Margaret and Paul set out on foot with Coo-Coo as their guide across the fields.

"Ellis, you behave now!" Alvina called out as the three passed the door of the estate kitchen.

"Yes, Ma," he said, and was soon several yards

ahead of Margaret and Paul on the path through the tall coconut palms. He stopped and waited for them.

"Look now," he said. "Easy for people to come along here, sun coming up."

It was, as Boots had told them, a mere fifteen minutes to the hill up to the sugar mill. At the top, Margaret breathed deeply and looked at the sky. Pale blue with pinkish clouds, the sun just coming above the horizon. Half a dozen stately frigate birds spread their wide wings as they circled the sea. The boats docked at the marina, tiny from this distance, rode quietly at their moorings. Prince Aziz's yacht was like a great mother hen surrounded by chicks. A dozen lesser yachts had been arriving and were anchored nearby.

Margaret went into the sugar mill. The stones of the makeshift fireplace were gone, and the ashes scattered. She placed Carolyn Sue's necklace in the deep chink in the wall. Then she poked at the pile of dried palm fronds with her toe. One long branch fell to the ground, and she saw that it had been concealing a two-foot square package securely wrapped in chicken wire and canvas. A good place to conceal the original red bundle with bracelet now replaced, the ring and the lock of hair. She didn't care to know what was in the package, since one sort of criminal activity was enough to deal with, but it was obvious enough if anyone was bent on looking. . . .

"That's done. Now . . ." She looked around. "No place of concealment here, but if you were to station yourself down behind the big bougainvillea bush, you could see anyone who came."

Paul shifted uncomfortably. "Is this necessary, Margaret?"

"We have to have a treasure hunt," she said. "We might as well make it worthwhile."

"Nothing will come of it," Paul said. "I am certain. The tropics have made us *pazzo*—crazy."

"Well, I have made certain other plans," she began.

"Good," Paul said. "I do not wish to know of them. I am going to Chatham."

"Whatever for?"

"Drinkin' a beastly cold beer with Bootsie," Paul said, with a grin. "Actually, I have some business in town. A little thing I want to get for Georgie. Do not try so hard to control my life. I understand now De Vere's reluctance to take you on on a permanent basis. I will catch a ride back to Indigo Hill before you know it." He started down St. Joseph's Trace to the main road.

Margaret said, "Coo-Coo, a man in love is not an easy man." She didn't want to explain to Coo-Coo that he and Paul were in love with the same woman. The problem was that nothing Margaret had seen for sale in Chatham could equal Coo-Coo's gold bracelet, and Georgina appeared to her to be a material rather than a sentimental girl.

"Listen," Coo-Coo said. "Boys beating pan, getting ready to play for Saturday night."

Margaret could hear a steel band practicing somewhere off in the hills.

"Coo-Coo," she said suddenly. "Take me down into the gully and show me where you found the red bundle."

He shook his head. "Is a bad place."

"Nothing can happen now," she said. "We know it was false obeah."

The boy sighed and led her to the top of the gully. The descent was like leaving a happy sunlit world and entering the abode of ghosts. Overhead was a canopy of leaves from the big mango and breadfruit trees that let barely any light through. A stand of slim bamboo grew from the floor on the opposite side of the gully. She could see a few tatters of paper still nailed to the trunk of the mango tree. It was damp and very quiet.

"Here," Coo-Coo said. "This is the place. I see a little piece of red sticking up."

"How can you tell the place?"

"Shoelace catch on that old root there. When I fall down, right in front of my eyes I see the red." He looked around nervously. "Is a bad, bad place."

Margaret agreed, and was glad to ascend into the sunlight. They crossed the fields again in the hot sun. At least it would be much cooler for the searchers in the early morning.

Halfway back to Indigo Hill, Margaret said, "Coo-Coo, I've changed my mind. I want to go back and look at the sugar mill again." Coo-Coo frowned. "You can go along. I know the way."

"Okay," he said, and free of the necessity of strolling in a leisurely manner alongside Margaret, he raced ahead and was soon out of sight.

Margaret turned back, walking as much as possible in the shade of the palms.

She had suddenly had a better idea.

Chapter 23

The goat had returned to the sugar mill when Margaret got back. Before she ducked inside the mill out of the sun, she surveyed the harbor below. Some of the boats had spread their sails and were moving with the wind toward open water. As Margaret watched, a helicopter rose from Prince Aziz's yacht, hovered, and flew toward the big island, which was merely a dusky blip on the horizon.

"Money, money, money," she hummed to herself. Inside the mill, she removed the red bundle and replaced it with Carolyn Sue's aquamarine necklace tied up in a headscarf she found in the bottom of her bag. Good enough for the treasure hunters.

Margaret thought for a moment, and then wrote out a brief message: *Look where you buried it.*

The goat was standing in the round doorway, chewing and contemplating Margaret like an old friend.

She went outside again. Clouds seemed to be piling up in the east, but they were still fluffy and white, not like the thunderheads she knew, but friendly Caribbean clouds.

Margaret headed toward the spot at the top of the

gully where she and Coo-Coo had gone down earlier. The sun had moved further to the west, and it was even dimmer than before.

There was a sudden muffled thump behind her, and Margaret gasped and turned. Then she almost giggled. A very large, ripe mango had fallen from the tree.

She found the place that Coo-Coo had indicated as the spot where he had found his treasure. Margaret had no tool to dig, but with hands and a stick she managed a shallow hole big enough for the red bundle. She pushed the dirt around it, leaving a bit of the red cloth showing. Then she stood up and brushed off her hands. This was better. Paul could keep watch on the mill with Boots close at hand. She would conceal herself somewhere here in the gully. As soon as Paul saw someone arrive well ahead of the other treasure seekers, he would send Boots to summon Lambeaux. When the person realized that the sought-after red bundle was in the gully, Margaret would be a witness to its retrieval. An uninvolved person would not come down here.

It was not an outstanding plan, but it was the best she could think of, even though she knew beyond a doubt that a second person was involved. Proving that, she thought, might be impossible.

She looked around the dim, quiet place. What will I do when things start happening? she thought.

The answer was easy. She would do nothing but watch.

Then she thought that was wrong. She needed to have something that would connect the person, the bundle, and the murder of P. Quince. She had to leave only the bracelet and the lock of hair, and keep the ring with the initial.

She started to pull the red bundle out of the damp earth and stopped.

The sound had been very faint, as though branches on the bushes at the top of the gully were being pushed aside. Frantically she tore apart the bundle, thrust the ring into her pocket and reburied the cloth and the bracelet. Perhaps Coo-Coo was returning, but she'd take no chances. It could also be the murderer. Like everything happening on Boucan in connection with Jimmie's party, this was happening too soon.

The sound of someone approaching was unmistakable now. She moved back toward the thick stand of bamboo at the other side of the gully.

Coo-Coo stumbled into the gully through the brush.

Rusty Keating was right behind him.

"Here's the boy, Lady Margaret," he said in a mocking voice. "He's telling me you're hiding the thing I want at the mill, but I don't see anything there I recognize. But I'm directed to come here. . . ."

Coo-Coo said, "Don't tell Red Man anything." The boy was holding back tears. "He grab me by the house when I comin' back, take me in m'lord's car, make me tell. Say if I don't, he kill Miss Georgie."

Rusty pushed Coo-Coo, and he fell facedown onto the ground. Margaret winced as Rusty put his foot on the boy's back and held him down.

"Nice little boy," Rusty said. "Known him all his life." He raised his voice. "Where are my things?"

"Take your foot off the boy and take two steps back," Margaret said. Maybe someone would notice the Jag at the sugar mill and investigate. Everyone knew everything on Boucan.

Rusty removed his foot, but he didn't move back.

"Come, Coo-Coo," Margaret said. He dashed to her side, and she put a protective hand on his shoulder, and thought fast. What could Rusty do to them? He had no cutlass to cut them down, he couldn't force them to consume toxic plants or a piece of fish barbecued over a fire made of lethal oleander wood.

Why couldn't she and Coo-Coo simply run? The boy must know ways out of the gully, and Rusty couldn't catch both of them.

Rusty would not catch either of them, if she had anything to say about it.

"Don't think of running," Rusty said. "I am one of the few people hereabouts who does carry a gun."

Margaret knew little about handguns, but that was unmistakably a gun in Rusty's hand.

Oh, really, she thought, they advertise escape from reality, and it ends up just like New York City.

"I need it for my business," Rusty said, "and this is business. Where are those things I want?"

"You can't shoot us," Margaret said. "People will hear. People know who has a gun. And a lot of people know I'm here."

Rusty chuckled. "Your Prince Paul thinks you're napping in your bungalow. No one else notices or cares. Just tell me where the objects are. When I have them, we'll stroll up to the mill, take the Jag to Arawak Bay, get into the zodiac that's waiting, and go out to sea. Not far, but there will be a terrible accident. Those boats sink in a minute, and I will manage to swim ashore. Life goes on as usual . . . for me."

"And the person you take your orders from," Margaret said.

"I work for myself," Rusty said. "My father and grandfather worked for . . . these people. I merely have business associates. Now, where is it?"

Margaret could feel Coo-Coo trembling beside her.

"Look! Is there in the ground!" he blurted out.

Rusty was momentarily distracted as he saw where Coo-Coo was pointing. He lunged for the red cloth.

Margaret grabbed Coo-Coo and ran toward the bamboo forest. The ground was soft and footing was bad. The bamboo grew close together so that she had to part it to get through.

"Run," she gasped. Coo-Coo was hanging onto her hand as she pulled him deeper into the bamboo. She could hear Rusty coming after them. Now Coo-Coo took the lead, dragging her deeper into the bush. The ground started to rise slightly, and then they were faced with a steep hill. Fallen trees blocked their path. Margaret tumbled once and felt a sharp pain in her knee. Coo-Coo managed with more grace.

"Path over there," Coo-Coo said. "Goes to the end of Mamee Joe's garden."

It wasn't more than a faint trail, and it was very steep. Coo-Coo was hanging onto vines and branches to pull himself upward. Margaret followed, expecting to hear shots at any moment, but the noise of pursuit seemed to have ceased. She concentrated on moving forward and upward. She was heavier and less agile than Coo-Coo, and the climb began to seem unendurable.

Coo-Coo paused and whispered, "I going ahead to look. The houses over just so."

"Be careful," Margaret said. "Rusty could have driven up St. Joseph's Trace. Is anybody at home?"

"All gone," Coo-Coo said. "Mamee Joe, Ma, Derrick at the big house. The others down by the guest house, even the babies."

Not good news, and the sun had set. Darkness had fallen on Boucan.

He motioned to her to keep quiet and peered over the edge of the gully. He ducked back quickly. "Fitzie from Arawak Bay up by the houses with the truck. Two more boys there and the Red Man."

Margaret thought for a moment. Rusty must realize

that more people than just Margaret would know about the objects from P. Quince. Indeed, Georgina had one of the bracelets. When he looked at the bundle, he'd see the ring was missing. He'd know Margaret or someone else had it.

Why didn't someone from the big house wonder where she was and look for her? But no. Indigo Hill was full of visitors, trying on costumes from the trunks, being served, eating and drinking. No one would notice that she and Coo-Coo were not about.

Why didn't Rusty Keating just make his escape?

Once more she answered her own question. Money probably, and the chance to affix the blame for all that had happened . . .

"We have to get to the big house quickly," Margaret said.

Coo-Coo looked back fearfully. "Can't go back through the gully," he said. "Too dark to find the way. Jumbies there too."

"Can we somehow go across the fields so they can't follow us? We daren't go along the main road."

Coo-Coo considered. "Is all bush after Mamee Joe's land until you get to the plantation and the back road to Indigo Hill." He peered over the edge of the gully again and ducked back. "Truck leavin', boys comin' this way. I don't see Red Man. Come, quiet."

They began to move nearly horizontally across the steep slope. Trees and bushes grew out of the embankment nearly at right angles. The darkness made it doubly difficult.

Margaret heard one of the men call out in an incomprehensible patois. Another answered. Coo-Coo froze, and Margaret followed suit. A beam of light swept the darkness above the gully. Then, after a time spent clinging to the hillside, the voices seemed to move away.

"Is okay now," Coo-Coo said. "I goin' first and you hold onto my hand. Quiet, quiet."

Finally they reached a point where Coo-Coo heaved himself over the top of the hill. Margaret followed. They were at last on flat ground. Margaret lay back for a moment, and wondered if her knees, heart, and fair English skin would ever recover.

Coo-Coo stood up cautiously. "Look now. You can see the lights."

High on the next hill, the big house at Indigo Hill was ablaze with lights. Between was a dark valley where she could make out the tops of many palm trees. Beyond that, on the back road to Indigo Hill, she could see the headlights of a single car racing along toward the house. Rusty in the Jaguar on his way to finish his business.

"Let's go," she said.

Coo-Coo and Margaret descended into the valley. She could still feel pain in her knee, but now they walked on flat land through the stately coconut palms in eerie silence. The sky was bursting with stars, and the sliver of the new moon followed their progress.

Coo-Coo hesitated at a stream.

"We can walk across," Margaret said. "It's not deep."

"Bad water," he said. "And you find cayman sometimes."

Margaret searched her memory. "Ah, right," she said. "Something like a crocodile." After this day, the last thing she needed was to be nipped or worse by a large reptile. "Isn't that a log over the stream?"

They managed the crossing without disaster.

Finally, they were climbing the hill to the back of the big house. They could hear a steel band playing. It sounded to Margaret like the Triumphal March from *Aida*.

Just before they reached the cookhouse, Margaret stopped and faced Coo-Coo. She put her hands on his shoulders. "You are my hero," she said. "Go to your mother now and stay with her and the others in the kitchen. No matter what she says about how dirty or late you are, you cannot say anything until I say so. Even if she punishes you. This is very serious. Do you understand?"

Coo-Coo shrugged. "Easy to understand. Man have a gun and he want to shoot me. I'm not talking to anybody."

Alvina was holding an enormous bowl of rice when they appeared. She scowled at Coo-Coo. "Boy, you in big, big trouble."

"He's a lifesaver, Alvina," Margaret said. "Be easy on him."

Alvina gaped at the sight of Margaret. "Madame, where you been, lookin' like that?"

Margaret looked down at her dirty clothes and scratched arms. "Taking care of business," she said. "Where is everyone?"

"Barbecue at the pool, trying on the carnival costumes."

"Everyone? Rusty Keating, Mamee Joe? Lady Alys?"

"Lady Alys still keepin' to her room. Red Man come up in m'lord's car, leave it out front. Mamee Joe here just now. . . . "

Margaret put a finger to her lips and Coo-Coo nodded.

As Margaret went into the house, she heard Alvina scolding the boy, but not too harshly.

No one was in the entrance hall. She went upstairs

to Lady Alys's room. If Mamee Joe was there, it might
be all right. She turned the knob gently and went into
the darkened sitting room. From this side of the house,
the steel band was only a faint melodic line of high
metallic trills with an underlying bass.

The door to the bedroom was open, and she could
see Lady Alys lying in bed, propped up on a pile of
lacy pillows with a lamp lighted beside the bed.

She went into the bedroom. On the fine cotton sheet
that covered Lady Alys was a square of red cloth, a
gold bracelet with gold nuggets at each end of the circle,
and a lock of dark hair. Next to them was a rectangular
gray metal box, open, with the key still in the lock.

She looked at the old woman. It was difficult to tell
if she was still breathing. Then Margaret touched her
hand. It was icy cold. The blood in Lady Alys's veins
had always been ice-cold, but she saw that a pillow had
fallen to the floor beside the bed. How simple to press
down and stop an old woman's breath. That wouldn't
trouble Rusty Keating.

Margaret left the bedroom. On the sitting-room side
of the door was an old-fashioned key in the lock. She
removed it, and locked the door from the outside. If
Mamee Joe returned, she'd surely take away the bracelet and the lock of hair. She would probably understand
what they meant, but she would be the loyal servant
until the end.

When Margaret reached the verandah, she saw the
Jaguar leaving. She didn't know if Rusty Keating had
seen her, but at least he appeared to be leaving alone.
She wondered if he was heading for Chatham and his
sailboat, or toward the village at Arawak Bay and a
zodiac boat that would speed him away.

It didn't matter. He had done Lady Alys's bidding in
order to keep his smuggling or whatever it was going.

Lady Alys had done more than her share to keep the family name clear on her island. A granddaughter had been killed because she wanted to seek revenge or help her mother or expose the illicit activities on the island. Lady Alys had lured a former daughter-in-law to the island and had her murdered in such a way as to make it look like a local crime, to keep her from blackmail that probably involved Jimmie's illegitimate daughter. She'd used her knowledge of Boucan's magic practices to instruct Rusty how to cast suspicion on the local people. She knew everything that there was to know about her island. And Rusty was forever her servant.

Cleone bustled out from the house. She had taken to her new position of importance.

"Is there some way I can ring Mr. Lambeaux?" Margaret asked.

"You could call the police station," she said. "Constable will know where to find him. Number is two three nine." She took a closer look at Margaret. "Oh, madame. You have an accident?"

"Just doing some exploring," Margaret said. "Could you ask Lord Farfaine, Prince Paul, and Miss Georgina to join me on the verandah right away? It's very important. Thank you so much."

Margaret sank down in one of the chairs at the far end of the verandah and listened to the happy crowd noises and the steel band around the pool.

Suddenly Mamee Joe was standing beside her.

"I saw the trouble for years and years," she said, "but she was my lady. My friend. Old ladies together, remembering how it used to be."

Mamee Joe didn't go into the house, but limped down the steps and disappeared into the night.

Chapter 24

Prince Aziz graciously offered Margaret the use of his helicopter to take her across to the big island.

"I have instructed the pilot of my jet, which is at the airport there, to take you on to New York at your convenience. No, no, it is not the least trouble."

Mr. Lambeaux, more grudging than gracious, permitted her to leave Boucan. "Irregular," he said, "but if we leave you loose on the island, we don't know what more trouble you're going to find." He accepted the charred stick from Mamee Joe's oleander bush and the handful of leaves. "I'm just hoping we get Rusty Keating back from whatever island he's gone to." Lambeaux shrugged. "He was more deeply into the business of arranging transfers of illicit drugs than I had suspected when I arrived."

Margaret looked at him. "So you were sent over for more business than just Clarissa's murder."

"In a manner of speaking. The death of the young woman before Christmas caused us to take a close look at that village, the comings and goings by land and by air. Those boys at Arawak Bay are facing some trouble, but they're saying Rusty telling them not to worry, is

229

all approved and nothing could happen to them. And he had the money and possessions to tempt them.''

"Approved? Then it is true that Lady Alys pulled the strings. . . .''

"Tacit support—let us leave it at that since she is dead. I should hate to see the old lady be remembered as a . . . drug kingpin.'' He looked around the beautiful grounds of Indigo Hill. "It takes a lot of money to maintain this as a private home. I hear from my connections that Lord Farfaine himself is not as wealthy as he likes to appear. Lady Alys had to do her share to keep the place.''

"She went as far as seeing that two murders were committed to protect her life here and the name of her family,'' Margaret said.

"We all feel for our families,'' Lambeaux said. "Lady Alys thinkin' about days when position have more meaning than character. Those women were threats. Marva's daughter understood that she had been sent away by Lady Alys, and she wanted her revenge by exposing the illegal activities. The former wife hooked up with the girl and was trying blackmail. . . . Rusty's forebears worked here, you know. It was a long tradition of serving Lady Alys's family.''

No wonder Lady Alys had not found Paul suitable. He was merely another of her servants, like Marva, who had fled. Perhaps Jimmie would find her one day and provide for her.

Margaret said, "I understand Rusty placed the false obeah signs to make it look local. Lady Alys would know all about them. I know he killed Miss Quince to stop her from nosing about Arawak Bay, and he befriended Clarissa—after Lady Alys had lured her to the big island and instructed him to find her and bring her over. I imagine he took her up to the sugar mill for a picnic, and saw to it that she ate food cooked over the oleander fire. . . ."

"And evidently assisted her demise further by stopping her breath when she was unconscious, just to make certain. . . ."

"Indeed?" Somehow, Margaret was not surprised. "He had the Arawak Bay boys carry her body in a trunk here in that old pickup. Surely they weren't aware . . . He left it overnight in the freezer house. I assume he then placed the body on the island the night Paul heard the boat."

"What is your question, Lady Margaret?"

"He must have put the chicken head in my bungalow, but why on earth did he come back in the night to hide Clarissa's papers?"

"Did he? They were innocuous, told us nothing." Lambeaux smiled. "Perhaps someone wanted to help us without actually accusing someone close. . . ."

Margaret thought guiltily of the letter from Lady Alys to Clarissa that she hadn't given to the police—so as not to be responsible for pointing them in her direction.

"Now Indigo Hill is Georgina's," Margaret said.

"In alliance with your young friend, do you think?"

Paul and Georgina had been sitting together by the pool all day, deeply engrossed in conversation. Paul had refused the opportunity to return to New York with Margaret and was staying on for at least the length of his commitment to Lord Farfaine, and perhaps a longer one to Georgina.

The celebrations at the house had, of course, been cancelled, although the island was proceeding with its planned street carnival to mark the end of the holidays. Jimmie had hidden himself in his rooms on the side of the house that looked down on the drive and the pool. Margaret imagined that Jane was pacing back and forth, wracking her brains to figure out how to escape, probably forever.

When Margaret left Lambeaux and went to the back of the house to see about her lift to the marina, she found Coo-Coo near the cookhouse, done up in a fantastic spangled costume and a painted face. He danced about excitedly upon seeing her. She suspected he might have transferred his devotion from Georgina to her.

"You comin' back just now?" he asked.

"Someday," Margaret said. "Have you ever wanted to go to America?"

"I've seen snow on the telly," he said. "I would like to see snow. You could fix it?"

"Very likely I could," Margaret said. "But your mother says you skip school too often. . . ."

"No more," Coo-Coo said. "School starting Monday. Goin' to school every day."

"Excellent," Margaret said. "I shall ask Derrick to send me reports."

Derrick was puttering morosely around the Range Rover waiting to drive her to get the launch to Prince Aziz's yacht.

"Is bad business for the island," he said. "Lady Alys gone and who's to keep the house goin'?"

"Georgina said something about turning Indigo Hill into a real hotel. She would need your help."

"I spent five years in hotels in America," Derrick said.

"There you are," Margaret said. "Talk to her and Paul about it. At least it would mean that Indigo Hill would continue to exist."

Tyrone Pace arrived at the Range Rover carrying his luggage.

"Prince Aziz is more a fan of soccer and thoroughbred racing than cricket," he said, "but he nevertheless offered me a seat on the helicopter to the big island. Madame Campos and Carlos have extracted invitations from him to join the party on his yacht.'' He grinned and shook his head. ''It is amazing the way some people are born with an instinct for survival in the best possible surroundings.''

There was only Mamee Joe left to see. Margaret found her sitting upstairs outside Lady Alys's door, as though she could not believe that the inhabitant of those rooms was gone forever.

''I'm so sorry, Mamee Joe,'' Margaret said.

''They sayin' the Red Man kill she with a pillow over her face,'' Mamee Joe said. ''But I know, I know. Is the shame and the pain that kill she. I goin' soon myself, I feel it. Is the end of the old days.''

Margaret slipped away quietly.

Paul and Georgina waited at the Range Rover to see her off. Paul had managed to find something in Chatham that replaced Coo-Coo's gold bracelet: Georgina was wearing a string of tiny pink Caribbean seashells around her neck.

''We will be in New York in a couple of months,'' Paul said. Margaret noticed the ''we.'' ''We have a good deal of thinking and planning to do.''

''Good,'' Margaret said. ''Keep me informed. Georgina, there's one matter that has puzzled me. On my first night here, an intruder appeared in my bungalow and left a bundle of Clarissa's papers.''

Georgina looked at the ground. Then she said, ''I found them in Grandmother's sitting room. I realize now that Rusty must have brought them to her after . . .'' She looked at Margaret. ''I didn't want to confront her, but I knew something wasn't right. I thought if someone else had them . . .''

''No harm done,'' Margaret said. She looked at the

handsome dark-haired couple and hoped they both had found what they'd been looking for.

As Derrick drove Margaret and Tyrone away, she looked out the back window for her last sight of Indigo Hill. Paul had his arm around Georgina, and looked very much like the master of the estate.

Chatham's main road was thick with costumed people, dancing and swaying to a steel band. The death of Lady Alys and the old days had passed them by without a second thought. When they finally managed to reach the marina, Prince Aziz's launch was waiting at the pier to take her out to the yacht. As she went aboard, she caught sight of Boots standing in front of the rum shop. He pulled off his old Mets cap and waved it.

"Derrick, wait." Margaret handed him a handful of local currency. "Have Boots drink a beastly cold beer in my honor."

"Margaret! You're back so soon?" De Vere's voice at the other end of the line was a welcome sound indeed. "I didn't expect you for a week. How was your holiday?"

"Lovely," she said. "Peaceful, relaxing. Paul seems to have found the woman of his dreams. The people of Boucan are delightful. I'll tell you all about it. Later."

Much later, she decided.

JOYCE
CHRISTMAS

Available at bookstores everywhere.
Published by Fawcett Books.